A RANGER'S TIME

A Novel by

EDWARD L GATES

Best Wishes —

Edward L Gates

Edited by Heidi M. Thomas

Copyright © 2015 Edward L. Gates

All Rights Reserved

Reg: TXu 1-921-250

United Stated Copyright Office

ISBN: 0996145702
ISBN-13: 978-0-9961457-0-1

Cover designed by the author

This book is dedicated to the loving memory of

The Bean.

Those who know him, know why …

Acknowledgements

Although the thoughts and words in this novel are strictly those of the author, this book would not and could not have been written without the help, direction, cooperation, friendship and understanding of a lot of people and institutions. Those directly involved, and whom I relied on the most, are listed below. There have been others who have helped shape this story; too many to mention here. To all those, forgive me for not mentioning you by name, but you have my deepest and most sincere heart-felt thanks. I count on all of you in my life, and will continue to do so.

First and foremost I want to thank family. My wife, Barbara, and my children Ed and Jon, were always in my corner. They always believed in me even when I had moments of self-doubt. Barbara is an endless source of encouragement and support. I want to thank her for being one of my toughest critics. Sometimes we didn't agree, but she always presented a different perspective that made me think of new possibilities and viewpoints.

None of this would have been possible without Dorothy Cora Moore (author of *The Atlanteans*). Your knowledge is boundless and I can't thank you enough for sharing it. It was your guidance and, most importantly, your encouragement that gave me the confidence and determination to take my scribblings to a new level. Your help and direction was invaluable. I will always be in your debt.

I especially want to thank my editor, Heidi M. Thomas, award-winning author of the *Cowgirl Dreams* Trilogy. She's not only a great author, but a brilliant editor as well. She took editing a step further, making suggestions that really tightened up the characters, the story line, and the story's overall flow. What makes her so invaluable is that she found the obscure continuity issues that were in this story. I couldn't have asked for anything better.

To Candace and Steven Gates, thank you for taking your time to review this work as it was being written. Your equine and historical knowledge was priceless. Gus was no more than a passing thought until you made him real and gave that added dimension to the story. Thank you for sharing your knowledge. And thank you for being my test reader and bringing to light historic deficiencies in the story. Your input and feedback was exactly what was needed to tighten up the story.

The Panhandle Prairie Historical Museum Research Lab – I want to thank the entire staff there, especially Milly and Warren for your cooperation, information, and kindness that I could never repay. Everyone there was more than accommodating in helping me fill in the historical aspects of early Amarillo. Your input brought an air of authenticity to this story.

Amarillo City Library – I owe a debt of thanks to the staff of the upper floor research area. Any questions I had were quickly and expertly answered. They brought to light books, records, maps, and information about historic Amarillo. The kindness and the historical information they provided helped build authenticity to this story.

Last, but not least, I want to thank The Prescott Review Group: Mary Ann Clarke, Judith March Davis, William T. Johnstone, and Dougal Reeves. All accomplished and brilliant authors in their own right. Thank you all for coming to my rescue on every chapter. I shudder to think how this book would have turned out without your invaluable insight and input. I am forever in your debt and at your service.

This book is a work of fiction. The characters in this book are fictitious, and any resemblance to any real persons, either living or dead, implied or otherwise, is purely coincidental. Certain names of people, businesses, and institutions in Amarillo in the late nineteenth century are a matter of historical record and are used throughout this story for the sole purpose of setting a scene. Their names are used strictly as a historical reference and nothing more. There is no mention of their actions and or character in this story and none are implied.

1

The Ranger

August, 1887

Somebody's going to die here. Charlie prayed it wouldn't be him. He slowly inched his hand to his holster and unhooked the leather hammer strap. *This was going to go real bad real soon.* Ranger Charlie Turlock nervously watched the eight men standing in front of the ranch house.

A hot, dusty August breeze swirled around him and fanned his dirty white duster. A bead of sweat escaped the sweatband on Charlie's hat and traversed the wrinkles that lined the weather-beaten face of this old Texas Ranger.

Charlie and fellow Texas Ranger Dick Adams escorted two deputy US marshals to Abe Walker's southwest Texas ranch to serve an arrest warrant on a saddle tramp named "Bull" Murphy. He was wanted in Wichita for killing a bartender.

Cattle baron Abe Walker leaned against a post on the front porch of his house. He stood with his right hand resting on his gun. Even in his mid-sixties, he was still a titan of a man. His six-foot, two-inch frame and broad shoulders gave him the air of authority. He too carefully watched everyone like a mountain lion ready to pounce. He wore the defiant smile of a man in control.

The four lawmen stood in the courtyard to Abe's right facing Bull Murphy, two other ranch hands, and foreman Mac Sherman. The men formed a disorganized circle. Their eyes shifted back and forth from one person to another. The tension was intensified by the oppressive heat and humidity. Marshal Williams, from Wichita, just announced his intention to arrest Murphy and return him to Kansas to stand trial.

"Well, I don't believe I like that notion, Marshal," Bull Murphy said. "I kinda like it here, so I don't think I'll be obliging you." There was a pause as Murphy looked at Mac Sherman and Abe Walker. He smiled at the four lawmen across from him. "I work for Mr. Walker here in the Pecos and everyone knows the only law in the Pecos is Mr. Walker's law."

The ranch hands and Abe Walker laughed. Walker sauntered along the porch railing to the top of the porch steps. "You got your answer, Marshal! I'm starting a drive soon and I can't spare any hands. I think you'd better leave now."

The two marshals looked at each other and began a short conversation that no one else could hear. No one wanted a gun battle, but at this point there was no getting away from it. Charlie thought he noticed a slight smile break on the corner of Marshal Hendricks's mouth.

"Oh, hell no," Charlie muttered. The deputy marshals turned back toward Murphy and drew their guns. But at the same time, everyone else drew theirs. At the first shot, the men scurried in all directions. Adams and Charlie joined the shootout.

Mac Sherman drew and fired at Marshal Hendricks, striking him dead center in his chest before the marshal could get his gun completely out of his holster. His chest erupted with a crimson discharge and the marshal collapsed. Marshal Williams fired twice at Mac but both shots missed. Then the marshal loosed a couple of rounds at Murphy dropping him instantly. Walker and the other ranch hands fired at the lawmen.

During the melee, Walker's 18 year old son, Jeremiah, came out of the house brandishing a Henry rifle. He shot Deputy Marshal Williams who crumpled to the dirt. Jeremiah then turned his rifle to Dick Adams and fired a shot that missed. Charlie raised his Colt and pulled the trigger. It was empty. He quickly pulled the Smith and Wesson from his belt and fired. The porch wall behind Jeremiah exploded with the boy's blood and he dropped to the floor. Seeing his son go down, Abe Walker dropped his gun, slumped to the porch floor, and cradled the body of his son in his arms.

Mac Sherman fired a shot at Charlie that barely missed his head but nicked his right ear. As an instinctive move, Charlie spun and fired in the direction of Mac. Charlie's bullet careened across Mac Sherman's forehead ripping the skin to the bone. It was a lucky shot. Mac fell to the ground. The shooting was over.

Charlie stood with guns in both hands surveying the scene. Thick grayish-white gun smoke shrouded the courtyard in front of Abe Walker's ranch house, and the acrid smell of blood and burnt powder filled the air. The echoing sounds of countless gunshots still rang in Charlie's ears.

"Dick? You hit?" Charlie hollered.

"No! No, I'm okay." Dick walked over to the two marshals lying on the ground. "How 'bout you?"

"Just a scratch. I'm fine," His right ear stung and burned. Charlie holstered his empty Colt and reached up to touch his ear. A thin streak of blood ran down his neck and was being absorbed by his collarless tan and brown patterned cotton shirt.

Charlie looked around as the smoke began to clear. Bull Murphy was down. Mac Sherman was down. Another ranch hand was wounded and being tended to by another hand who never pulled his gun. One of the marshals was dead and the other was badly wounded. Abe Walker sat on the porch holding the lifeless body of his only son and heir in his lap. His hands and arms were covered in the boy's blood.

Time seemed to stop for Charlie. He couldn't move. The carnage before him would be forever etched into his memory.

"You killed my son!" Abe Walker shouted at Charlie. "You'll pay for this, Ranger!"

Charlie pointed his gun at Abe Walker and cocked the hammer but couldn't pull the trigger. He felt dark and empty inside looking at Abe holding his dead son. Visions of a dead young traveler from Charlie's past flashed in his brain. He just stood and looked at Abe. He couldn't quite make out all that Abe was saying over the ringing in his ears, but he got the message just the same.

"You hear me, Ranger?" Abe shouted again. "You're a dead man! I'm gonna gun you down, you bastard!"

Charlie refocused on the situation before him. He kept his revolver in his hand and walked over to check the bodies. He kicked the gun away from Murphy and checked his breathing. There was none. Then he walked over to Sherman's body. The ringing in Charlie's ears began to subside. Charlie kicked Mac's gun away. Mac's face was awash in blood, but he stirred. The foreman opened his eyes and looked up at Charlie.

Sherman reached up and touched his bloody forehead. "Damn you, Ranger! I'll get you for this. You're a dead man."

Charlie turned and walked away without a word.

"I owe you! We'll meet again, Ranger," Mac threatened. Charlie never looked back.

Dick Adams helped the wounded Marshal Williams onto his horse while Abe persisted in his verbal assault of the lawmen. Charlie glared at Abe as he walked by the porch but didn't say anything. He and Dick loaded the body of Marshal Hendricks onto his horse and tightly secured it. Then Dick got on his horse, pulled his gun and kept it leveled at the ranchers while Charlie mounted Gus, his grey dappled gelding. He walked the horse closer to the porch. Abe stood and stared at the Texas Ranger. Charlie saw the hate and anger through the tears in the rancher's eyes.

"I'll leave you to bury your boy. You can leave Murphy for the buzzards and coyote's for all I care." Charlie turned Gus to leave but stopped and looked back at Walker. "It didn't have to be this way. You could have stopped it. This is all on your hands, not mine."

The rage was plainly visible in Walker's reddened face as he stepped to the edge of the porch and pointed his finger at Charlie. "Your time is up, Ranger," he managed to squeeze out through clenched teeth. "I'll take your life for my son's life. I'll find you! I'll find you and gun you down like a dog."

Charlie nudged his horse and walked away leading the horse carrying the body of Marshal Hendricks.

That night, Charlie, Ranger Adams, and the wounded marshal rode into the town of Pecos with the body of their murdered companion. Charlie and Adams left the two marshals in Pecos in the care of the local lawman and doctor.

The next morning the two rangers headed east toward Lubbock to rejoin their battalion. They crossed the Pecos River and rode in silence all day and into the night before they were safely out of west Texas Indian Territory. When they finally camped, the two sat around the fire in silence. Charlie stared hypnotically into the fire, watching the flames dance among the logs, while he made meaningless doodles in the dirt with a small stick. He ran the shootout over and over in his mind. Every shot, every cry of pain, every movement of every participant played in slow motion. He could still smell the gun smoke and hear the deafening blasts of each shot.

"I don't think I can do this anymore," Charlie finally said never looking up from the fire.

"What do you mean?" Dick asked.

"I'm getting too old. Ain't got the stomach for it anymore." Charlie paused and with a violent thrust, threw a small stick into the fire. "Hell, Dick, I just shot down a young boy."

"That boy shot down a US Marshal and tried to kill me," Dick retorted. "Hell, Charlie. You saved my life and probably that marshal's life." Charlie didn't answer. "And then you took out that foreman with one shot," Dick continued. "I never saw a shot like that! You put a bullet in his head from over fifty feet away! That was really some shot."

Charlie glanced up at Dick and snickered. "I never saw him." He looked back into the fire. "I just turned and fired. It was nothing but pure luck."

"Just the same, it was one hell of a shot."

The two sat in silence for a while longer. Charlie raised his head. "I've been doin' this for over twenty years, Dick. I'm 47 years old and I'm tired. My body can't take all this saddle time anymore. I can't keep up with you young fellas." He paused for a moment. "I don't know what I'd do, though. The rangers have been my whole life. I guess I'll talk to Captain McMurry when I get back to Lubbock. This may be my last year as a ranger."

"You're a legend, Charlie," Dick said. "McMurry ain't gonna let you just walk away. I'm sure he'll find something else for you to do in the battalion."

"Yeah. Maybe so."

Dick watched Charlie stare into the fire. "You think Walker will follow through with his threat?"

"Yep, I do," Charlie said. "He's a hard case. He'll never forget this or me. It'll fester in him over time. Yeah, he's gonna hunt me until one of us is dead."

"You should've killed him on the porch."

"Yeah, I reckon so," Charlie said. "Just couldn't do it with him holding his boy."

Four days later, Dick Adams and Charlie Turlock rode into Lubbock, Texas and reported in with Captain Sam McMurry. The captain was a small, thin man with graying hair and a full bushy moustache. As a quiet, soft spoken man, he was renowned for his ability to arrest men with little or no gunplay, which earned him the nickname of "Soft-Voice" McMurry.

Dick went into the captain's office before Charlie. After a short visit, he came out, shook Charlie's hand and said goodbye.

"Where you off to?" Charlie asked, a little surprised.

"Austin. Gonna see my family for a spell and join up with the battalion there."

"It was a pleasure riding with you, Dick. You're a good man."

Dick Adams smiled at Charlie and shook his hand one more time. "Good luck to you, Charlie," he said and walked out to the street. Charlie watched him mount his horse and ride out of town.

"What's this I hear about you quittin' the company?"

Charlie turned around to see Captain McMurry standing behind him with a smile on his face and an extended hand. Charlie returned Sam's smile, shook the captain's hand and the two walked into the captain's office and sat down.

"Gettin' too old, Sam. I can't take all that time in the field anymore. I'm tired, not as quick as I used to be. I can't see very good anymore and I can't hear as good either."

6

"What do you want to do, Charlie? If you want to stay with the rangers, I can get you in on a desk job if you want."

"Nah, I'm not a politician. That's your job. I wouldn't be any good riding a desk. I don't want to leave. Hell, I don't know what I'd do with myself. Don't you have any local, easy assignments I could do?"

"Actually, I think I do. There's a new settlement up north around the Frying Pan Ranch. I think they're calling it Amarillo. Anyway, there's been a string of rustlers and mavericks raiding them ranches in the area. The bosses are fit to be tied. Local law can't deal with it. They've been asking for some help guarding their cattle. They want those raids stopped ... at any cost, if you get my meaning." Charlie nodded. "I'm sending you up there with a couple of other rangers to do whatever you need to do to discourage any further trouble. Got it?"

Charlie couldn't have hoped for anything better. He was relieved and excited about this new prospect. "When do we go?"

"The other group left yesterday. Get some rest, restock, and head out tomorrow. It'll be a good assignment, Charlie. You'll be able to put your head on a pillow every night." Captain McMurry grinned.

Charlie nodded. "I appreciate this. Where am I staying?"

"The ranchers will put you up. Check in with them. I'll probably pull them other rangers out of there after a while. You stay as long as you need to."

Charlie stood up to leave.

"One more thing," the Captain said. "You'll be working along with the local lawmen in Amarillo. Make sure you keep them informed of what you're doin'. I'm going to have you run prisoners up to the Colorado Territorial prison every once in a while. It'll be a good break for you."

Charlie thanked the captain again, and walked out of the office with a new sense of serenity. Captain McMurry followed Charlie out to his horse. "You still ridin' this ol' crow-bait plug?"

"What do ya' mean? Gus here's a good ol' horse. Been with me a long time." Charlie stroked Gus's neck. "Hell, he knows me better than I do. He ain't as strong or as fast as he used to be, but neither am I. He's got more game than a lot other mounts. Nah, I think he and I will probably go out together."

Charlie climbed into the saddle, waved to the captain, and headed up the street to the livery to get Gus boarded for the night. The next morning he'd head north to Amarillo. Patrolling cattle sounded like an easy, low impact assignment. And it would probably keep him far away from Abe Walker. He was at ease.

.

2

Upton

June, 2220

Russell trembled with nervous anxiety. He feared something
would go wrong this time. This would be his third attempt and with
each trip he'd gotten a little more nervous. His first two time jumps
were without incident. In fact they were somewhat exhilarating, in a
strange sort of way. Having one's atoms disassembled and then
reassembled in another place and in another time was a little daunting.
There were so many things that could go wrong, and Russell worried
about each one of them.

"Relax," Michael said. "You've done this before and never had
a problem."

"That's easy for you to say. You're not the one being ripped
apart," Russell replied.

Russell Hicks, a young scientist specializing in theoretical
physics and astrophysics, was one of three technicians assigned to the
top secret time travel and teleportation project. These black projects
are owned, operated, and funded by the government. But no one knew
exactly who in government. The lines connecting the DARPA projects
to any government agency were blurred at best. Officially, they don't
even exist. The National Lab in Upton, New York housed the time
project, although, no one would admit it.

Michael O'Riley and Steven Marcohen were the other two techs. Steven and Russell graduated together and were hired by the government right out of college. Michael, the "old-timer" of the project, had been there the longest and was designated Lead Technician because of his seniority.

Russell looked at his reflection in the glass wall of the time chamber. "I look like an idiot in these clothes." He wore a tie-dyed tee-shirt, dark blue jeans that were a little too tight, and white vinyl gym shoes.

Steven tried to hide his snicker. "No, no. You look… fine." He turned away trying to hide his laughter.

"Yeah, go ahead and laugh, Steve. Next time we'll send you back to the cavemen!"

"It'll be fine, Russell," Michael said with a smile. "The archive chips reported that in 1992 people wore these… these… What are these called?"

"Tee-shirts!" Steven said.

"Right, tee-shirts and jeans," Michael continued. "Did you dose?"

"No. I don't like the way that stuff makes me feel."

"The meds are supposed to relax you, Russell. That's what they're for. Everybody doses. At least every once in a while."

"Thanks, but I'll pass," Russell said. "I'll be fine."

The lab door opened and a man in a grey suit entered and walked toward them. Russell looked at the clock; 9:20 PM. His time jump was scheduled to execute in ten minutes. Civilians were not supposed to be in the lab outside of the day shift. As he got closer, Russell recognized him as Paul Camber, a sales representative for one of the hundreds of companies contracted with the government to supply project parts.

"What the hell is he doing here?" Russell whispered to Michael.

"Go check the power panels," Michael said. "I'll handle this guy."

Russell and Mr. Camber met a month earlier. He left their meeting with a cautionary feeling about this salesman. He had a

10

feeling that Camber was not to be trusted. Paul Camber saw Russell and looked away. Michael stopped Paul and the two briefly talked.

Russell waved his data cell over a sensor in each power panel and the information appeared in a virtual display above that panel. With the data results captured in his cell, he moved to the next panel. He was engrossed in his data retrieval and hadn't noticed Paul Camber had left.

"Russ!" Steven called out. "It's time."

Russell took a deep breath and walked over to Steven. Michael joined them.

"Let's go over it again," Steven said.

Russell rolled his eyes. "How many times do we have to go through this? Like Mike said, I've done this before."

"It's a good idea, Russ," Michael chimed in. "We need to make sure we all know the plan."

"Okay, okay. I'm supposed to check pollution levels in 1992. And then slightly disrupt a specific event to see if there is a butterfly effect across time, right?"

"Exactly," Michael said. "In August of ninety-two a young boy won first place at the Amarillo Fair for his animal. He went on to hold political office in Texas. We want you to change the outcome of him winning that first prize and see if it makes a difference in his future, or anyone else's future."

"How will you know?"

Steven explained. "We recorded the major happenings in the boy's life period. We also recorded what happened to the two runner's up. Those files are sealed away. When you get back we'll record them again and then unseal the pre-recorded files and check for any differences. Now get ready."

"You got six hours," Michael added. "Then we're bringing you back, whether you're finished or not. Got it?"

Russell nodded and smiled at Michael but the smile was not returned. In fact, Michael never raised his eyes to look at Russell.

"Just do what you need to do and then find a place to hide until we retrieve you." Michael walked over to his console and sat without another word.

"What's got into him, all of a sudden?" Russell said under his breath.

Steven shook his head and shrugged his shoulders. "Who knows? Don't worry about it. You know how moody he gets. It's time." Steven walked to his console leaving Russell standing alone in front of the glass chamber that housed the time travel apparatus. Russell took a deep breath and set his ID chip and his data cell in a lockbox. He entered the glass chamber and climbed the two steps leading to the titanium platform. Two six-foot concave disks were mounted on the platform, one silver and one gold. They faced each other and were about three feet apart leaving enough room for Russell to stand between them. Russell positioned himself between the disks and looked through the glass walls at Steven. He looked at Michael, who normally would be watching. Michael sat at his console with both hands on the controls and his back toward Russell.

Steven slipped on his eye protection and gave Russell the thumbs-up. Russell wanted to step away and halt the jump. He couldn't shake the feeling that something wasn't right. He reluctantly returned the thumbs-up signal to Steven. Steven turned to his console and Russell watched the red digital timer across the room start the countdown. When the counter reached one, Russell closed his eyes and held his breath. There was a bright flash of light, a loud snap of electricity, and the glass chamber was empty.

3

Encounter

June, 1892

For the next few years, following his meeting with Captain McMurry, Charlie worked for the bosses of the five major ranches surrounding Amarillo in the panhandle. He got to know all of them fairly well. Mr. Stewart, the ranch manager at the LIT, told Charlie he could bunk in an old deserted buffalo hunter's cabin on the LIT property. The cabin sat atop a wooded bluff overlooking the ranch lands just four miles north of Amarillo. The Amarillo River flowed close by so the cabin always had a good supply of water. This cabin became Charlie's home.

The prisoner trips to the Colorado Territorial Prison became more and more frequent. But he didn't mind. It was easy work, not very dangerous, and it got him away from the ranches and Amarillo for a while. It was a good respite from his routine duties. He would collect prisoners from the jails of neighboring towns and transport them to the territorial prison in Cañon City in the Colorado Territory. Charlie found the trips to Cañon City relaxing.

He loaded the prisoners on the Atchison, Topeka, and Santa Fe railroad in Amarillo and rode it all the way to Cañon City. He normally had around five or six prisoners to contend with. By the time he picked them up and chained them to the floor in a special-built prisoner rail car, the fight was out of them and they were fairly resigned to their fate. All Charlie had to do was sit on a nice cushioned stool for two days and watch the prisoners with a coach gun across his lap. In Cañon City the prison wagon was always there to meet the train. Charlie marched the men off the train and into the wagon. He exchanged signatures and paperwork with the guards and then he was done.

For the first few trips, he would stay in Cañon City anywhere from a day to a week until the next train came by heading back to Amarillo. The waiting was the worst part of the trip. He was bored. While riding the train to and from Cañon City, he longed to be out on the trail again. He missed the solitude and peacefulness of the prairie.

By his fourth trip, he was tired of train travel. This time he loaded Gus into the stable car and brought him along. After the exchange of prisoners with the guards, he and Gus would make their week-long excursion back to Amarillo. He wasn't in any hurry to get back and it wasn't likely he would be missed. These return trips through the prairie gave him time to reminisce about his life and time to think about what future he had left. Charlie made a prisoner trip about every two or three months.

The sun was almost set on this hot June day in 1892. The heat that bore down on Charlie all day long was finally starting to dissipate. He stood next to Gus on a bluff overlooking the town of Tascosa at the end of the Dodge City Trail in the Texas panhandle. This was a bad time to be here. After three long, rough days on the trail, the last place he wanted to be was in Tascosa at night. Usually, on his trips back to Amarillo, he'd stop here for supplies, food, or maybe a drink. This trip was different. He was in a hurry to get back to Amarillo. In his haste, he ended up here a half day sooner than normal.

Charlie knew all too well of the chaos that broke loose in this old cattle town after dark. What little law there was usually turned its back on the ruckus caused by the cowboys and outlaws that frequented the saloons and brothels. He was in no mood to deal with that hell hole tonight. He was tired and sore and all he wanted to do was bed down.

14

He rode wide of the town along the Canadian River bank and crossed the river at Bridge Street. On the other side of the river, he rode a few miles south along the bank through the tall switch-grass and cottonwood trees until he came to a small clearing next to a bend in the river. Charlie unsaddled Gus, removed his bridle and let him roam off to drink and graze while he set about building a fire. There was something comforting about a fire's flickering glow: a source of warmth, relaxation, and light. In the dark lonely plains, it was the perfect companion.

Charlie set out his bed roll near the fire and hung his gun belt over the saddle horn, making sure it was easily accessible. Darkness had engulfed the Great Plains and a cold night was approaching. Charlie sat on a rock next to his saddle and stared into the fire sipping his coffee. The trip from Cañon City, along the Montana Trail to Amarillo was a tough four-day trip for any seasoned rider. At his age, however, it usually took him a good six or seven days. It had taken everything he and Gus could muster to get to this river in just three days.

Charlie hadn't forgotten the orders he got from his new battalion captain, Bill McDonald, before he left Amarillo. He had warned Charlie that Abe Walker was driving his herd up from the Pecos and was heading toward Amarillo. The captain wanted Charlie to get back to Amarillo as quick as he could to help the local lawmen.

Seeing Abe Walker and his cowboy thugs again was a meeting Charlie would rather avoid. In fact, he had purposely and affectively avoided it for the past few years. Walker's last words from their first meeting rang vividly in Charlie's ears. Issues were left unsettled. The next encounter would likely be someone's last. He worried it might be his.

Watching the fire had a hypnotic effect on Charlie. He lost track of time as he watched the flames dance in and around the cottonwood logs. He thought about his age. He'd always believed he could stay young forever. At 51, he could no longer turn his back on his daily aches and pains, his diminished vision, his tiredness and his lack of stamina. To make matters worse, he recently noticed a slight tremble in his hands.

Charlie longed for the vitality and strength of his youth. He wondered if the decision he made when he was young was the right one. He thought about the trouble he caused and the reason he disappeared. He'd been running away from his past his whole life. Over the years he thought about going back, but deep inside he knew that once he left, he would never go back.

Being a Texas Ranger had been Charlie's life. He loved his job, and he was good at it. He poured another cup of coffee, moved to his bedroll and sat on the blanket. He just couldn't see himself doing anything other than what he had done most of his life. His job kept him active. It made him feel useful. He needed a purpose to his life, and his job served that purpose.

Charlie liked his time riding the trails back to Amarillo with Gus, reminiscing of past glory days as they went. All he could reminisce about on this trip, however, was the last time he and Abe Walker crossed paths five years ago.

Charlie remembered that day like it was yesterday. He picked up a small stick and poked it into the dirt over and over. He remembered every shot of every man. He could never forget that awful smell of dust and burnt gunpowder mixed with the odor of all that blood. Over the years he heard about the horrible scar Mac Sherman now had on his forehead. Charlie was certain Mac thought of him every time he looked in a mirror. Most of all, however, the regrettable vision of shooting down Abe's son, Jeremiah, had never left Charlie, even after all these years.

Retirement from working as a Texas Ranger for the past 25 years didn't seem like such a bad idea anymore. When he got back to Amarillo he would talk to the captain about his options; that is if he survived the inevitable confrontation with the cattle baron and his crew. Charlie stood and stretched. He tossed his small stick into the fire. *I should have killed that old man along with his boy.*

He soon shook his thoughts away, and let out a short whistle. Gus walked over near where he was sitting. In all Charlie's years with his horse, Gus had never gotten used to being around a fire. He would come no closer than the ring of light the fire emitted. The larger the fire, the farther he stayed away from it.

Securing the front legs with a hobble just outside the firelight, Charlie stepped back away from the blaze to admire the sky.

"No moon tonight, Gus," he said. "Stars look pretty bright." He patted Gus on his neck, and the gray returned the affection by nudging Charlie's shoulder.

"Good night, ol' pal." Charlie crawled into his bed roll and loosely pulled his blanket over him. As hard and uncomfortable as his bedroll was, his aching body welcomed the reclining position. He rolled on his side to watch the fire. The crackling sounds of a campfire and the soothing babbling of the water rolling over the rocks always soothed him. Before long he was sound asleep.

Charlie woke with a shudder. Had he heard a noise or did he dream he heard something? It took a moment to get his bearings and then he froze. What and from where? His ears strained in the stillness. Nothing. He propped himself up on his elbow and listened more attentively, trying to hear the slightest sound.

Charlie looked over at his horse. Gus was staring intently at him, his eyes wide and his ears pointed, and then gave a low neigh. Something was troubling him. Over the years Charlie had become acutely aware of Gus's slightest movements and noises. He furrowed his brow. *He senses something.*

Charlie got off his make-shift bed and pulled his Colt from the holster. He slowly walked to Gus and put a calming hand on his nose.

"What is it, boy?" he whispered. "What ya' hearin'?"

Charlie backed himself along Gus's side, and out of what little light the dying fire emitted. He didn't want to make himself a target for whoever or whatever might be lurking in the dark.

Gus snorted, and tried to back away from whatever he was sensing, but Charlie grabbed the rope on his halter and held him close.

"Easy there," Charlie urged quietly. He squatted amidst the sagebrush, still clutching the rope in one hand and his Colt in the other. He stared out into the blackness where Gus was facing. Charlie thought this might be one of Walker's advance scouts looking for water and grazing land for tomorrow. But then he reconsidered that notion. It couldn't be. They wouldn't be this far north yet, and they

17

surely wouldn't be riding in the middle of the night. Charlie had to get Abe Walker off his mind. Maybe it was some outlaw from Tascosa out here to do no good. Either way, he stayed out of the fire light.

He listened for any discernible noise in the quiet of the night. He still could not hear or see anything.

Gus snorted again. Charlie had never seen him agitated like this. Gus has been exposed to every kind of critter and varmint there was. He had been around gun battles, chases, and hunts and none of that ever bothered him. However, something was scaring him now. He stared wide-eyed at Charlie.

A slight breeze came out of nowhere. A hot wind started at ground level and seemed to rise up and around them in the cold night air.

Gus shook his head and snorted, his nostrils flared as he tugged to get free of Charlie's grasp. His eyes got wider and his ears were laid back.

The breeze quickly turned into a wind. It raged stronger and stronger. Gus kicked at the wind and pulled hard to break free. Charlie stroked Gus's neck and tried to comfort him to keep him secure. The wind became like a tornado. He grabbed for Gus's rope and reached out for a nearby Mesquite tree for added support and to help keep Gus close.

A blinding bluish light flashed in the prairie. Followed immediately by the loudest clap of thunder Charlie had ever heard. The shockwave knocked him flat on his back, still holding onto Gus's rope. Then, the unsettling calm returned. Charlie sat up and picked up his hat and his gun. He looked around and saw nothing. He heard nothing.

"What the hell was that?" he questioned out loud.

Gus stood calm beside him. The campfire had been blown out and only hot red embers remained in the pit. Charlie put some more wood on the fire and fanned the embers with his hat until the flames started up again. He strapped on his gun belt, holstered his Colt, and walked back over to Gus.

"What do you think?" Charlie stroked the gray's neck and patted his side. "You all right?"

Just then Gus swung his head up and to the side and looked out in the direction the flash had occurred. His ears perked straight up and forward. Then, Charlie heard a snap and the rustle of brush from where the horse was looking. Gus lowered his head and gave out another low warning neigh.

"I heard it too, boy," Charlie said.

Once again Charlie backed out of the fire's light, and squatted near Gus, looking out into the blackness. He watched and waited.

Then he heard another snap, louder this time. Charlie jumped a bit at the sound. The footsteps were getting closer now. Someone, or something, was coming toward the campfire.

Without any warning, a male voice pierced the darkness.

"Anybody there?"

Charlie drew his gun and turned to face the sound. But he kept silent. He backed a little farther into the darkness. Then the rustling and steps stopped.

"Hello? I'm coming in, okay? I don't mean any harm, all right?"

The footsteps started up again. Charlie could only watch and wonder. Following a rustle of sagebrush, a figure, highlighted by the firelight, came out of the darkness.

Charlie's heart pounded so hard it felt like it would explode out his ears. All he could think about was Walker's cowboys. The anxiety of facing any of Walker's men paralyzed him. His mouth was dry and he found himself not breathing. Every muscle in his body felt constricted. His hand shook as he fully cocked his gun and watched the figure approach the camp.

As it advanced into the fire's light, a young man finally came into full view. He stopped at the fire's edge and looked around at the seemingly deserted campsite. Charlie could see this boy was not one of Abe Walker's cowhands and he certainly didn't come from Tascosa. The tension that gripped Charlie only moments before, evaporated. He was mesmerized by this boy's appearance.

Charlie guessed the stranger to be in his early twenties. He had a tall, slender build with reddish brown hair cut short on the sides and left longer on top. He was dressed like no one Charlie had seen in this part of the country. The man had on a tight shirt that was brightly colored in no particular pattern. It had no buttons, no collar, and sleeves cut way above the elbow. His pants were like Strauss's dungarees, but colored a dark blue that looked way too tight. Charlie tipped the brim of his hat back and shook his head. *Nobody could ride a horse in trousers that tight.*

Then he noticed the boy's shoes. They had no heels, no side panels, and no spurs, and almost looked like moccasins, except they were pure white with laces on the front. Charlie shook his head in disbelief. He could only stare in amazement at this young man.

"Hello, anybody here?" the young man called out.

Then the stranger noticed Gus and walked toward him. Charlie watched him coming closer, and in one motion he rose, stepped out of the darkness, and pointed his revolver in the young man's face.

"That's close enough, boy!" Charlie growled.

The stranger was so startled he jumped back, stumbled and fell down. He kept staring up at Charlie, who was barely lit by the fire.

"Who are you and what are you doing in my camp, boy?" Charlie grumbled.

"I ... I ... Jesus!" he stammered.

"Your name 'Jesus', boy?"

"Huh? ... No! ... I mean ... What's going on here?" the stranger asked.

"Well if it ain't Jesus, who are you?" Charlie demanded.

"My name's Russell," the boy said.

"Russell? That's your name, boy? Russell? What kind of name is that?" Charlie demanded.

"My name is Russell Hicks." The young man stared straight into the gun's barrel. "Can you point that thing somewhere else?"

"Hicks?" Charlie repeated, wanting to be certain he heard it right. "Russell Hicks?" The name touched a nerve in Charlie's memory. He repeated the name silently. *Where did I hear that name before?*

"Yeah," Russell replied.

Charlie studied him and could see that he posed no real threat. He un-cocked and holstered his gun. The young man scooted backward a little.

20

"Now, Russell Hicks, what are you doing in my camp, in the middle of this prairie, in the middle of this night?" Charlie stepped closer and frowned, waiting for an answer.

Russell just stared at him with a frightened look on his face. Charlie stared back at him as if looking completely through Russell to what lay behind him. Charlie was trying to find that name in his past. Then it struck him. It was from his childhood. He had met a Russell Hicks when he was a boy. But the Russell Hicks he met was a frail, old man. Charlie filed the memory away and focused his gaze on Russell's face.

"Who are you looking for, boy?" Charlie demanded. "Are you working for Abe Walker?"

"Who? I don't know anyone by that name. I'm trying to ...". Russell stopped speaking and looked around. He appeared unsure of where he was. The expression on Russell's face showed Charlie that this boy was very confused.

"What's today?" Russell finally asked with a frantic note in his voice.

"Today?" Charlie leaned back surprised by his question. "Today is going to be your last day if I don't get me some answers."

"No. I really need to know what day this is," Russell demanded.

Charlie wasn't sure about this young man. "Well, Russell Hicks, I don't rightly know what day it is exactly. Let's see, it was a Sunday when we got to Cañon City. I remember that because the church bells were ringing. Let's see now ..."

"No, no, not the day, the date, the date. I need to know the date! What year is this?"

"Well, it's sometime around the end of June. I know that, and the year is 1892," Charlie answered.

"Damn it!" Russell jumped to his feet and turned his back to Charlie. "Damn, damn, damn it! We missed it! This can't be happening! I'm off a whole frickin' century!"

Russell kicked a small rock and stomped around screaming obscenities and talking crazy about *it* being all wrong.

"Hold up, boy," Charlie said.

But Russell kept on with his tantrum, saying things Charlie didn't quite understand. Things like, this is the wrong time, and the wrong century, and they'll never find him again.

"I said you'd better stop this right now!" Charlie said a little louder.

Yet Russell continued on with his outbursts. Finally Charlie drew his pistol, pointed it skyward, cocked the hammer and pulled the trigger. Russell jumped, and then turned back staring wide-eyed at Charlie. The loud retort shattered the night's stillness and seemed to hang in the air until Charlie finally spoke. "I told you to hush up, boy. And I mean it."

Russell froze, still stunned from the explosion that shocked him into silence. After a short eye-to-eye glaring, Charlie continued. "You feel like explaining your presence to me now? Or do I bury you here tonight?"

Russell's complexion turned an ashen gray as a wisp of smoke drifted out of the barrel of Charlie's gun. He opened his mouth as if to say something but closed it again. Charlie saw the fear in his eyes. He motioned for his visitor to sit down, which Russell did immediately. Charlie holstered his gun and picked up his tin cup and poured himself a luke-warm, stale cup of coffee. He tossed his canteen into Russell's lap and sat on a rock near the fire.

Despite his shaking hands, Russell uncorked the canteen and took a drink, never taking his eyes off Charlie. The two sat in silence for a few moments. Russell was intently staring at Charlie.

"What you lookin' at, boy?"

Russell looked away and just shook his head. A glint of firelight reflected onto Russell's face. He looked down and saw the reflection was from the badge on his vest. "You ever seen a badge like this?"

Russell shook his head again. After a moment he looked at Charlie and broke the awkward silence. "Are you some kind of enforcer or something? A policeman or something?"

"Enforcer?" Charlie looked at the boy with a slight grin. He hadn't heard that term since he was a boy. "I'm a Ranger, boy. A Texas Ranger."

"Oh," Russell managed. "What's a Texas Ranger?"

Charlie glared at him. "The Rangers are a Texas militia. We work for the governor. But, I'm still wantin' to hear about you, and you're wasting my time." Charlie sipped his coffee, waiting for his answer.

"I think I'm lost," Russell finally said. "I think I'm in a lot of trouble."

"Where's your horse? You didn't just walk out here. So, how'd you get out here?"

"You wouldn't believe it." Russell took another drink from the canteen.

"Try me," Charlie encouraged.

"You're going to think I'm crazy, and then you'll probably kill me."

"I think you're crazy now. I'm still deciding about killing you."

Russell was fidgeting, apparently trying to stall for time. Charlie sat patiently waiting for what he imagined would be quite a story.

"Okay. You wanted it, so here goes." He gazed into the fire. "You're not going to believe this." He took a quick glance at Charlie. "But I came from a long way off. A really long way off."

He paused and watched Charlie for some sort of reaction. Charlie sat still and waited. "I actually came here from a … a … another time."

Russell looked at Charlie once more, turned away, and then moved a little closer to the fire.

"I came here from the future," he blurted out.

Charlie sat motionless. Russell froze.

"The future?" Charlie shook his head. "The future?" he repeated.

"Yeah, the future!" Russell turned back to face Charlie. "I know it sounds crazy, and I know you don't believe it, but I swear it's true."

He was almost pleading for Charlie to believe him. There was a long pause as he waited for some kind of reaction.

In a slow, calm voice, Charlie asked, "So what did you come here for?"

23

"That's just it!" Russell said, "I'm not supposed to be here. Well, technically I guess I'm in the right space, but I came to the wrong time! We were aiming for 1992, not 1892! I'm a whole century off!"

Charlie shook his head. He couldn't take his eyes off Russell. He swallowed as if he was trying to keep his insides from spewing out. Something about this Russell Hicks made Charlie very uncomfortable. Old feelings and memories of his past were flooding his mind. It was a cool night, but he could feel the beads of sweat on his forehead. Charlie stood and finished his coffee. "You're loco, boy." He looked over at Gus. The horse looked away. "He thinks you're loco, too."

"I swear to you, it's the truth."

"You need to leave here, boy, and I mean pronto," Charlie said.

"I can't," Russell said.

"Well, you just came here. You ought to be able to just leave here," Charlie reasoned.

"It doesn't work like that. I'm stuck here until an operator moves me."

Russell's words seemed to strike a sudden note of finality in his own mind. He hung his head and stared into the fire, as if suddenly realizing the gravity of his situation.

"Where you from, boy?" Charlie tried to change the subject.

"I'm originally from Connecticut, but I've been living and working in Upton, New York," Russell answered.

"Upton?" Charlie recalled a distant memory of that name.

"It's the government's National Lab facility out on Long Island," Russell said. "We've been working on the development of time travel there for years. One of their clandestine projects that officially doesn't exist."

"Upton," Charlie repeated. He just shook his head while Russell continued to stare into the fire.

"Did you come here for any particular reason?" Charlie asked after a brief silence.

The question was apparently a surprise to Russell. He frowned and had a questioning look in his eyes. "Reason?"

"Yeah. People go places for reasons," Charlie said. "Why did you come here? Are you looking for anyone in particular?"

"No, no it's nothing like that," Russell explained. "I was going to the nineteen-ninety's for two reasons, actually. I wanted to find out how polluted their environment was. And, I was supposed to test a theory about what affect a disruption in the past could have on the future."

Charlie let out a sigh of relief and relaxed. "Well, I don't care about any of that. All I know is that you can't stay here. I don't need you around me right now. You have no idea what a mess of trouble you just rolled into. And you are just one more problem I don't have time for. The question is what am I going to do with you?"

"Wait," Russell said. "Do you understand anything I just talked about?"

Charlie leaned in closer to Russell and glared at him. "I think I know who you really are. I've been looking over my shoulder for 30 years, wondering if that stranger eyeing me is the one or not. Whether I know what you're talking about or not don't matter. It don't change nothing. You still can't stay here."

Russell's eyes widened. He had a shocked look on his face. He just stared at Charlie and then suddenly shivered from the cold night air.

"Put that blanket around you." Charlie pointed to his bedroll.

Russell pulled the blanket around him. He looked at Charlie. "Thanks." He stared into the fire, watching the flames lick back and forth among the logs, apparently trying to grasp the situation he'd been thrust into.

Charlie untied his duster from behind his saddle and draped it over his own shoulders to guard against the cool night air. He too stared into the fire.

Charlie mumbled to himself under his breath. "I've been trying to hide from you all my life."

Charlie continued watching the fire, never once looking up to see if Russell was watching him or listening to him.

If Russell heard the old lawman mumbling, he never acknowledged his words. The two sat silently watching the fire dance in the night. Charlie now had this boy to deal with. What to do with him? His thoughts of Russell were soon replaced with the consuming thoughts of his upcoming meeting with the cattle baron. He couldn't shake the fear of facing Mac Sherman and Abe Walker. Yet, as the fire created dark shadows that danced among the trees, he knew the unavoidable showdown was coming … and soon.

4

The Trip Home

As the sun crested over the eastern hills, a beam of sunlight crept across Charlie's forehead and struck his eyes. He sat up, startled awake. He had slept on the ground next to his saddle. *The sun's up. Why was it so late in the day?* His conscious mind pulled together the events from the previous night. He looked over at his bedroll and it was still occupied by that stranger. *What was his name? Oh yeah, Russell, - from the future.*

He cursed the light. Usually by the time the sun rose, he had broken camp and had been on the trail for a while. Now the day was going to be longer than he wanted. The trip home over the prairie would be during the hottest part of the day.

Charlie wasn't sure when he'd fallen asleep. The last thing he remembered was staring into a dying fire pit. Over the years, Charlie's body became trained to wake in that gray dawn just before the light of the sun begins to push away the dark. That, of course, assumed he got a reasonable amount of sleep the night before. Last night was not a reasonable amount of sleep. Last night was not a reasonable night.

He struggled to pull himself up out of the dust. The aches and pains of an older worn out body were intensified from sleeping on the cold ground. He stretched to loosen as many muscles and joints as he could. A snap in his neck, a pop in his knee, and a sharp pain in his shoulder all brought back memories of the hard times of his younger days.

He made his way to where Gus stood. He patted the horse's neck and removed the hobble. Gus walked off to the river to drink and graze a while before the trip home.

The fire had died down to just smoke and hot cinders. A few tongues of fire occasionally spurted from a burnt log in the pit. Charlie refilled his coffee pot at the river and poured the last of his crushed coffee beans into the pot. Then he set it dead center on the hottest coals he could find.

From his saddlebags he retrieved his last can of peaches and a folded up oilcloth that contained his loose food supply. It held four hard-packed corn biscuits that he called "dodgers", and some chunks of jerked beef. He poured a cup of lukewarm coffee for himself and sat down on a rock by his saddle. He dipped a dodger in the coffee and chewed on the biscuit while he watched his unwelcomed guest sleep. *What to do with this boy?*

He was sure Russell would wake up with all the commotion he was causing. But there he lay, with the sun shining bright in his face, sleeping as if it were the middle of the night. He finished his biscuit and pulled a knife from the sheath on his belt and cut open the top of the can of peaches. After eating a few of the peaches, Charlie couldn't wait any longer. He stood up and nudged Russell with his boot. "On your feet, boy. The day's half gone already."

The sleeping stranger moved a little under the blanket and then groaned. Charlie laid another boot on him, a little harder this time.

"Come on, you. Time to get moving," Charlie said a little louder.

Russell opened his eyes and looked around. He squinted from the bright sunshine and appeared a little confused. He looked up at Charlie and seemed to remember the night before and where he was.

"What time is it?" Russell asked.

"Are you starting that again?" Charlie said. "It's late. We should have been on the trail hours ago. Let's hurry up."

He watched Russell struggle to his feet and look around. Charlie continued to break camp. Since he only had one tin cup with him, Charlie finished drinking his coffee and then refilled the same cup for Russell. Charlie tossed the oil cloth to Russell. In it Russell found the dried corn biscuits and a few chunks of seasoned dried beef. Charlie told him it was his food for the day.

Charlie pointed to the fire pit. "There's a cup of coffee and some peaches sitting on that rock next to the fire." He poured the rest of the coffee from the pot into the fire pit, rinsed the pot, and tied his gear up with his bedroll.

Russell picked up the cup and took a sip and quickly spit it out. Charlie looked over at Russell with a frown.

"What's the matter?" Charlie asked

"This is the worst coffee I ever tasted. There's chunks of soggy beans floating in it."

"That's all the coffee you'll get," Charlie said. Russell choked down the next sip and shuddered as he swallowed.

"You make one hell of a cup of coffee," he said barely under his breath.

Charlie smirked. He threw a blanket across Gus and led him back to the campsite. Putting on the bridle, he picked up the saddle and threw it across the blanket and cinched up the straps. Then he loosely tied the reins to a nearby mesquite tree.

"One more thing and then we go." Charlie strapped on his gun belt.

"Go? You mean leave here?"

Charlie emptied his two canteens onto the fire to extinguish any remaining hot coals, and then went to the creek to refill them with cool, fresh water.

"I have to be in Amarillo as soon as possible. That's my order." Charlie hung the two canteens on his saddle horn and picked up Gus's water bladder. He looked Russell square in the eye. "Yes! We're leaving here. And right now!"

Charlie filled Gus's water bladder and tied it to the saddle just below his rifle scabbard.

"I can't go. They'll be looking for me here. I have to stay in this space! If I leave they'll never find me." Russell gulped down the last of the peaches.

"You can't stay here, boy. You'll never survive," Charlie said. "This sun will kill you, especially dressed like … like … well, whatever it is you're dressed like."

"What's wrong with the way I'm dressed? This is historically accurate to what young people wore in the 1990s."

"Well, they must not be riding range a hundred years from now." Charlie picked up his saddle bags, stopped, and gave Russell one more questioning look.

Russell didn't move.

Charlie shook his head. "Well, I can't force you to go. You do what ya' like. You'd just slow me down anyway. It's probably best that you stay away from Amarillo, with what's coming."

After tying down his saddle bags, Charlie swung up into the saddle. Russell stared up at him, confusion in his face.

"You coming or ain't ya'?" Charlie said. Russell didn't answer. "Suit yourself." He turned Gus upstream and started walking him back toward the trail to Amarillo. After a few steps Gus stopped.

"What now, you old plug?" Charlie tried nudging him on, but Gus stayed still. The horse turned slightly and looked back at Russell as if to tell Charlie that he shouldn't leave the visitor here.

"Well, you'd better come along or this old horse won't move a step," Charlie said. "You're lucky, boy. He likes you."

"Give me one minute." Russell took a stick and scratched *AMARILLO* in the dirt next to the fire pit and then walked over and joined Charlie and Gus. They left the clearing together and headed back to the southbound trail.

Charlie rode Gus while Russell walked alongside. Charlie stopped and looked up at the sun. It was already getting hot. He took off his jacket and tossed it to Russell.

"Are you crazy?" Russell said. "I'll burn up in that thing."

"You'll burn up without it," Charlie said. "If you don't cover up that lily-white skin of yours that sun will cook you. Now take it and put it on."

Reluctantly, Russell slipped on the oversized jacket and turned the collar up to protect his neck from the sun.

"You ever been on a horse?"

"No. There aren't a lot of horses left where I come from. People don't ride horses anymore. They travel around in PTU's." Russell looked at Charlie. Charlie didn't change his expression. "PTU's are personal transportation units. Some still have old cars, but most are being phased ..." Russell again looked up at Charlie and shook his head. "Never mind."

"Well I'll be damned," Charlie finally said. "No horses. You hear that, Gus? You're going to retire." Charlie had a pretty good idea what Russell was talking about, but he kept quiet and just let Russell talk. It had been thirty years since he heard a lot of those terms. Charlie thought that maybe this so-called time-traveler didn't hear his mumblings last night. At least he was hoping so.

Charlie looked down at the boy. "Well, you sure can't walk to Amarillo in those ugly old shoes you got on. Charlie pulled his foot out of the stirrup and offered it to Russell. Here, step on this stirrup and swing yourself up behind me. Gus can carry both of us for a while."

Russell hoisted himself up on Gus and sat on the edge of the blanket behind the saddle. With each movement of the horse, Russell would squirm and let out a grunt.

"Something wrong?" Charlie asked over his shoulder.

"These pants are scratching my legs."

"Well, it's better than walking - at least for now." Charlie smiled.

After riding for a little while Russell asked "How far do we have to go?"

Charlie pointed to a far off crest that rose off the prairie floor. "You see that ridge along the horizon up ahead?"

"Yeah, I see it. Is that where we have to go?"

"Well, there's another ridge just like it and twice as far on the other side of that ridge. We have to go over that second ridge and then down through a small valley after that," Charlie explained.

Russell let out an audible sigh. Charlie lowered his eyes and shook his head. *What did I get myself into?* This was going to be a very trying day for both of them.

"There's a good sized creek that runs along the base of that second ridge," Charlie said, "with the coolest and freshest water in these parts. We'll rest up there."

After riding at a quick lope for a while, Charlie and Russell both dismounted and walked, giving Gus a much needed rest from the burden of two riders. Russell had been talking about bending space, worm holes, and time theorems. He kept rattling on and on about the dimensional matrix that made time travel possible. In fact, he talked most of the morning away. Charlie just let this stranger ramble on to help pass the time.

By midday they had crossed over the first ridge. Sweat poured off Russell. His face was bright red and he was beginning to stumble. During the past few hours they had taken turns riding single on Gus, then letting him walk free, and then doubling up on him.

Charlie kept an eye on Russell. This was dangerous country for a seasoned outdoorsman. It was almost always fatal for the novice. Charlie poured some water onto his neckerchief and wrapped it around Russell's head to cool and shade him.

They were at the south base of the first ridge looking over the dried bitter grasses and clusters of sagebrush that covered most of the flat terrain. There was nothing else. There was no movement except for an occasional hot dry breeze.

Charlie handed Russell one of the two canteens. The young stranger took a long swallow and then handed it back. Charlie took a small sip, put the wooden plug back in, and hung it from the saddle horn.

"That's all you're going to drink?" Russell asked.

"For now. Not sure if any of the creeks we'll pass will be running or not," Charlie said. "There was a pretty good snowfall this past winter so we should have a good water supply on the way. But, just in case, I'll drink as little as possible."

Up to this point, Charlie had been pouring water from Gus's water bag into his hat and letting the gray drink a bit from the hat. It was just enough to fend off dehydration and cool him down a little.

They started to walk across the flat land between the two ridges. The heat rose from the prairie floor, distorting the grass and brush and giving the impression of it being under water. The heat mirages were so thick they reflected the color of the sky and it looked as if there was a giant blue sea just out of reach.

Charlie had been walking alongside Gus for quite a while before he finally stopped and rested his feet. The sun had moved a bit off to Charlie's right.

"Must be around two," he mused. "Time to make tracks."

Russell was almost unconscious from the heat. He was barely able to hang onto the saddle horn to keep from falling off.

"I hate to do this to you, Gus, but you have got to get us to that ridge. Poor Russell here don't look so good."

"I'll … be … fine," Russell said between short breaths.

Charlie climbed onto Gus behind the saddle. He put his arms around Russell's ribs to grab the reins and tapped the horse with his heels. "Heeya!" he yelled, and Gus took off at a run.

After a while, Charlie could feel Gus laboring under the weight of the two riders and the intense heat. But he needed him to make up some time.

When they were halfway to the second ridge, he pulled up on Gus's reins and slid down off the side. Gus was winded He blew hard and white foam formed around his mouth. Charlie pulled Russell off and laid him down on the dirt with his head on the shady side of a sagebrush. It was enough shade to keep the sun from directly hitting his face. He pulled the two canteens and took a long swallow from the first canteen. He soaked Russell's neckerchief and then poured some down his throat. Russell choked a bit and then took another swallow.

"You doing okay?" Charlie asked.

"I'll make it," Russell said. "Thanks for the water."

Charlie stood and left one canteen with Russell. He pulled the near-empty water bladder off his saddle. He poured the remaining water into his hat for Gus who downed it in seconds.

"That's all you get for now," Charlie said softly. "Can't risk you gettin' sick on us." He patted the horse's nose.

They sat on the floor of the ancient lakebed for a few minutes to give themselves a rest and to give Gus a chance to catch his breath. Gus walked around a bit and Charlie poured a little more water from the second canteen into his hat and Gus again slurped it up. Then Charlie announced that it was time to go. Russell said he felt pretty good and would try walking for a while so the three headed off toward the second ridge and the promise of a drink of cool creek water. Charlie and Russell again swapped out riding Gus and walking. However, after just a short while, Russell became affected by the heat and ended up riding most of the way.

By the time they reached the base of the second ridge, Russell was barely conscious and was slumped forward in the saddle. Charlie had walked most of the way on his own He was just about out of energy, out of wind, and dead on his feet.

Gus smelled the cool water and began to pick up the pace. A smile formed on the cracked lips of Charlie. A tear formed in his eye from joy and relief. He knew he was as good as home now and kept up with Gus's hurried pace.

"This is it, Gus," Charlie shouted as he hurried to the creek full of clear cool water.

He pulled the empty water bag off the side of the saddle and the two empty canteens and knelt down by the creek.

He shoved his head under the water and let the soothing coolness of the water spread throughout his body. He drank a few handfuls of water, filled each canteen and then dunked the water bag into the water until it was full. Gus walked over to the creek and started to drink. Charlie pulled him away and poured some water from his water bag into his hat and let him sip some water from it. He poured some water over Gus's neck and head to help cool him down. Charlie pulled Russell off the horse and set him along the southeast side of the rocks in the shade. He dipped the neckerchief that Russell was wearing into the creek and laid it across the boy's head. Charlie handed him a full canteen of cool water.

"Here you go, boy. You can drink all you want, there's plenty more. Just drink it slow with small sips."

Russell took a couple of big drinks and choked.

"Easy, boy," Charlie cautioned, "Your tongue swells up in the heat and makes it hard to swallow. Sip it easy or you'll get sick."

Charlie led Gus into the creek and continued to cool him by letting him sip a little water and then dumping a hatful of water over his body. When the horse seemed to be cooled enough, Charlie sat down next to Russell and drank from the other canteen. The two sat in silence just taking in the cool water and resting in the shade.

"I've got a cabin just this side of the town," Charlie said. "It's an old buffalo hunter's cabin. It ain't much but it keeps me dry and comfortable."

"How ... how ... far is your place?" Russell asked between breaths and swallows.

"Not far, now. Maybe another hour or so."

Russell nodded and took another sip from the canteen.

"Just over this ridge the prairie turns into a valley of sweet range grass. It's beautiful," Charlie smiled at the thought of the valley he just described. He never gets tired of seeing the grass in the valley swaying in the breeze.

"Sounds nice," Russell said.

"Yeah. The stream that flows here feeds that valley. Just before we get into Amarillo there's a little trail that cuts off to the left and heads up into LIT territory. That's where my place is."

"LIT territory?" Russell asked.

"It's a big ranch," Charlie explained. "A few years back, a bunch of smaller outfits banned together and formed these organizations. They took over all the land. There's the LIT ranch to the west, which we just rode through. Then there's the LX ranch, which is a little east of here and just north of Amarillo. The Frying Pan ranch is a bit further east. There's a couple of others."

"And your cabin is on the LIT Ranch?" Russell asked.

"Well, it's not really my cabin. Years ago, all this area used to be overrun with buffalo. Thousands of them. Hunters would come here from all over, and when they killed their fill, they'd move on. Some of them built some small cabins to stay in during the hunt."

"How'd you get the cabin?"

"The Rangers got sent here a while back to stop mavericks and cattle rustlers. We got to where we were real friendly with the ranchers. I got to know the ranch manager pretty well so he told me I was welcome to use the old buffalo cabin. I've been there ever since." The two sat watching the sun get lower in the sky.

Finally Russell broke the silence. "You mentioned some trouble last night and again this morning. What kind of trouble are you talking about?"

"It don't concern you," Charlie said gruffly.

Russell let his question drop. Gus nudged Charlie in the back. It was time to go.

"Damn horse must be in a hurry." Charlie stood and stretched. The sun was low enough to head toward the cabin without Russell drawing too much attention. The three climbed the ridge.

At the top of the ridge Charlie and Russell both climbed on Gus. The horse walked with ease now, rejuvenated from the water, the rest, and relief from the sun's heat.

Charlie was thinking about his cabin and the comforts of home. He was thinking about Amarillo. He wasn't worried about his surroundings anymore, and he hadn't thought about Abe Walker or Mac Sherman all day.

As they started their easy descent from the top of the ridge the valley rich with range grass came into view. The grass swayed in the breeze like ripples on a lake.

"This is beautiful. Just like you said." Russell looked over the valley and all around. Then he chuckled.

"What's so funny?" Charlie asked.

Russell pointed to the dust cloud on the horizon in the southwest. "That's what our skies look like all the time where I come from."

Charlie looked off to where Russell gazed and his thoughts of home evaporated. The calm, contented demeanor quickly changed to concern. "Damn!"

"Is that a dust storm or something?" Russell asked.

Charlie ignored the question.

"Abe Walker. Son-of-a-bitch! He got here quicker than I expected. This ain't gonna be good," Charlie said out loud, not really meaning it for anyone's ears.

"Who's Abe Walker? And what does he have to do with that cloud?" Russell asked.

"That's not a cloud, boy. Its cattle, thousands of them kicking up dust. And they all belong to Abe Walker. You wanted to know what trouble is? That's it. There's always trouble when Abe and his crew get near a town."

"You know this fellow?" Russell's brow creased.

"Yeah," Charlie said solemnly, "We've met." He spurred his horse forward.

Gus occasionally tried to step off the trail into the grass to eat a bit. Charlie coaxed him back onto the trail and toward his cabin. After seeing Abe and his cattle drive approaching, getting back seemed more urgent.

By the time they reached the turnoff to Charlie's cabin the sun was set and everything was awash in a blue-gray hue. Just light enough to find their way up into the rocks and trees. They were finally home. What a trip. Four long hard days on the road and a new visitor who gave Charlie a new challenge. With Abe Walker and his crew only a day or so out, and with his new 'guest', Amarillo will be an interesting place tomorrow.

5

Cabin

Charlie didn't care about the appearance of his home. The old buffalo hunter's cabin fit the description of a shelter, but that was about it. It was crude and small. He never figured on entertaining house guests so the upkeep of the place was of no concern to him. It kept him warm and dry and that's all he needed.

The structure was tucked up among the cottonwood trees just up the hill from the Amarillo River. It wasn't all that much of a river, more of a creek. In drought conditions it occasionally would run dry. In the rainy season it could become a raging torrent.

Outside, along the left side of the cabin, between the back wall and the side of the hill, Charlie had fashioned a stall for Gus. He built it into the side of the hill, and extended an outcropping of wood planks from the hillside to the side of the house. It was large enough for Gus to lie down in and stay out of the weather.

It was almost dark when they entered the cabin of rough-hewn logs sealed with mud and small stones. A stale musty odor of a closed up space hung in the air. Charlie struck a stick match and lit a lantern that was sitting on a small wooden table in the middle of the room. Charlie walked across the mismatched, flat, river-bed rocks that made up the floor of his small rectangular home. He opened the inner shutters covering the only two windows and pushed open the outside shutters to get some air circulating. One wooden chair sat next to the table and a wooden stool rested against the back wall. By the look on Russell's face it was plain to see that he was surprised at Charlie's meager living conditions.

"You're really livin' high style here, aren't you?" Russell said.

"I don't need much. Stay inside here and keep quiet. I've got to take care of some things." Charlie went back outside and led Gus to his stall along the left side of the cabin.

Gus walked under the outcropping and looked into his empty grain bin. He gave a long, low snort at Charlie.

"I'll get ya' some oats later. You just hold on a minute." Charlie pulled a log across the make-shift corral entrance. He grabbed an old wooden bucket and headed down to the stream at the bottom of the hill to get water. It was a small river that was too shallow and moved too fast to have any fish in it. But it was a great source of fresh water. Charlie brought back a full bucket, emptied it into Gus's trough, and went back for a second bucketful. When he returned, he pulled off the saddle and bridle and poured the water over Gus to clean and cool him down.

After he wiped him down and brushed him, he dug a full shovel of grain from a wooden barrel he kept covered on the side of the house and poured them into Gus's grain bin. The horse ate them in a few bites.

Russell sat in the chair by the table and looked around the inside of the cabin. Other than the table, chair and stool, a small hand-built rope bed holding a thin straw mattress stood along a side wall. It was crude and looked as if it were fashioned out of old support timbers or railroad ties. Russell curled his lip. *That can't be comfortable.* He wondered where he was going to sleep.

At the foot of the bed sat an old, badly worn leather-bound trunk with a rusty padlock securing its lid. In the back corner of the cabin stood a small round iron stove. A coffee pot sat inside an iron skillet that rested on top of the stove. Along the back wall was the only real piece of furniture in the place, a nicely finished washstand with a marble top. A wooden bucket sat on the floor next to the stand and a metal bowl on the marble top. A small, cracked mirror hung from a string above the washstand.

Russell heard Charlie attending to Gus outside. He walked to the stove, opened the small metal door and stared at the remnants of past fires. Where he came from, fires were started with the flick of a switch, a controlled chemical reaction rather than the actual consumption of any fuel, like coal or wood.

When Charlie returned to the cabin he stopped at the open front door and watched Russell stare at the cold empty stove. He smiled. "That's a stove. When there's something burning in it, it heats the place up."

His voice appeared to startle Russell for a moment and the young man turned and backed away from the stove.

"I ... I wasn't sure. I ..." Russell stammered.

"It's no big mystery, you know. You put some wood in it and light it up. Ain't you ever built a fire, boy?"

"NO!" Russell shouted. "I never built a fire! And my name is Russell! Not Boy!"

"You're gettin' kind of touchy, here." Charlie paused and gave Russell an icy stare. He saw the fear, the hurt, and the anger in Russell's and eyes. He too was cold, sore, hungry, and tired, and he was sure Russell was even more so. The meager corn biscuits and dried beef had done little to satisfy their hunger. Charlie was sure that the last twenty-four hours demanded more physical exertion from Russell than he had ever done in his entire life.

"All right, it's Russell." Charlie said with a calm voice. "But remember, you're the one who came here. I didn't invite you."

Russell hung his head and looked away from Charlie. Charlie could see that his last remark hit a nerve.

Charlie stepped to the stove and threw in some paper, dried twigs, straw, small kindling, and a couple of larger sticks. He held a small stick over the top of the lantern and within seconds the tip was ablaze. He carefully lit the kindling in the stove and after a few moments a fire was beginning to blaze. Russell seemed spellbound as he watched the process.

"That's all there is to it." Charlie closed the fire door on the stove.

"Oh, I see," Russell mumbled. "The only fires I know about are enclosed technologically controlled chemical fires. I've never seen any actual open flames."

The small room was beginning to warm. Charlie pulled the stool away from the wall and sat down at the table across from Russell and stared at him.

"What's wrong?" Russell asked.

"What's wrong? Everything! All of this is wrong. You don't belong here."

"Do you?" Russell snapped.

The comment took Charlie by surprise. His eyes widened and he paused for a second. How much had Russell figured out about him?

"You be careful with me, BOY!" Charlie warned. "Now I want to know why you're really here. I want to know what I'm supposed to do with you. And, I want to know how I'm going to get rid of you."

Russell stood up, cast an angry look at Charlie, and moved a little closer to the warmth of the stove. Charlie watched as Russell's expression changed to a solemn look as the seriousness of his situation appeared to sink in.

"It was a mistake." Russell lowered his head and his voice. "It really was just a mistake. You can do what you like. I'll never get back anyway. I'm dead any way you look at it."

Charlie let out a heavy sigh. He remembered his own past of being alone and lost in a strange place. He reluctantly had to rely on the help of strangers. Charlie began to feel a little sorry for this time traveler. He let the subject drop until later. Until he got the answers he was looking for, he'd have to keep an eye on Russell.

"Come on and sit down. I'll fix up something to eat." Charlie offered the chair to Russell and smiled.

Charlie kept the remnants of a large smoked ham butt wrapped in an oil cloth and stored in a wooden box on a shelf near the stove. He cut two large slices and dropped them in the iron skillet and added a little water. From another box he pulled a stale bread loaf and cut two large pieces.

"Use this to sop up any meat drippings. The bread's too hard to eat otherwise," Charlie said.

Russell watched Charlie cook. The smell of ham steaks filled the room and caused his digestive system to start rumbling.

"Who's this Abe Walker guy?" Russell asked.

"He's a hard case. A fella you don't want to mess with. That's who he is," Charlie said.

"Why?"

"Because he'd kill ya' just as soon as look at ya'. He's a big bug in the cattle business. He came through a lot of tough times, and he lives by his own rules; always has. Trouble is he tends to push those rules on the people he comes in contact with along the way."

"Why is he coming here?"

"Hell. You sure got a lot of questions," Charlie said. "Well, he's coming here to sell his cows. He used to take his herd to Wichita or Dodge. That's where his cattle got sold and shipped by rail all over the country. That's where the money was."

Charlie turned the ham steaks over, added a little more water to the pan, then set the stale bread chunks on top of them in the skillet so they would steam and soften a bit. Russell came back to the table and sat down, intently listening as Charlie told his story.

"But, in the last few years, with two railroads coming through here, Amarillo has built up a top notch cattle business. Now it's finally big enough to handle Walker's herd. He gets as much money here as he would in Wichita and it saves him another few weeks or so on the trail."

"Why is he so mean?"

"He had a tough time of it. That kind of life would make anybody mean." Charlie sat on the stool watching the ham steaks cook and occasionally looking at Russell. "Abe came through Texas heading west with his wife and baby boy after the war, sometime in the seventies. I'm not sure exactly when. He and his family were part of a small train heading to California. He had a good bull and a few cows with him." Charlie stood and checked the steaks. "Way I hear it, as he came through Texas he began picking up strays along the way. He picked up so many, in fact that by the time he reached the Pecos, he had pulled together a pretty good sized herd. He decided to pull out

42

of the wagon train and settle right there along the Pecos River. That area was right on the edge of Indian Territory. At that time, he was one of only a few white men that ever came west to the Pecos."

"Just him and his family?" Russell asked.

"Yup. Just them," Charlie answered. "Like everyone else that came west, they were looking to make a new life. At that time, the only people in that part of the country were tribes of Navajo and Ute Indians and a few locals trying to scratch out an existence from some very rough country. Neither group was very friendly to the whites moving into the area. Texas was just a fledgling republic. They were getting used to their independence from Mexico. There was still a lot of bad blood between Mexico and Texas, and no law there. The army and the few towns and outposts were miles and miles away."

"My God, how did they survive?" Russell asked.

"He did what he had to do. All them settlers did," Charlie said. "It was that or die. This country is not very hospitable. He had to fight the weather, the land, marauding Indians, and bands of Mexican banditos. It was a daily struggle and it made him a very hard man. He didn't like or trust nobody."

Russell just shook his head. "That must've been rough. How anybody could go through that every day? It's unbelievable."

"It got worse," Charlie said. "Abe lost his wife in an Indian attack a couple of years in. That loss made him a very bitter man and even more ornery, if that was possible. Then it was just him to raise his only son, Jeremiah."

"How did he get so many cattle?" Russell asked.

"Walker wasn't the only one to come out to the Pecos. There were a couple of others and they all just claimed as much land as they could homestead. They had huge cattle empires with thousands of head of cattle on hundreds of thousands of acres. These big ranchers sort of banded together and watched out for each other. They made their own rules as they went. Their law was the only law in the Pecos valley and they dealt it out at will and harshly."

"I can't believe someone could live like that." Russell said again.

"Well, you'll never forget how hard today's ride was on you," Charlie said. "Well, imagine working and living in that every day."

Charlie set down a knife and a metal pie pan that held a thick ham slice and a steamed chunk of bread. Russell gave a crooked smile to Charlie as a thanks for some hot food.

"The outside of that ham steak is cured and packed in salt to preserve it. You might not like that part." Charlie stabbed the steak with his knife and took a bite from it.

Russell didn't seem to care. Salt or no salt, he ate like he was starving.

Charlie continued his story. "Eventually, like everywhere else, settlers, farmers, smaller ranchers, and traders, started moving into the land west of the Pecos. They were all trying to carve out a piece of land and a new life for themselves. These newcomers started little settlements that grew into towns. This was another thorn in Abe's side. He liked his solitude and hated people. At first, the cattle barons tried to force them out of the area, but they still kept coming. So, since they couldn't force them out, they decided to control them. The cattlemen set up their own people as law and government officials. They set up their own banks, supply stores, saloons and any other business they could think of to try and drive the settlers out of business and out of the area."

"Why didn't the government step in and do something?" Russell asked.

"There wasn't any government. The army was too far away to be of any use. The only law was the cattlemen's law. Eventually the town folk got tired of it. They wanted their own elected government, statehood, army protection, and other things civilized people demand. There was a huge power struggle. Most of the other cattle barons just sold off and moved out. Walker decided to stay. A lot of them sold off their herds and land to Abe. In some areas of Walker's land you can see from one horizon to the other and it would all belong to Abe Walker."

"That's hard to imagine," Russell said

"Over the years, Abe never changed. He kept to himself and ran his land with the same iron-fisted law he first brought to the Pecos. That's all he knew. And when he traveled anywhere, his law went with him. His cowhands are all hard working, hard living men. Most of them have shady pasts. Abe has a lot of gun hands who are not afraid

44

of a fight. Most of the older ones were seasoned ex-army from both sides in the War. When they get to a town and let loose it's usually at the expense of some people and property."

"How'd you get involved with him?" Russell asked.

Charlie explained the story of how he and the deputy marshals first came into contact with Abe Walker. Abe blamed Charlie and all lawmen for the death of his son and vowed he would take an eye for an eye.

"So, how often do they come here?" Russell asked.

"It's been a couple of years, I guess," Charlie recalled. "I wasn't here the last time they came through. But I heard that a couple of Abe's cowhands got drunk and started a gun fight in Amarillo. A lot of bullets were fired and a lot of those shots went wild. One bullet wounded a woman and another one killed her son. They were just walking by outside. The town was outraged. City Marshall Cook arrested the two gunmen, but Abe came in that night and took the two hands back to camp with him. They broke camp the next day and no one has seen either of them two cowboys since.

"What happened to them?" Russell asked.

Charlie let that question hang. He stopped at this point and looked at his bed.

"Well, morning has a way of sneaking up on us around these parts. We'd better get some sleep." Charlie stood and grabbed the bedroll and his saddle. "You sleep here on this bed. It ain't much, but it's softer than the floor."

"What about you?" Russell asked.

"I'll be all right. Gus is pretty warm and he won't mind the company at all."

With bedroll in hand he shut the two inside window shutters and blew out the lantern. The glow of the fire burning in the stove seeped out along the edges of the fire door and gave a strange red glow to the cabin's interior. Charlie stepped out and shut the door behind him. In the darkness he felt his way around to the make-shift corral. Gus stirred a bit but then settled down after realizing who was coming to visit.

Charlie had a plan. He had to get to town first thing in the morning. He had things to do before anyone knew he was back.

EDWARD L GATES

6

Doc Morgan

The sun shone through the crudely hewn slats that made up the old shutters in Charlie's cabin. A sudden breeze blew against the house and rattled the door. The noise jostled Russell from his sleep. He looked around and shaded his eyes from the light. Morning did come quick, just as Charlie mentioned. He felt like he'd hardly slept at all.

Outside he heard the birds chirping and the sound of water flowing along the bottom of the hillside. He could hear the breeze as it drifted through the tree limbs and scattered the fallen leaves across the ground. However, he didn't hear any movement from Gus's corral. He wondered if Charlie was still asleep.

He rolled on his back and stared at the thatched roof above him, reflecting on the previous day. It was still all so surreal. He was hoping this was all a bad dream and he would awake in his apartment in his complex. He had time-jumped before, but this was the first time there'd ever been a problem. He was rationalizing his situation and was sure that his operators were working on the problem from the other side of the time matrix. Surely they wouldn't let him hang in another time dimension. They wouldn't assume the worst and just write him off that quickly as a casualty of a flawed dimensional matrix. Would they?

He was rolling over in his mind the possible causes of the blunder that landed him in the old west during the 19th century. He sat up in bed. Wait a minute, could they have done this intentionally? He was now wide awake. He wondered why someone would do that to him.

The fear of never being able to return to his own time overwhelmed him. A warm flush of blood coursed through his body and beads of sweat emerged on his forehead. What would he do? He was trying to imagine his life in this time. The anxiety of being stuck in a place and time that was so foreign to him consumed him. He was finding it difficult to breathe. He didn't know the first thing about survival practices. Charlie was right. He'd never survive out here by himself.

He thought about Charlie. He smiled thinking about Charlie. What a character he was. His anxiety began to abate. What did he say when they first met? "I know about you." Russell wondered what good ol' Charlie meant by that.

Russell pulled his tired, sore body out of the bed and stretched his back. His entire body ached from the uncomfortable trip to the cabin from the Canadian River. Sleeping on that bed didn't help at all. How these people survived day after day in these conditions was a wonder to him. What a horrible bed, he thought. He slept better on the ground of the prairie the night before. He pulled open the shutter and let in the daylight. He picked up one of his shoes from next to the bed and slipped it on but didn't see the other shoe. It must have been kicked under the bed. He reached under the bed, but couldn't feel it. He got down on his hands and knees and looked, but it wasn't there. He stood and looked around the cabin, but it was gone. He scratched his head in thought. *Where the hell is my other shoe?*

Charlie sat atop his grey gelding in the early morning shadows of the livery stable watching the townspeople coming and going through the different establishments. There were too many people around to take a chance on being recognized. Mornings were the busiest times in Amarillo. People came to town early to get their business done before the heat of day made it too uncomfortable.

Amarillo had a central street, named Polk Street that ran perpendicular to the rail tracks and featured a row of businesses along

48

both sides of the dirt thoroughfare. A few cross streets intersected this central street and led to residential areas around the town. Amarillo was not a very large city in 1892. Its population was only around 600 people, and a good number of them still lived about a mile away in the original settlement which had become known as Old Town.

On the west side of town, along the railroad tracks running around Wild Horse Lake, was nothing but stock yards and corrals. They stretched all the way around Old Town and all along the rail line as it turned north.

Livestock was the main commerce in Amarillo. The brokers dealt in all kinds of livestock, but mostly cattle. Herds from all around the south and the west came through Amarillo to be shipped by rail. It was the best place to ship livestock to all parts of the country.

There was virtually no breeze this morning, so dust from the stockyards hung thick in the air. The sun filtering though these dust particles turned the air a golden yellow and cast a bronze hue over the entire town. With no breeze, the stench from the stockyards was almost choking.

Charlie knew that as soon as he was spotted in town, Captain Bill McDonald would find some task to assign to him. He didn't have time for that right now. Charlie maneuvered Gus out of sight behind the livery barn. He wanted to get his business done and get back to his cabin before anyone knew he had returned from Cañon City.

Charlie walked Gus along the back streets of Amarillo trying to be as inconspicuous as he could. He kept thinking how he would have been better off leaving the time traveler out there on the prairie. Let him fend for himself. Maybe Russell was right. Maybe they would have found him there and brought him back to where he belongs. Maybe he'd never be found. Maybe Russell was stuck here with Charlie in 1892. He shook his head at this notion. He couldn't think about that now. He had enough to worry about without this new set of problems. He hadn't counted on Russell to deal with.

Charlie walked Gus across the rails and turned west toward the stock pens. Right before the pens was a small row of three buildings. The building on the west end of this row was the office of livestock broker J.J. Billingsly. The office in the middle was a telegraph office, and the building on the east end of this row was Doc Morgan's home and office.

Nobody was sure whether Walter Morgan was a real doctor or not. He came to the Old Town settlement about four years earlier and set up shop as an undertaker. Since they didn't have a doctor at the time, people started coming to see him with their ailments and injuries. They figured he had to know something about the body if he was an undertaker. He patched them up as best he could. Things worked out pretty well for him and his patients, so pretty soon everybody started calling him 'Doc'. He had the best of both worlds. If his treatments didn't work out for his patients, he would eventually bury them. Two years ago, a Doctor Cornelius, Tuck Cornelius's father, set up a practice. However, some people still came to see "Doc" Morgan. Charlie was one of them.

Charlie pulled Gus around the back of Doc's office and tied him to a rail alongside the building. The doctor was out back working. Doc Morgan was a short, thin man somewhere in his forties with close-cropped black hair. He didn't have a family. Rumor had it that he left a betrothed on a farm in Indiana and headed west, never looking back.

Doc was wearing his signature black trousers, white shirt, with no collar, and had the sleeves rolled halfway up his arms. He also sported an unbuttoned black vest. The man owned a black fedora hat that he kept in his office, but Charlie could never remember seeing him wear it.

He was sawing wood planks to construct lids for two freshly made coffins leaning up against the back wall of his office.

"You had a bad week, Doc? Or you expecting some kind of trouble?" Charlie quipped. His question obviously startled the doctor who jumped. He dropped the saw and turned around.

"Damn it, Charlie! You shouldn't sneak up on a fella like that." Morgan put his hand on his chest, stepped away from the wood planks as he appeared to try and gather his composure. "Damn near scared me to death!"

"Sorry, Doc. I wasn't meanin' to rattle ya'," Charlie walked over and shook the doc's hand.

"You just get back?" Doc Morgan picked up his saw and put it on top of the plank he was cutting.

"Got back last night and went straight to the cabin. So, why the coffins?"

"No reason," the doctor said. "Just bored. Been too damn quiet around here. Nobody's sick and nobody's dying. I just needed to do something." After a minute he asked "So what brings you here? You feeling all right?"

"Oh yeah, yeah. I'm fine, just fine," Charlie answered quickly.

There was an awkward moment of silence. Doc Morgan was waiting for Charlie to say what was on his mind. Charlie didn't know exactly how to ask. He had practiced his speech all the way into town from his cabin, but now it all went away.

"Well, Charlie, What is it? 'Cuz I got to finish these lids," the doctor finally said.

"I got this friend," Charlie began. "He came to visit me last night at the cabin. And uh, he … he comes from a far way off. Ya' see?" There was another pause. Doc Morgan looked a little queer at Charlie, but Charlie continued. "Anyway, he's got these clothes that don't really fit in out here in these parts."

"What do you mean 'don't fit in'?" the doctor asked.

"Well, Doc. They just ain't right. They don't fit the boy right. He's kind of a shave tail and … well, they just ain't right for this part of the country."

"Well what the hell do you want me to do about it? I ain't no tailor, here."

"I know. I know," Charlie said. This was a lot harder conversation than he had imagined. He was still searching for the right words; saying what came to mind next.

"Well, doc, I was just wondering … if maybe you … uh, well, maybe you still had some clothes from some of your clients that didn't go home and maybe didn't need them clothes no more."

Doc Morgan gave a little laugh. "How big is this fella?" he asked.

"Well, he's a thin boy, but a couple inches taller than me."

"Why don't you take him down to the mercantile and get him something new?" the doctor suggested.

51

"Well, Doc. The kid sticks out like a bruise as it is. I don't want him wearing nothing new. You got something in there or not?"

"Take it easy, Charlie," Morgan said. "There's a few old clothes in a bag on the shelf in the back room. They're pretty ripe, though. You'll have to do something to 'em before he can wear them."

"Thanks, Doc. I owe ya'," Charlie replied.

Charlie opened his saddle bag and pulled out Russell's shoe. He started heading to the back door of Doc Morgan's place when the undertaker noticed the shoe.

"What the hell is that, Charlie?" Morgan asked.

"Can you believe this? It's one of his shoes!"

Doc Morgan walked over and took the shoe from Charlie's hand. He was staring at it apparently in awe.

"Well I never," the doctor said. "I've never seen anything like this. What kinda hide is this? That's the softest thing I ever felt ... and light as a damn feather. Where'd you say this friend of yours is from?"

"I didn't say. And I ain't rightly sure. I think it's some other country or something," Charlie said. "He tried to explain it to me last night, but I didn't understand it."

Charlie took the shoe back from the doctor and went inside the building.

Doc Morgan's back room was used as an embalming room, operating room, examining room, and storage room. A large stained wooden table was in the middle of the room and a smaller table took up half of one side wall. That table had a couple of fancy wooden boxes on it that Charlie knew held the doc's instruments. On the bottom shelf was the black canvas bag that Doc Morgan referred to. Under a shelf next to the bag, were a few pairs of boots and a couple of old shoes. That's what he was looking for. Pulling the bag off the shelf, he dropped it on the table in the center of the room. He picked up two pairs of boots and set them on the table next to Russell's shoe and selected the pair that was closest to the size of the shoe.

Charlie untied the rope that had the bag somewhat sealed and pulled the bag open. The disgusting odor of old dirt, rotting bodily fluids, decaying tissue, and death immediately filled the room. Charlie coughed and gagged and pulled away from the bag of clothes, trying to catch a breath of fresh air. He was going to need a minute or so to get used to that smell before he went back into the bag.

"I told you they was ripe," the doctor said as he stepped into the room from outside.

"By God you weren't lying." Charlie coughed again. "That's the foulest thing I think I ever smelled in my life. What do you keep these things for, anyway?"

"Well, mostly I just forget they're there. When I finally get around to cleaning up this stuff, I usually just burn them. Sometimes, if they ain't in too bad a shape, I'll send them over to the Chinaman and clean them up and give 'em away to some folks that could use them."

Charlie shook his head and pulled the bag off the table and took it outside into the open air. He dumped the bag out onto the ground and started separating them. All of the clothes were pretty old. Some were torn up so bad they weren't able to be worn. There were a few woman's clothes, but mostly men's. All had some kind of stains on them from blood, dirt, and who knows what other bodily fluids. He picked out a pair of pants that he thought might fit the time-jumper and a couple of shirts that were not too badly ripped up or stained.

"You want these others back in the bag?" Charlie asked.

"Nah. Just leave 'em there. I'll go through it now," The doc said. "It'll give me something else to do today."

Charlie rolled the pants and shirts up and stuffed them into one side of his saddle bags. He went back in and grabbed the boots and Russell's shoe and stuffed them in the other side of the saddle bags. He shook hands with the doctor and got Morgan's assurance that he would keep this just between the two of them. He mounted Gus and took off to the north to get as far away from town as he could. He was going to make a wide swing east away from town to get back to his cabin. He had to figure a way of getting these clothes cleaned up and on Russell before anyone found out that he was here.

Russell had looked everywhere for his other gym shoe. He was getting frustrated. He sat on the stool with one shoe on, racking his brain. Charlie, he finally thought. Charlie had to have taken it. He jumped up from the stool and pushed the door open.

"Charlie?" he hollered as he turned the corner of the cabin and headed for Gus's stall.

"Where's my shoe!?" he demanded. He stopped when he noticed that Charlie and Gus were gone. *Now what!*

7

Abe Walker

Driving three thousand head of cattle north from the Pecos valley is a long, hard, dirty endeavor. For Abe Walker, who was now in his sixties, this trip was particularly rough. In his prime, Abraham Silas Walker was a towering figure with rust-red hair and a fiery temper. He stood well over six feet tall with massive shoulders, a barrel chest, and large strong arms. Just his physical presence intimidated those around him.

Now, Abe was a sickly old man; a mere shadow of his youth. His massive shoulders and torso had all but disappeared, and his shoulder-length hair was thinner and mostly silver highlighted with wisps of reddish-brown streaks. His eyesight had become clouded and distorted, and his demeanor had gotten worse, if that was possible. The death of his only son and heir a few years ago only made the anger and resentment grow stronger and deeper within him. He vowed revenge for the murder of his son and that's all he's been able to think about since he started this drive. He means to see that promise carried out before he dies.

The herd was a day outside of Amarillo. Abe sat astride a large palomino that stood sixteen hands and rode alone alongside the massive herd with a red bandana covering his nose and mouth to protect from the dust. Being so close to Amarillo brought to mind his vendetta with Charlie Turlock. The last time he was in Amarillo, Charlie was nowhere to be found. This time he was counting on settling a long overdue score with the Ranger.

Mac Sherman, Abe's ranch manager and foreman, galloped forward to ride alongside his boss. Mac was Abe's right hand man and Abe counted on him for everything. He made sure Abe's ranch ran like a well-oiled machine. He was also a problem solver; any problem at all. Mac had a way of making trouble vanish.

"Pretty soon we'll be outside Amarillo, Mr. Walker," Mac said. "You want to graze them here or push 'em north of town?"

Abe lowered his bandana. "Naw, keep 'em rolling. We'll bed them in that grass valley just north of town for a few days. That should fatten them up before we corral them." Abe pulled on the reins of his palomino. As if they were joined together, Mac reined in his horse as well.

Sherman was a hard man who came west from Missouri. Rumor had it that, in his youth, he rode with Captain Bill Quantrill during the war. When things got too hot for Quantrill's Raiders he headed west trying to escape his reputation and any wanted posters that might be out on him. Abe Walker met him in a saloon in Tucson. Mac was involved in a ruckus in a bar and seemed to handle it with a very cool poise and confidence. That impressed Abe, and he hired him on the spot. Mac quickly became the man Abe counted on in a fix. It wasn't long before Mac became foreman and then ranch manager.

Abe looked at the scar that ran across Mac's forehead. It was impossible not to notice it. The anger that was already festering in him rose like molten lava as he remembered the day Mac got that scar, courtesy of a slug from Charlie Turlock's revolver. It was the same day Charlie shot and killed Jeremiah. He knew the memory was as fresh in Mac's mind as it was in his. Abe had seen the pain and anger in Mac's face every time Mac saw his reflection in a mirror or in the gawks of someone's stare. Like himself, he was sure that Mac was aiming to even the score with Ranger Charlie Turlock.

"I don't want any trouble in Amarillo, Mac, and I mean it. At least not until we unload this herd. No trouble of any kind." Abe gave

his foreman a slight nod to put a final emphasis on his last remark.
Abe wanted to make sure he understood. Mac nodded his
understanding. Abe touched his spurs to the side of the palomino and
started off at a walk. Mac followed alongside.

"The trouble we had a few years back will still be on people's
minds. That marshal will be looking for any reason to pester us," Abe
continued. "Any reason at all. He's a tough man and I made him look
bad the last time we were here." Abe paused. "He won't forget that.
He'll be ready for us this time. The last thing I want here is a war
before I get these cows sold."

"You want me to go in and ... uh ... *talk* to him?" Mac asked.

Walker snickered under his breath. Abe knew Mac's way of
"talking" to people was pretty one-sided. And if the conversation went
on a little too long, someone got hurt; and it was never Mac. Mac
Sherman was a dead shot with a killer instinct. He entered any fracas
with a calm head, which made him even more deadly. Mac learned
early on that the first person to lose his composure was the first person
to lose the battle. He always came out on top.

"No, best to leave him be, at least for now," Walker replied.
"Just tell the men. I can't afford to lose anyone on this drive at this
point. I need every one of them, especially now that we're so close."
Abe pointed his finger at Mac and frowned. "If I have to come get any
of them, they're gonna wish I hadn't. You tell 'em that, Mac."

"Yes sir," Mac said reluctantly. Mac was as true to Abe as a
person could be. But he also looked after his men. Walker was well
aware that these men worked long and hard to bring the herd this far
and they deserved to have some fun in town and relax. He knew Mac
would have a hard time delivering his message to the men.

Abe always backed his hands no matter what. He and Mac
never let anything get in the way of his boys cutting loose. Whatever
trouble they caused, Mac would always take care of it later. But this
time was different. Abe had to get his business done first. Later he
would tell Mac exactly why.

"What about the ranger?" Mac asked after a short pause.

The last time they were in Amarillo, Mac spent the better part
of his time trying to find Charlie. Just by coincidence, Charlie

happened to be out of town at that time, running prisoners to Cañon City.

"Turlock will get what's coming to him in due time. You'd better be careful. I think Turlock already proved that he's nobody to mess with, Mac. And I certainly can't afford to lose you now," Abe said.

"I owe him, Mr. Walker," Mac said firmly. "He's mine as soon as our business is done."

He shot Abe a look and gave a quick nod that told his boss he was done talking. With that he lightly kicked his horse and took off at a quick trot, leaving Abe Walker in his dust.

Abe pulled his bandana back over his nose and mouth and turned his palomino to the left, heading to the other side of the herd. He looked to the west and watched the sun on its descent toward the top of the distant mountains. Time was getting on, but they still had a few more hours of daylight. Abe was pleased that they had made such good time getting to this point.

He pushed his crew hard and they responded. They would head for a watering hole a little northwest of where they were, just alongside the grass valley north of Amarillo. Abe caught up to the flank rider and, over the noise of the herd, hollered an order.

"Turn 'em up! Turn 'em up!" He began swirling his hand in a circle above his head and pointed to a ridge off to the north.

The rider gave an understanding nod. He then took off at a gallop and headed for the front of the herd, relaying his boss's commands to the other riders as he passed them. In a few moments, with the crew of cowboys chanting and whistling, the single mass of thousands of longhorn cows made a slow guided turn to the left and headed up the rise toward a fresh water lake just on the other side of the crest. The lake was fed by a stream north of Amarillo, the same stream that had replenished Charlie and Russell on their way back to Charlie's cabin.

As the herd neared the top of the ridge the lead cows smelled the scent of the water. That was all they needed to get there on their own. Abe galloped to the top of the ridge and stopped to watch as the cattle slowly moved up the ridge as a single unit. It was poetry to him.

He never got tired of seeing that sight. With no one around him, he sat back in his saddle, pulled his bandana down to his neck, and smiled.

Abe looked off to his right, and stared at the horizon to the south-east. His brief smile quickly turned into a frown. Just a short ride out in that direction was Amarillo. He was not looking forward to venturing into that town. He fought the urge to bypass the town completely and continue on to Dodge. But Abe knew his crew hadn't seen a glass of whiskey or a pretty girl for months. He knew they were all itching to get into town and bust loose. He hoped his words to Mac would hit home. But he also knew some of these roughnecks would do whatever they wanted regardless of the consequences. He was not looking forward to dealing with any problems. He didn't have the time or the inclination.

Abe and Mac hadn't set foot in Amarillo in more than three years; not since the killing. Now, this town had a new mayor and a new council. If there was trouble, it wouldn't be easy to bribe them over to his way of thinking, as he did before.

Even if he could, there was Marshall Cook, and he wouldn't back down a second time. And, of course, there was Mac. Eventually he and Ranger Turlock were going to cross paths with each other. As much as he didn't want that meeting to happen, he knew he couldn't prevent it.

Maybe it was his age. Maybe it was his health. Whatever it was, he had a bad feeling about this trip to Amarillo. He was not looking forward to the next few days. His mind and probably Mac's too, was already set in what had to be done. Charlie Turlock had to pay for what he did. The inevitable confrontations were in the wind. He just hoped he was still around to pick up the pieces after it was all over.

As he sat on the ridge staring at the southeastern horizon, he lowered his head and turned back to watch the herd move over the crest of the rise in search of water. The lead cows were on a quick march to the edge of the lake. As always, the rest of the herd followed the lead cows wherever they went, and his smile returned. He pushed the thoughts of Charlie and Amarillo out of his head and enjoyed the sights of his cows. He relished in the thoughts of all that he built; this herd, the fortune he amassed, and empire he built. All for his son; his only son gunned down by a lawman. Goddamn that Turlock!

New Clothes

Russell sat outside on the ground, leaning against the front wall of Charlie's cabin. He sat staring at the stream that flowed along the bottom of the hill, amazed at how clean and pristine the water appeared. In his time there were very few streams left at all. The ones still there ran in various colors depending on what polluted soil they flowed through.

He'd heard about streams like this in his history studies but never thought he'd be fortunate enough to actually see, smell and taste one. He breathed in deeply through his nose and savored the scent of the trees and the land around him. No pollutants, he thought, just the clean, crisp air. However, he did notice the faint sour aroma from the stockyards some miles away, but it was not distracting. He had to remember this so he could explain it to everyone when he got back, if he ever got back.

Russell looked around the grounds outside the cabin. With only one shoe on, he couldn't stray very far. Walking was a chore. He had already stepped on sharp sticks and stones with his sock-covered foot.

Charlie walked alongside Gus as they approached the cabin and saw Russell limp around the grounds.

"Don't wander too far," Charlie said. Russell jumped at the sound of Charlie's voice.

"Charlie! Where have you been?" Russell demanded. "You shouldn't sneak up on someone like that." He took a few quick steps toward Charlie and stepped on another stick with his shoeless foot. "Damn!" he hollered. "Where's my shoe, Charlie?"

"Come on. Hurry up. I got some boots for you," Charlie said.

"What? I don't want any boots. I want my gym shoe back," Russell protested.

Charlie went to Gus's coral and grabbed the water bucket. He handed it to Russell along with his other shoe.

"Fill it with water and bring it over to that old tree stump there." Charlie pointed to the stump of a long ago felled tree. Russell slipped on his other gym shoe and headed down to the stream for water.

Charlie dumped the contents of his saddle bags on the ground by the stump. The stench from the clothes had subsided a bit, but it was still quite overpowering. He went inside, started a fire in the stove, filled the coffee pot with water and set it on the burner plate on top of the stove. He removed a well-used soap cake, a tin of saddle soap, and an old rag from the washstand and set them on the table. Charlie went back outside and waited for Russell.

"My God! What is that smell?" Russell asked, as he returned with the water.

"Take that pile of clothes and dump them in the bucket and make sure they all stay under the water. That'll cut the smell for a while until the water gets hot enough to wash them."

"Wash them?" Russell asked.

Charlie brought out the water bucket from inside the house. When the water in the coffee pot was hot, he added it to the half-filled bucket.

"Take those clothes out of the cold water and put them in this hot water bath. When they're good and soaked, you can start rubbing them down with that soap bar." Charlie pointed to the small soap cake on the table.

"Are these your clothes?" Russell asked.

"Nope," Charlie said, without looking up. He soaked the rag he had pulled from the washstand and went back inside without saying another word. Charlie sat down on the stool with the saddle soap and began cleaning the boots he had just brought home.

The boots were worn, but still in good shape. By the wear shown on the inside heels and ankles, Charlie surmised that the boots were worn by a cowboy, or someone who spent a lot of time on horseback.

When he finished cleaning one boot he set it on the table. Real nice, he thought, and began cleaning the other boot. He watched Russell outside push the clothes back down in the bucket.

"The more often you push them down in the water, the cleaner they'll get."

"You want me to wash your clothes?" Russell asked indignantly.

"Not my clothes," Charlie answered. After a pause he added, "They're your clothes."

Russell stared at Charlie with a look of disbelief.

"There is no way in hell I'm wearing these ... these things!"

Charlie put down the boot he was scrubbing and raised his eyes to meet Russell's.

"Look, boy!" Charlie spoke slowly, trying to control his temper. "I don't know what you're doing here. And frankly, I really don't care anymore. But you are here right now and that's not going to change anytime soon. So you'd better get used to it."

The two stared at each other for a while in silence. Charlie could see Russell's brow furrowed with defiance. Charlie's resolve stiffened and he rose and stepped toward Russell.

"If there's one thing I know," he continued, "it's that you can't go around these parts dressed like you are. The last thing you want to do is draw attention to yourself. If you don't want to wear these things then I'll just take you back out to the river and leave you there to fend for yourself. You savvy?"

Russell stood in the doorway staring back at Charlie and by the look on his face it was plain to see that he knew Charlie's words rang true. Charlie waited for a reply, but Russell didn't say a single thing.

"And that's the most explaining I ever did to anyone in twenty years!" Charlie went back to working on the boot. Russell grabbed the bar of soap, walked out of the cabin, and scrubbed each garment.

Charlie finished rubbing down the boots getting them fairly clean. They were still pretty worn, but he thought it was probably better they looked that way.

"How many times do I wash these things?" Russell asked.

"Till they don't smell no more," Charlie answered. "Then you dump them in that other bucket of cold water and rinse them out the same way until the water runs clear."

Russell stood holding a crumpled, dripping, white shirt. In disgust he threw the shirt back into the bucket and the water splashed up and soaked the clothes he was wearing. Charlie chuckled and turned away.

As Russell worked on scrubbing his new clothes, Charlie opened the old trunk at the foot of his bed. He pulled out an old, well-worn hat he had used only a few years before and set it on the bed. He knew Russell would not fit into any of his old clothes, except for maybe a vest he had. A nickel-plated Smith & Wesson .32 revolver sat on top of a stack of neatly folded old clothes in the trunk. Charlie slid the pistol into his belt along his back.

The old leather vest with rawhide fringes along the bottom was still in pretty good shape. Some of the fringes were missing and there was a small tear near the left pocket. Other than that, it was wearable. He hung the vest over the back of the chair and nodded approvingly. *That should fit the boy.*

Charlie turned back to the trunk and was about to close the lid when he paused. It had been a long time since he had gone through this vault of his past. A few newspapers containing stories of Ranger exploits where he had been involved, some small gifts that he received during exchanges with the local Indian tribes. All fond memories from his life in the nineteenth century that no one else would ever see. He didn't even know why he kept them. Some sentimental attachment, he guessed.

Then Charlie noticed the canvas bag at the bottom of the trunk. He had kept that bag locked up in the trunk for these past thirty years. The memory of his escape as a youth flashed back in his mind like a

64

lightning bolt in a dark sky. The bag contained his past and it wasn't pleasant. He reached to pick up the bag but then changed his mind. *Its fine where it is*. He didn't need to hold it to have those memories come back, and he was not sure he wanted them back.

He felt guilty about running away when he was young. He always planned to go back, but could never muster up the nerve to do so. Charlie sat down on the side of the bed overwhelmed with emotion as the haunting picture ran through his mind of the night a man died on his watch. He questioned if all this really turned out the way he thought it would.

"You all right?" Russell asked.

The question snapped Charlie back to reality. He hadn't noticed that Russell had re-entered the cabin and was watching him from the table.

He pushed the lid of the trunk shut, and tossed the dirty old hat to Russell.

"See if this will fit that head of yours."

The hat was a little tight, but Russell said it would work fine.

Charlie stood and nodded his approval at Russell. "When those clothes are dry, we'll head to town to get some food and supplies."

Russell's eyes beamed. The excitement of going to see the old west town of Amarillo was plain to see. Then a sense of dread shot through Charlie's innards like an arrow. He couldn't see anything positive coming from a trip to town with this time traveler. Something was bound to go wrong.

9

Amarillo

Russell again felt the clothes he'd washed earlier and hung to dry over a rail fence around Gus's corral. They weren't completely dry, yet, but he put them on anyway. He just couldn't wait to see Amarillo in 1892. The pants were a little big in the waist, but an old pair of Charlie's suspenders kept them from falling off. The length, on the other hand, was a good fit. The white cotton shirt was tight across his chest and neck and he couldn't button the collar button. The sleeves were way too short, so he rolled them up to just below the elbow. Charlie's old vest fit fine, but it was heavy and made his damp clothes feel even wetter. Russell chose to carry it until his shirt dried completely.

"I feel like an idiot in these things," Russell said.

Charlie smiled and set his old hat on Russell's head. "You'll do," he said. "Walk slowly in them boots. It'll take a little while for you to get used to them. I don't want you stumbling all over. Then you would look like a fool."

Russell stood in the doorway and watched Charlie turn the corner toward Gus's stall. As Charlie instructed, he cautiously took a step to follow Charlie around the outside of the cabin and felt his foot slip a little inside the boot. There was no arch support. It appeared to him that either boot would fit either foot. There was no left or right boot, just two of the same.

Russell braced himself along the wall of the cabin as he gingerly walked around in the boots. As Charlie said, this was going to take some time to get used to.

Charlie rode up alongside Russell atop Gus, removed his foot from the stirrup, and offered his hand. "Grab hold and climb on. Time for us to get some chow."

Russell stepped up on the stirrup and swung himself onto Gus's back behind the saddle. Charlie clicked his tongue and Gus started off at a slow walk down the path toward Amarillo.

It was around noon when they left the cabin and the sun was straight up in the sky. As they left the shade of the trees, Russell could feel the sun drying his clothes. It was a welcomed heat.

"When we get into town, we'll be doing a lot of walking. I want you to keep your mouth shut when we get around people," Charlie ordered.

"What for?"

"You have to stay as unnoticed as possible. If people ask, I'll tell them you're a friend from back East, and that you stopped for a visit on your way to California. I want you to play as dumb as possible. It should be easy for you. Just don't open your mouth if you don't have to."

"What am I going to California for?" Russell asked.

"I don't know, boy! Figure something out yourself."

The ride to Amarillo was only a few miles. Russell kept looking around at everything. He seemed to be having trouble containing his excitement. Charlie looked to the west at a huge dust cloud rising off the prairie. "Abe's here already," he said, not meaning it for anyone's ears. He knew where Abe was heading. He knew that by this evening the grass valley northwest of town would be covered with Abe's cattle. *It all starts tonight.*

They rode into town from the northeast but the remnants of the original Oneida settlement to the west, by the Amarillo River, were in plain sight. People and businesses were still in the process of moving to the current site of Amarillo, about a mile in from the river on higher ground. Although somewhat faded, some of the houses were covered in yellow paint from the celebration of when Amarillo was awarded the county seat a few years earlier.

By the time they got to the outskirts of Amarillo, Russell put on Charlie's vest and his old-west ensemble was now complete. In town, Charlie put Gus in the livery stable and exchanged pleasantries and small talk with Tuck Cornelius, the proprietor. Gus was going to get new shoes by the local blacksmith, and then groomed by Tuck personally. He'd be well cared for and well fed today. A pampering he more than deserved.

As the two walked down the raised wooden sidewalk into town, Russell watched the people making their way about. Fascinated with the clothing that everyone wore, he looked at his own clothes and was satisfied with Charlie's selection. He realized that Charlie was right in his assessment. Russell blended in with the masses.

Russell read every sign as he passed the various businesses that lined the street. Some buildings, like some of the homes, were covered in a faded yellow paint. Others were ornately whitewashed with green or red trim. Yet, some were just unpainted weathered wood.

Russell kept checking his gait, trying to take measured steps so as not to stumble. He was still getting used to wearing those ill-fitting boots. "Where are we going?"

Charlie didn't answer. They walked past the White & Tipton Hardware store and Russell had to stop and look. He was fascinated with the tools, and the bags of seeds and feed, and household items on display in the windows and out on the sidewalk. He wanted to go inside the store but Charlie kept walking. They passed by Taylor's saloon and another mercantile store. Charlie stopped and opened a non-descript door and the two walked into City Marshal Cook's office.

A small, narrow room, not much bigger than Charlie's cabin, shared side walls with the mercantile on one side and Hanna's Eatery on the other. The smell of Hanna's cooking permeated the marshal's office and made Russell's stomach rumble. A young, stocky man, with a wide-brimmed hat that hid most of his face, sat in a chair with his feet propped up on a small table. Marshal Cook sat across from him at his desk and looked up as Charlie and Russell entered.

"Why, hello, Charlie!" The marshal smiled as he rose to greet them. "You just get back?"

"Got back last night." Charlie shook the marshal's hand, and looked over at the young man across from Cook. "Howdy, deputy."

Deputy F.G. Johnson acknowledged Charlie's greeting with a nod, but didn't say anything. He looked at Russell and nodded a greeting. Russell nodded back.

City Marshal Amos Cook was a tall slender man, in his mid-40s, with wide shoulders and a thin waist. He had a long narrow face and soft gray close-set eyes. His short-cropped hair was mostly dark brown with grey patches along the temples. It matched the bushy untrimmed mustache that hid most of his mouth.

"I saw Walker's herd just west of here. They should be bedded down by this evening," Charlie said.

"I know," the marshal replied. "I'm afraid it's going to be a busy night. Especially with the new ordinance the council passed."

"What ordinance?"

"A few years back, Dodge City passed an ordinance that no one was allowed to carry a firearm in the city limits. A little tough to enforce, but it seemed to cut down on a lot of trouble," Marshal Cook explained. "I thought it might be a good idea to have the same law here. The council passed the ordinance a few days ago while you were gone."

"Those boys ain't gonna like turning over their firearms," Charlie warned.

"Well, then they got a choice. They can leave, spend their time in jail, or die. And I don't rightly care either way."

Charlie chuckled.

Russell wasn't paying much attention to Charlie's conversation with the marshal. The interior of the marshal's office had caught his interest. There was no color. Everything was old worn, grey wood. The walls, the ceiling, and the floor had never been painted. The one desk and the small table in the room, as well as the two wooden chairs, were well used and looked a dirty faded grey. The single wood cabinet that hung on the wall behind the marshal's desk had two doors that could be locked, but they stood wide open. The cabinet held three rifles and there were empty slots for five more. A large, thick wooden door on the back wall opened to a small cramped room made of stone. At first, Russell thought this was a storage room, but noticed a cot inside the open door and bars across the small opening in the back stone wall.

"Well, Amos, you'll have your hands full enforcing that law," Charlie said.

"You gonna be around later?" the marshal asked.

"Well, truth be told, I don't want to be. I got the boy here and I don't want him around any trouble."

"Who's your friend?" Marshal Cook looked at Russell.

"This here is Hicks, Russell Hicks. He's a friend from back East. He's here for a short visit. On his way to California."

"Hicks?" the marshal repeated. Russell offered his hand to the marshal who shook it and smiled. "Well, welcome to Amarillo, Hicks. How long you staying?"

"Don't know," Charlie quickly answered for Russell. "I guess till he gets tired of being here."

With that, all three laughed, and Charlie ushered Russell toward the door.

"We're gonna get some grub and then I'll show Hicks around the town," Charlie said.

"Have you seen Captain Bill, yet?" Marshal Cook asked.

"Not yet. I was going to stop in there after we eat. Why?"

"Well, he was looking for you yesterday. That's all. He had to send a couple of Rangers to Waco. I guess he's running out of Rangers," the marshal said with a smile.

Charlie walked out the door with Russell ahead of him. Marshal Cook followed them outside onto the sidewalk. He stopped and slowly looked around the streets as if imagining the anticipated arrival of Abe Walker and his cowboys. A grimace appeared on Marshal Cook's otherwise congenial face. Charlie knew what he was thinking.

"Don't worry. I'll be around for you, Amos," Charlie said.

The marshal acknowledged Charlie's remark without a word and the two shook hands as they parted company.

"Who's Captain Bill?" Russell asked as they walked a little while.

"He's my boss," Charlie began. "Captain Bill McDonald. He's in charge of Company B of the Frontier Battalion of the Texas Rangers. He just took over about a year or so ago. He was a political appointment by the new governor. I don't understand it. Ol' Soft-Voice McMurry ran this group just fine for years. Couldn't see any reason for him to go. New governor, new appointments." Charlie stopped and looked over at Russell. "Sorry. I didn't mean to go on like that. It's not your concern."

"I take it you're not too fond of Captain Bill," Russell said.

"He's okay. He ain't no Sam McMurry. Let's grab some food." Charlie opened the doors to Hanna's Eatery, next to the City Marshal's office. The windows in the faded whitewashed double doors were adorned with red and white checkered curtains. The smell of hot food being cooked made Russell's mouth water.

"Charlie!" A shout of happy recognition came from a short, rather rotund lady standing behind a small counter. "It's real good to see ya'," she continued in a slight Swedish accent.

Charlie returned the greeting with a smile and a wave. At this hour, the restaurant wasn't crowded and they sat at the first table they came to. Hanna waddled her way through the tables and chairs and gave Charlie a big hug.

"Good to see ya', Charlie. When did you get back?"

"Got back last night."

"Hello. I'm Hanna." She looked at Russell with a warm welcoming grin. "Who's your friend?"

"This here's Rus ..." Charlie began.

"Hicks," Russell quickly interrupted. "Russell Hicks." Russell smiled at Charlie defying Charlie's earlier order to keep his mouth shut.

"That's right. Hicks is from back East," Charlie confirmed.

"Well, glad to meet ya', Hicks. You boys want to eat?" she asked.

"What's on today?" Charlie asked.

"I got me some good steaks today, Charlie."

"Well, bring us a couple beefsteaks and two coffees," Charlie ordered.

"Coming right up." She turned and headed back toward a door behind the counter along the back wall.

"She's a nice lady," Russell observed.

"Hanna's a fine lady," Charlie said. "None better. She came out here about four years ago with her husband, Walter. They had a small spread down by the river in Old Town. They farmed a bit and raised hogs. Walter died from the fever a couple of years back. She couldn't do the farm by herself so she sold the farm and the hogs and set up this place. Good food, good people."

The interior of the diner was simple wood siding that had been whitewashed some years before and was in desperate need of another coat. A short counter ran partially along the back wall with three stools in front of it. Six tables stood around the small diner in no apparent order, five of which would sit only two or three patrons. The one exception was a large round table in the middle of the room that had six chairs around it. Only one other table was occupied this afternoon by two men drinking coffee.

Hanna brought back two thick ceramic mugs filled with hot black coffee. Russell stared at the mug, a little hesitant to sip the coffee after he remembered the campfire swill Charlie brewed up the night before.

"Don't worry," Charlie said. "It's much better coffee than mine."

Russell smiled and took a welcomed sip. Thank God, Russell thought, it actually tasted like real coffee.

"Steaks will be up in a minute, boys." Hanna smiled and returned to her position behind the counter.

Russell watched Charlie watch the people walk by on the sidewalk outside the restaurant. Charlie looked as if he was expecting something to happen. The two sat in silence. The steaks came with two large potatoes and a generous helping of beans. They were the biggest slices of meat Russell had ever seen. He commented on the portion size, but Charlie ignored him. As hungry as he was, Russell could only manage to eat half of his steak and only one of the two potatoes. He set his fork down and leaned his chair back.

"So, what's next?" Russell finally broke the long silence. Charlie just looked at him.

"You sure aren't much of a conversationalist around food," Russell commented.

"We're going to Solomon's Store and pick up some supplies. Then we're going to the Ranger's office down the street." He smiled at Russell and gave a little wink. "And if there's time, we might be able to stop at the hotel and have us a drink before we head back to the cabin."

Russell kept looking out the window and fidgeting with the fringe on the leather vest. He was excited and anxious to get started. He wanted to see it all. He wanted to experience a lifestyle he had only read about in historical research.

Charlie stood and walked over to Hanna. They exchanged a conversation that Russell couldn't hear and Charlie paid for the meals. He walked back past the table and picked up his hat. "Let's go."

The two left the restaurant, crossed the street, and walked along the sidewalk until they came to Solomon's General Store. Like the hardware store, it had two large windows where a number of goods were displayed like canned goods, hats, soap cakes, and other items. A few boxes outside on the sidewalk displayed fresh produce for sale from local farmers. Russell was awestruck. It looked like a museum display to him. He was having a hard time realizing that these were real everyday goods and not historical artifacts.

Russell stood in the doorway and gawked at the floor to ceiling shelves that lined the two side walls inside the store. They contained everything from canned goods to tools to household items to clothing; pretty much anything one could imagine. Russell entered the store and the worn pine floor planks creaked under him with each step. A musty smell greeted him as he first entered. He walked slowly taking it all in, not wanting to miss a single item. Russell caught the sweet aroma of peppermint as he walked by a display case featuring jars of various candies that lined the top of the case. Baskets and metal buckets and tubs hung from various hooks along a ceiling beam. A collection of various shovels and picks and forks were neatly stacked in the front corner of the store.

Charlie was talking to the store clerk at the counter and placing his order for matches, coal oil, coffee, ammunition, canned fruit, dried fruit, beans, some hard candy, and some other things that Russell didn't hear. Russell was too busy looking at everything in the store. He was fascinated by all the different varieties of goods in such a small space. There were two large wooden display cases in the store. One stretched along the back of the store and contained different bins holding grains, flour, dried beans, sugar and coffee. The other case ran along the right side of the store and was filled with cigars, handguns, ammunition and boxes and sacks of other items. The center of the store contained racks and tables all featuring different wares for sale like cookware, tools, blankets and tack items. The left side of the store was a long counter containing clothing and bolts of fabric. He felt a hand on his shoulder.

"Let's go," Charlie announced.

"This place is great!" Russell said. His eyes beamed with excitement as he moved away from Charlie and began reading the labels of some of the canned goods. "I want to stay here and look around some more."

"No," Charlie said. "I got some things to do and it's already late in the day. We have to come back later and pick up the order. You can look around some more then."

The excitement drained from Russell's eyes and he lowered his head in disappointment as he followed Charlie out the door. They walked down the sidewalk for two blocks, passing a couple of saloons, the office of the *Amarillo Champion* newspaper, the First National Bank, and a number of other businesses and residences. Russell wanted to go into every business, but Charlie kept prodding him along.

They finally came to one of the few brick buildings in town on the corner of an unnamed side street and Polk Street, the main thoroughfare. The front door was painted white and had a large brass star nailed to the door. A brass plaque, attached to the brick next to the front door, announced that this was the Amarillo Ranger Outpost for Company "B". Two long benches lined the sidewalk on either side of the front door of the Ranger's Office.

"This where you work?" Russell asked.

"Yeah, we're just a small company, part of the Frontier Battalion sent here. Our division is headquartered a little ways from here in Quanah. There's only about six or eight of us here at any given time."

"They move you around?" Russell asked.

"Not much. Not me, anyway, I guess they figure I'm too old to be any good at anything, so they pretty much leave me be." Charlie smiled at Russell and patted his shoulder.

"Sit down out here." Charlie pointed to one of the benches. "I got some business inside. I shouldn't be too long."

He opened the front door and before he went inside issued one last command.

"Don't go anywhere and don't talk to anyone." With that, he went inside and closed the door behind him.

The interior was a large open room with white plastered walls and dark wood trim. The left side held two doors with frosted glass panels. One of them had the word COMMANDER lettered on it. There were two desks in the room; one against the back wall, cluttered with stacks of paper. A large map of Texas hung on the wall above the desk. The other desk was against the front wall, next to the door.

Two other rangers in the office, both sitting at the desk by the front door, greeted Charlie as he came in.

"Cap'n Bill will be glad to see you," one ranger said. "He's been looking for you for two days."

"Well, no sense keeping him waiting." Charlie opened the door to the commander's office and walked right in.

When Charlie came out of his meeting with Captain Bill McDonald, he met with the other two rangers and told them about his discussion with the captain. He was being assigned to work with Marshal Cook until Walker and his crew were gone. Something he knew already. Just before Charlie left, one of the rangers handed him a telegram.

"I almost forgot. This came for you last week. Been sitting on this desk ever since."

Charlie opened the telegram. It was from a Frank McCrudy who Charlie took to the prison in Cañon City five years earlier. The telegram had said that Frank had been released two months ago.

Charlie looked at the two rangers who intently watched Charlie read the telegram.

"Whatcha think?" Charlie asked.

One ranger shrugged his shoulders and kept quiet, but the other said "Ain't Frank McCrudy that fella you testified against a ways back?" The first ranger slapped him on the shoulder to quiet him.

"Did everybody read this?" Charlie asked. The rangers lowered their heads and looked away. "Yeah, I testified all right, but not against him. I testified for him. He was innocent. Never should have been sent up. Poor guy was in the wrong place at the wrong time."

"Sounds like he wants to see ya'."

"I paid Frank a visit just about every time I dropped off prisoners. Nice fellow. He said when he got out he'd let me know where he was. He appreciated what I tried to do for him. He said I got an open invitation to visit him once he got out. Looks like he landed in Trinidad. Must be doing some mining."

"Where's Trinidad? I never heard of it," said the second ranger.

"Ain't much. It's a small mining town in the southeast mountains in the Colorado Territory. Maybe someday I'll look him up." Charlie folded the telegram and stuck it in his vest pocket just before he headed for the door.

Russell did as Charlie asked and sat on the bench outside the ranger's office watching people move about the town and interact with each other. The sun was getting lower in the west and the town was in a mix of dark shadows and ribbons of bright sunlight peeking between the buildings. Men with guns walked into the marshal's office and walked back out without them. No problems here, Russell thought.

Russell felt relaxed. He'd thoroughly enjoyed this day. Charlie had been in the office for a while, but it didn't matter to Russell. He watched a short man in a suit hurry up the sidewalk and walk into Marshal Cook's office. A minute or two later the man exited and walked away. Russell thought little of it until he saw Marshal Cook and Deputy Johnson come out of their office, each carrying a large shotgun. The two walked side by side down the street toward the ranger's post.

A feeling that something wasn't quite right swept over Russell. He looked up and down Polk Street but didn't notice anything out of the ordinary. He watched the marshal and his deputy pass in front of the ranger's building and turn down the side street. Marshal Cook stopped on the side street directly across from Russell and moved to the shadow of a building across the street. Hidden in the shadow of the building, the marshal stared down the side street. The deputy stepped onto the sidewalk where Russell was sitting and walked past him down the sidewalk of the side street. The deputy stopped and stepped into a recessed doorway of the building behind the ranger's office. Russell walked around the corner of the sidewalk and looked down that side street to see what the marshal was looking at.

Russell felt his eyes widen with surprise as he watched a band of riders slowly coming toward Amarillo in what appeared to be a loose, haphazard formation. Marshal Cook opened his shotgun, checked the loads, and snapped the barrels closed. He wondered if he should get Charlie.

10

Cowboys in Town

It was late in the day when Charlie left the ranger's office. The bench where he left Russell was empty, and a moment of panic set in. His mind raced with concerns as to where his time traveler had wandered off to and what kind of mischief he got himself into. He looked up and down Polk Street but didn't see him.

Charlie turned and walked around the corner and saw Russell standing on the sidewalk leaning against a support post. The boy was staring up the side street to the west. Charlie breathed a sigh of relief.

"I thought I told you to stay seated," Charlie scolded as he walked over to Russell.

Russell didn't acknowledge Charlie. He kept staring up the street.

"Look, I'm talking to you …" Charlie stopped when he saw what Russell was staring at. The two stared in silence together for a moment.

"I'm guessing that's Abe Walker and his crew that you've been talking about," Russell said calmly.

Charlie never took his eyes off the assemblage of riders approaching the town. He just nodded an affirmation.

"I think you'd better get out of sight." Charlie pulled Russell away from the post and back around the corner. He opened the front door to the ranger's office and gently pushed Russell inside. Two rangers sat at the front desk.

"Keep him in here," Charlie ordered as he closed the door. Russell quickly moved to a window to watch Charlie and Marshal Cook confront Abe and the team of cowboys.

Charlie watched Marshal Cook step out of the shadow of the building and into the middle of the side street holding a double barrel shotgun across his chest. He stopped the caravan of cowboys and began explaining to them the new city ordinance outlawing guns within the town's limits. They didn't appear very receptive to the idea. Abe Walker's gaze swept around the street and surrounding buildings and came to rest on Deputy Johnson on the sidewalk with his shotgun leveled. He didn't notice Charlie who was carefully sizing up the situation from around the corner of the ranger's office.

"Looks like you're a bit outgunned here, Marshal," Abe taunted. "Just you and that deputy all you got? Now are you telling all of us that we got to turn in our guns?"

"You turn in your firearms or you turn around," Marshal Cook said sternly as he repositioned the shotgun so the stock butt was resting on his hip.

Charlie stayed in the shadows but moved closer to the street so he could survey the scene without being seen.

"I don't believe I like either of them choices, Marshal. Now why don't you just crawl back to your little office and let us enjoy your town for a while. We won't be here all that long," Walker said.

"The order stands," Marshal Cook said coldly.

Charlie watched the marshal make his point, but it was clear that his point was not being received very well. The cowboys were beginning to get restless. Abe and Mac, his foreman, were taunting this law officer and the lone deputy. Abe and Mac started their horses at a walk toward the marshal. Marshal Cook pointed his shotgun skyward and fired one barrel. The blast startled the horses and the two men pulled on the reins to bring their mounts under control.

"I'm only going to say it once more!" Marshal Cook shouted. "You turn your guns in or you get out of this town ... Now!"

Abe Walker lowered his hand to his gun and stared defiantly at Marshal Cook, his anger plainly visible in his face. He looked again at the deputy and back to the marshal, leaned forward, and rested his forearm on his saddle horn. "Well now, we got ourselves a standoff here, Marshal. You and your boy, there, both with only a shotgun and a holstered pistol against all of us. I don't believe it's going to go your way."

"Damn it, Cook. You're gonna get yourself killed," Charlie whispered to himself. Against his better judgment, Charlie pulled himself out from around the building's corner. He unlatched the hammer strap on his holster and walked out onto the sidewalk in clear sight of everyone.

"Hello, Abe," Charlie gave Abe an icy stare. "It's been a while." He stepped off the sidewalk onto the dusty street and walked toward the marshal.

"Not long enough, Ranger," Abe said returning the cold gaze. He straightened himself back up in the saddle and kept his right arm alongside his pistol.

"You got a problem here, Amos?" Charlie looked at Marshal Cook.

"Just explaining the new law."

Charlie looked up at Mac Sherman, seated on his red roan next to Abe, glaring at Charlie.

"Howdy, Mac." After a pause Charlie added "I see you're wearing your hat a little lower these days."

"No thanks to you, Turlock!" Mac growled, and reached for his gun.

The marshal leveled his shotgun, aiming it directly at Abe Walker, and Charlie quickly put his hand on his gun and hollered, "HOLD IT!" Everyone froze. "We don't need to do this!" Charlie continued loudly.

A tense, silent moment hung in the air as all parties, uneasy to make any move, exchanged nervous glances.

"Don't do it, Mac," Charlie commanded. "It takes a certain knack to pull a gun from a sitting position and I don't think you're that good."

It was a bluff, but it was enough to get Mac thinking. That's all Charlie wanted. Just a moment to think and not react. Mac stared at Charlie and swallowed, and for a split second his eyes dropped away and then re-focused back on Charlie. That was the signal Charlie wanted to see. He had bluffed him.

"Let's all just relax," Charlie said calmly, never taking his eyes off of Mac or his hand off his gun.

"Marshal?" Charlie finally said so the marshal could continue.

"You're all welcome in town," the marshal kept the shotgun focused on Abe, "but not packing your weapons. You can check them at my office, and you can pick them up on your way out of town. Or, you can turn around and head back to your camp. And if you don't like either of those choices, then some of you will never see your payday."

The aggravation showed on Abe's face as he listened to this lawman challenge him. The cowboys watched Abe to see what he would do. The tension was thick all around. He turned and looked at his crew, and then back to the marshal; his irritation plainly visible.

"You know we could take you all down in just a second, Marshal. You can't get all of us," Abe warned.

"You'll never clear leather, Walker. I can promise you that," Marshal Cook sighted down the barrel of the shotgun pointing at Abe Walker's chest.

"You might be right, Abe," Charlie chimed in. "We probably wouldn't get all of you. But I can promise that you and Mac would be the first two to go." Abe Walker frowned and squinted his eyes. His face reddened and it was clear that he was getting more and more angry. "You gonna risk losing all your cattle, Abe?" Charlie continued.

Abe kept his eyes fixed on the barrels of Marshal Cook's custom Greener shotgun. They must have looked like two cannons pointed at him. But Charlie knew that Abe couldn't lose face and he couldn't show any fear to his men. Abe never took his eyes off of the Marshal but cocked his head so his men could hear.

"Well, there you have it, boys. I don't want any trouble before we get the cows sold. We came too far. I need all of you to finish this drive." Abe unbuckled his gun belt. "But it's up to you. Right now, I could really use a drink." Then he started to laugh.

He walked his palomino forward, dropped his gun belt in the dust at the feet of the marshal, and continued between Charlie and Cook on his way to the saloon next to the hotel.

Mac and the rest of the cowhands stayed in place. Mac was still glaring at Charlie as he slowly lifted his hand off his gun.

"This ain't finished, Turlock," Mac snarled.

"It is for now," Charlie replied still keeping his eyes on Mac and his hand on his gun.

Mac walked his horse forward, following Abe's lead, and the rest of the cowboys followed Mac. The marshal blocked the horse's path with his shotgun.

"You want to unload?"

Tension hung in the air as Marshal Cook and Mac Sherman stared at each other; neither looking as if they would back down. The marshal cocked the hammer on his shotgun, took a step closer to Mac, and pointed the barrel of the shotgun at the foreman's mid-section.

"I got one barrel left. You take that rig off now, mister, or I'm gonna open you up." The marshal spoke in a low, stern voice. Charlie stood by, keeping his eyes on the rest of the cowboys.

Like Abe, Mac started to laugh. He turned back to see if his men were watching him. They all began to laugh with him. Mac unbuckled his gun belt, but instead of dropping it, he kept it in his hand.

"We check these in at your office?" Mac asked.

The marshal nodded and pulled his shotgun back and un-cocked the hammer. "You first." It was over.

Charlie turned and headed toward the marshal's office. Mac walked his red roan up the street after Charlie, still holding his gun belt in his hand. The rest of the band of cowboys followed suit. Deputy Johnson fell in behind the group of riders, keeping his shotgun ready, and picked up Walker's gun belt from the street. Marshal Cook walked along with the caravan of cow-punchers.

Charlie was the first to enter the city marshal's office and he sat down at the small table. Marshal Cook came in next and sat down at his desk. One by one the cowboys filed into the office, deposited their weapons and walked down to the hotel's saloon to join their boss. Deputy Johnson came in and set Walker's gun belt on the table with the rest of them and announced that all of the cowboys had come in.

Charlie and the marshal counted fourteen guns turned in, including Abe Walker's. There should have been fifteen. Charlie hadn't seen Mac Sherman come into the marshal's office.

"I appreciate your stepping in back there," Marshal Cook said to Charlie.

"Don't mention it," Charlie said, but his mind was elsewhere. "We're missing one, Amos." He headed for the door.

Just then Russell came bursting through the open door and almost ran into Charlie. In spite of Charlie's orders, Russell must have snuck out of the confines of the Ranger's office.

"That was amazing!" Russell exclaimed. "You just backed them all down. I never saw anything like that." His eyes blazed with excitement.

Charlie brushed him aside, walked out onto the sidewalk, and looked around for Mac Sherman. Charlie was very much on edge. With a determined killer like Mac armed and on the loose, Charlie feared for his life. His mind was swirling with the possibilities of Mac's whereabouts. He didn't have time for this boy right now. The sun was setting as Charlie scanned the streets and sidewalks. It was too dark to recognize anyone at a distance, especially with his failing eyesight.

Russell followed Charlie out onto the sidewalk still going on and on about the altercation he witnessed. Charlie finally grabbed him by his shirt, pulled him close, and stared at him, nose to nose. The action startled Russell and he immediately became quiet.

"Can you hush up for just one minute?" Charlie asked quietly.

Russell nodded.

"You think you can do something for me without causing too much of a ruckus? Because I got a job for you." He had to get Russell out of harm's way.

Russell nodded again without saying anything. Even in the dim light Charlie could see the fear in Russell's eyes. Charlie released his grip on Russell's shirt, pulled a ten dollar eagle gold piece from his vest pocket and handed it to Russell.

"I want you to go back up to the livery and get Gus. Tuck said it would be four dollars. Then walk Gus over to the store and pick up our bundles. Then wait for me there," Charlie instructed. "You think you can do that?"

"Sure. No problem." Russell jumped off the sidewalk and took a couple of quick steps before Charlie called him back.

"Do it slowly," Charlie instructed. "And try not to draw any attention to yourself."

Russell nodded and ambled up the wooden sidewalk toward the north end of town and the livery.

Marshal Cook joined Charlie out on the sidewalk just as Russell walked away. "What's wrong, Charlie?"

"It's Sherman. He didn't come in with the others," Charlie said in a quiet somber tone. "He's gonna kill me, Amos. The bastard's gonna dry-gulch me and shoot me down."

"Well, then we'd better find this Sherman fella first." The marshal gave Charlie a slight smile. Not feeling very jovial, Charlie half-heartedly returned the smile. Looking around the streets, Charlie spied Mac's horse tied at the hitch next to Abe Walker's horse outside the hotel.

"His horse is at the hotel." Charlie pointed. "He's got to be close by."

"Let's start at the hotel then. I think we'd better stay together," the marshal said.

The marshal ordered Deputy Johnson to stay inside with the guns and then closed the door to his office. He and Charlie walked toward the hotel. Charlie's senses were heightened. With each step he expected something to happen, but didn't know what. He and the marshal walked together, side by side, carefully studying each person they encountered and hesitating at each dark corner they approached.

When they reached the hotel, Marshal Cook stayed outside while Charlie went in and looked around in the saloon. Abe Walker was at a faro table and most of his hired hands were milling around. But there was no sign of Mac Sherman.

Russell paid the livery attendant and walked Gus down the street toward the general store. So far so good, he thought. Gus's ears were pointed and he seemed a little reluctant to follow Russell. But, he seemed to like Russell and went along with a little coaxing.

In the dusk, the air was starting to get cooler. Russell pulled down Charlie's old hat a little tighter on his head. Holding on to Gus's reins he tried buttoning Charlie's vest across his stomach as he walked, but gave up because it was too tight. Just then, the still evening solitude was shattered by a single gunshot. The impact of the bullet was so intense that Russell's legs buckled and he was driven off his feet. It was as if he had been kicked in the side by the horse. The bullet tore into Russell's right side. The sharp burning pain instantly radiated through his body and took his breath away. The pain was excruciating and he cried out.

A lone figure walked out of the shadows clutching a handgun. A smile slowly crept across his face as he approached Russell's body lying in the street.

Russell could not catch a breath. As hard as he tried, his lungs wouldn't function. He could feel the pounding of his heart in his chest and felt it skip a beat. He was losing consciousness. He was dying. Fear and panic set into Russell's mind as rims of darkness began to cloud his vision. He looked up as the gunman approached, but couldn't recognize him in the dark. The pain was too much for him to bear. Russell was struggling to remain awake and a second later, his body gave out and Russell drifted away.

"I got you, Turlock, you son-of-" Mac stopped in mid-sentence when he saw that he had shot the wrong man. He backed away and looked around as people began to congregate. Two figures ran up the middle of the street toward him. Charlie and Amos both pulled their guns as they ran but didn't fire because of the crowd and Gus in the area. Mac fired a shot in the lawmen's direction and took off running for the shadows of the buildings.

Charlie and the marshal soon reached Russell's motionless body. Gus stood over Russell with his head bent down near the boy's head, nudging him. Charlie pulled the vest open and lifted up the blood-soaked shirt to see the wound. Blood poured from a gaping hole in his side. "Oh God, no." Charlie pulled his bandana from around his neck and pressed it over the wound. Charlie felt a faint heartbeat. He was still alive.

"Get Doc Morgan up here!" the marshal shouted to a young man who was standing on the sidewalk. "Now!"

The young onlooker took off on a run toward Doc Morgan's place.

Charlie, overcome with anger and distress, raised his head and in desperation yelled. "I'll kill you Sherman! You hear me, Sherman? You're a dead man!"

Hanna was one of the people who came out of her restaurant after hearing the shot. She walked over and placed a hand on his shoulder as Charlie knelt over the motionless body of his friend.

"You can put him in the back room here, Charlie," Hanna said. "You men, there, get him off the street and bring him to the back. I'll show you."

"Stay with the boy," Marshal Cook said. "I'm going after Sherman."

With his gun in hand, the marshal headed in the direction Mac Sherman had fled.

Charlie and a couple of men picked up Russell and gently carried him through Hanna's Eatery and laid him on a small cot tucked away in the back corner of the kitchen. Hanna grabbed a clean towel and placed it over the wound to try and slow the bleeding. Charlie could only watch helplessly. Charlie paced the small kitchen wringing his hands. All he could think about was his remorse for sending Russell off by himself. He felt responsible for Russell getting shot. He wanted to run after Mac but knew he needed to stay with Russell. Charlie was filled with guilt because he knew it should be him lying on that cot instead of Russell. *Where the hell is Doc Morgan?*

11

Russell

The back kitchen of Hanna's restaurant was small and confined with a large wooden prep table, cabinets, shelves, and a large iron stove. Since she only served meals in the mornings and afternoons, she had plenty of light in the kitchen from the large window in the back wall above the cot. Tonight, however, the only light was from a taper candle in a brass holder covered with a hurricane globe. Hanna sat on a small stool next to the cot where Russell lay and pressed another towel against his wound. She had already soaked two towels with blood.

Charlie paced around in the small kitchen. His mind raced with different worries. Perhaps that boy never found Doc Morgan, or maybe Mac had stopped him along his way.

He heard a shot followed by another. Charlie ran through the front of the restaurant and went outside only to hear the sound of a galloping horse heading up Polk Street. Charlie watched Marshal Cook run from an alley onto Polk Street and aim his handgun at the retreating horseman only to realize his target was out of range. The marshal holstered his gun without firing and joined Charlie. Charlie went back to the kitchen. Mac Sherman had escaped once again. Charlie's blood began to boil. He could feel the rage inside of him intensify. *I'll kill that Sherman.*

Hanna looked up at Charlie with a concerned look on her face.

"Why don't you go outside and get some air? You can't do anything for him in here."

"Has the bleeding eased any?" Charlie asked.

"No." Hanna lowered her head and turned to look at Russell. She shook her head and turned to Charlie with tear-filled eyes. "He doesn't look too good, Charlie. He's not breathing right."

Just then Charlie heard footsteps coming through the restaurant. Doc Morgan entered the tiny kitchen and walked past Charlie directly to Russell lying motionless on the small cot.

"What do we have here?"

"The boy's been shot, Doc. He needs help right away."

Doc Morgan pulled the candle closer to Russell. "Do you have any more light, Hanna?"

Hanna nodded and left the kitchen. She soon returned carrying a hurricane oil lamp and a sheet from her bedroom, and set it on the table. The doctor pulled the lamp closer to him and turned up the wick for more light. Hanna tore the sheet into strips for the doctor to use.

"Is he gonna be alright?" Charlie's voice quivered.

"I don't know, Charlie. Looks like he lost a lot of blood."

"He has to live, Doc," Charlie demanded.

"I'll do everything I can, Charlie," Morgan said.

"You don't understand. He HAS to live! He just has to," Charlie impatiently said. "You have no idea what could happen if he dies back here. The ramifications of him not getting back have never been ..."

Morgan and Hanna stared at him with blank looks on their faces. Charlie stopped. For a moment he'd forgotten where and when he was. Charlie's cheeks flushed with embarrassment. "Sorry. I don't know what I'm saying."

Hanna gave Charlie a tender smile and a reassuring pat on his arm.

"I know you're worried, Charlie. Like I said, I'll do everything I can." Doc Morgan gave a nod to Charlie and went back to attending to Russell. "Let's see what we're working with, here."

He pulled away the towel Hanna had placed over the injury and tore open the blood stained shirt. He pushed and probed the wound to locate the bullet and see what damage was done.

"We got two holes here. Looks like the bullet went through," Doc Morgan said. "But it looks like it splintered his lower rib. There's bone fragments inside. It must have hit the rib and deflected out."

The doctor pointed to a wooden bucket on a side table. "There's a pump out back. Fill that bucket up with water and bring it in here."

Charlie grabbed the wash pail and quickly returned with the vessel full of water. He set it on the floor near the bed where Doc had opened his instrument bag and was working on Russell. He probed the wound and removed as many small bone fragments he could find. Morgan pulled a brown bottle and a clear glass vial from his bag.

"What's that stuff?" Charlie asked.

"This here is pure grain alcohol." The Doc handed the glass vial to Charlie. "I get this over at Taylor's Saloon. There's a gal there named Ethyl that brews her own shine. It's good pure alcohol. This is what it looks before she cuts it; clear, like water."

"Cuts it?" Hanna asked.

"This stuff will more-an-likely kill ya' if you drink it straight up. So, she waters it down some and adds some honey or burnt sugar or some spices to flavor it and then adds some tobacco chunks and who knows what else for coloring," Doc explained. "In its pure state, it's good for cleaning up wounds."

"What about this?" Charlie picked up the larger brown bottle.

"It's a calcium chloride solution. It's supposed to keep the infection down." Doc tore a clean linen cloth into strips and folded one into a small pad. He poured the alcohol from the vial onto the pad and wiped down the wound.

"It's a good thing this boy's knocked out, else he'd be screaming bloody hell with this stuff on him," Doc said.

Once the wounds were cleaned to Doc Morgan's satisfaction he pulled a coiled string and a hooked needle from his bag. The bleeding appeared to have diminished.

"I use a violin string." The doctor smiled at Charlie. "It's easier to get instrument strings here than it is to get catgut sutures shipped in."

Charlie watched as the doctor pinched the wound together and looped the hooked needle through the skin and pulled the string taut.

"They're both made with the same material," the doctor said while suturing. "I tried making some here, but I used up all my lye and I couldn't get the intestines scraped completely clean. They just wouldn't separate well enough. So I used my violin strings."

After Doc Morgan stitched both wounds closed, he took a clean pad of folded linen and poured some of the calcium solution on it and placed it over the wounds.

"I'm gonna need you to hold this boy up while I wrap these strips around him."

Charlie stepped forward and gently pulled Russell up by his shoulders and held him until the Doc finished the bandaging.

"You got a place for him to stay?" Morgan asked.

Charlie shook his head no.

"He can stay right here for as long as he needs to," Hanna offered.

"Is he gonna be all right?" Charlie asked.

Doc Morgan washed his hands in the bucket of water and dried them. "Well, we'll see. He should live, as long as the infection stays away. Hopefully he won't bust that wound open again and bleed out."

Charlie gently laid Russell back down on the cot and brushed a few strands of hair away from the boy's face.

"Don't worry about him, Charlie," the Doc said quietly. "Hanna will get him cleaned up after he wakes up."

"You bet I will," Hanna replied.

"I can't thank you enough, Doc," Charlie said. "What do I owe you for this?"

"Nothing right now, Charlie. We'll talk about it later." The doctor smiled. "I like the kid's clothes. They kinda look familiar. I think he'll need some new ones after this. I can't help you with that anymore." He gave Charlie a wink.

Charlie smiled and shook Doc Morgan's hand.

"Keep him quiet. Keep him down. He probably won't want to eat, but try and get something in him. Maybe some soup or something. I'll check on him in the morning." The doctor left Hanna's and stood outside on the sidewalk for a moment before heading off back to his office.

Charlie's mind raced with different thoughts and emotions. He didn't realize until now how much he really cared for this young man. *He can't die. Not here.*

"Why don't you go home, Charlie?" Hanna suggested, interrupting his deep thoughts. "Get a good night's sleep. I will take good care of Hicks, here."

"No, I think I'll stay in town while the boy is here." Charlie paused. "I do have to find Gus, though, and get him bedded down."

"I'm fine. You go." Hanna waved her hand at Charlie as if pushing him toward the door.

Charlie walked through the restaurant and stood outside on the sidewalk for a few minutes taking in the cool evening air and enjoying a moment of peace. He carefully scanned the streets and wooden sidewalks looking for anything out of the ordinary. By this time, night had engulfed Amarillo and visibility was limited to the dark outlines of buildings. It was uncommonly quiet for an evening with cowboys in town. Charlie guessed that the shooting had tempered everyone's spirit, at least for the time being. A light was on in the marshal's office so he went to visit Amos.

"How's the boy?" Marshal Cook asked as Charlie entered.

"Doc got him all patched up. Wait and see. I'm gonna keep him at Hanna's until Doc says he can be moved." Charlie paused and sat in the chair across from the marshal's desk. "Where's Mac?"

"Gone," the marshal said. "I went after him behind those buildings, but he must have doubled back in the dark, got his horse and left town."

"You didn't go after him?" Charlie stood, raising his voice.

Marshal Cook leaned back in his chair. "Hold up a minute, Charlie, its pitch black out there. You know this land better than anybody. You can't see anything out there," Marshal Cook leaned forward and looked at the paperwork he had been working on. "Besides, we both know where he went."

Charlie nodded and sat down. He was nervously tapping his heel on the floor. He felt as if he was going to crawl out of his skin. The anger over the shooting and losing Mac was making him a nervous wreck. He had to settle down. His initial thought was to go out to Walker's camp looking for Sherman. But he had to think straight.

The marshal was right. Riding out in the dark would be nothing but chasing shadows. And he was sure Mac went back to join the skeleton crew that Abe left with the herd. He knew where to find him. Charlie was too nervous and upset to sit. He stood and walked around inside the small office.

"Tuck took Gus back up to the livery," the marshal told Charlie. "He said he'd keep him there as long as you need."

"Tuck's a good man. I'll catch up with him tomorrow." After a minute he noticed the deputy was gone. "Where's Johnson?"

"He's walking around town between the hotel and the bowery. That's where those cowboys seem to congregate."

"Any trouble yet?"

"Naw, not yet. It's too early. They ain't liquored up enough yet."

Charlie paced in silence. It helped calm him. Charlie stopped and looked inside the empty jail cell. He had an idea.

"We gotta get Mac to come back into town," Charlie said.

"Now just how you planning on doing that?"

"We keep his boss here."

"His boss?" the marshal asked.

"Yeah. You throw Abe in jail. With him locked up he won't be able to sell his cows and pay off the cowboys. Mac will have to come in to get Abe out of jail."

Marshal Cook shook his head. "I don't know about this, Charlie."

"Abe will sell those cows tomorrow," Charlie persisted, "and once he does, we won't see him or Mac again for a long time."

"That'd be just fine with me."

"We have to end this, Amos. Mac has to pay for shooting Russell. And we'll never get another chance like this."

Before the marshal could answer, Charlie walked to the marshal's desk. "How about getting a drink with me?"

Marshal Cook shook his head but didn't answer. Then, as if reading Charlie's mind, the marshal leaned back in his chair and smiled at Charlie. "Yeah, I think a drink might be a good idea right about now. How about the hotel's saloon?"

"Just the place I was thinking of." Charlie grinned as he pulled Cook's hat from the peg on the wall and handed it to the Marshal.

12

The Arrest

Marshal Cook and Charlie began a leisurely walk along Polk Street toward Henry Sanborn's 40-room Amarillo Hotel. The hotel wasn't even two years old at this point, but it had already established itself as a grand place where people came to not only stay overnight, but to just pass the time. It attracted politicians, traders, ranchers and all kinds of businessmen from all around the area. The hotel was becoming the business center of Amarillo.

As Charlie and the marshal walked along the sidewalk, they heard the laughter and music filtering out onto the streets from the various establishments around town.

"It always starts like this," Amos said. Charlie looked at the marshal but didn't answer. "The evening. It always starts with everyone laughing, having a good time and a few drinks. A few hours from now they'll be paired off hollering at each other and starting fights."

"Well, that's when you earn your money," Charlie said as they reached the hotel.

The marshal just smiled. Outside the hotel, Deputy Johnson sat on a bench with his shotgun across his lap.

"Go on back to the office and wait for me. We'll take this watch for a while," the marshal instructed.

Deputy Johnson tipped his hat and headed back to the marshal's office to watch over the cache of guns they'd collected from the cowboys.

The two lawmen entered the hotel and stopped at the front desk to speak with the clerk.

"Any trouble here tonight?"

The clerk shook his head and looked across the lobby into the crowded saloon.

"No trouble, Marshal. But they're all a little squirrely after the shooting tonight," the hotel worker reported. "You'd better walk easy."

"Squirrely, huh?" The marshal looked over at Charlie. "Let's get that drink."

The marshal headed across the lobby toward the adjoining saloon and Charlie followed close behind. They stood just inside the doorway surveying the crowded barroom.

The saloon was not only one of the finer establishments in town, it was also the largest saloon in town. The bar stretched along the entire back wall. A small stage sat in the front corner of the room opposite the hotel lobby entrance. An out of tune piano sat on the stage being poorly played by a somewhat sober musician.

Cigar smoke hung thick in the air and the smell of beer and Ethyl's rotgut whiskey filled the room. A number of round tables scattered throughout the barroom were occupied by those enjoying libations, while a few other tables had their occupants engaged in a card or dice game. The house gambling was situated along the front wall of the saloon and included a numbers wheel, a few faro tables and a couple of hi-lo birdcage games.

Charlie spotted Abe Walker seated at the end of the faro table furthest from the door. Looking at the small stack of chips in front of the cattle baron, it was obvious to Charlie that Abe was having a bad night gambling. A few cowboys stood around him watching the table, while the rest of his crew were scattered throughout the saloon.

Marshal Cook and Charlie walked through the crowded barroom and muscled their way up to the bar. The bartender greeted them and asked what they wanted.

"Coffee," the marshal ordered and then looked at Charlie.

"Give me a beer." Charlie watched Walker lose another bet.

"I can't just arrest a man for no reason, Charlie."

"Oh, believe me, you'll have a reason," Charlie offered, "and I don't think it will take long, either."

The bartender set a glass of warm beer and a hot cup of coffee on the bar. Charlie dumped a few coins on the bar from which the barkeep took what he was owed and left the rest. Charlie took a few sips of the beer and turned back around to watch the crowd.

"How you want to handle this?" Marshal Cook asked.

Charlie took his gun belt off and set it on the bar in front of the marshal. Then he pulled his spare pistol from his belt and handed it to Marshal Cook. "Watch these for me. You'll know when to step in."

Charlie took a long drink from his beer, set the glass on the bar, and walked through the crowd toward Abe. The closer he got, the more he had to keep his anger in check. Abe was concentrating on the bets he just played on the queen and didn't see Charlie approach. But the cowboys around him did. One of them whispered in Abe's ear, and he looked up and glared at Charlie. Abe frowned and puffed out a breath of disgust turning back to the faro board.

"Doesn't look like it's your night," Charlie said.

The dealer pulled a queen for the player's card, and Abe won his last bet.

"Luck seems to be changing." Abe collected his winnings. He looked closer at Charlie. "No gun." He gave a slight snicker. "I'm busy. What do you want, Ranger?"

"Mac," Charlie said abruptly.

"Ain't seen him." Abe placed a few more bets on the board appearing uninterested in Charlie.

"You're a liar."

Walker jumped to his feet and gave Charlie a defiant look but didn't move any closer. His face was red with anger. Charlie took a few steps toward Walker. The cowboys around Abe moved a little closer as well. Abe took a deep breath. After collecting his composure, he sat back down and watched the dealer draw a card he hadn't bet. He slammed his fist down on the table in frustration of losing another round. He looked at Charlie who grinned at his misfortune.

"I heard your boy got himself killed, tonight." Abe smiled at Charlie. "What a shame. Dangerous town. You never know what'll happen."

Charlie's blood boiled and he took a step toward Abe but one of the cowboys stepped in front of him and blocked his path. Charlie stopped and regained his self-control. Abe said "killed". He didn't know Russell was still alive.

"Now you know how I feel, lawman! Eye for an eye, I'd call it." Abe raised his voice a notch.

"That boy was just walking down the street! He didn't hurt anyone!" Charlie matched Abe's volume. "Your son shot a Deputy US Marshal and was trying to kill a ranger."

"You killed my boy!" Abe hollered as he leapt to his feet and charged Charlie.

Even though Charlie expected some sort of attack, the old cattle baron's quickness and agility took him by surprise. Abe threw a right cross at Charlie, who ducked and backed up. He moved quickly, but his chin still caught a glancing blow from Walker's fist. It didn't hurt, but Charlie stumbled backward into the crowd, somewhat supported by them long enough to regain his balance.

Just as quickly, Abe was on him again and threw another punch, this time connecting solidly with the left side of Charlie's head. Charlie almost blacked out and the force of the blow caused him to lose his balance again. This time the crowd had moved away and he fell to the floor. Charlie struggled to his feet in a crouched stance, expecting another blow from Walker at any time. Focusing on Walker's legs, Charlie charged him knocking him into one of the faro tables and then onto the floor.

From a kneeling position, Walker threw another punch at Charlie that missed wildly and Charlie answered with a solid punch of his own to Abe's chest. Walker grabbed his chest and rolled onto his side gasping for air. Abe couldn't breathe. He rolled from side to side. Finally a breath came with a raspy, fluid sound. Then he coughed. He coughed a second time a little harder and then a third time even harder. When he finally got a good breath, he looked up at Marshall Cook holding his revolver.

"I think you two ought to come along with me." The marshal pointed his revolver at the front door.

Abe Walker and Charlie slowly got to their feet. Blood trickled down Walker's chin from the corners of his mouth. Charlie frowned. He'd only hit him once and it wasn't in the face. Marshall Cook marched the two out the front door of the saloon. The three walked up the street to the marshal's office where he locked Abe Walker in the stone jail cell.

"You all right?" Amos handed Charlie back his guns and his belt.

"Yeah, just saw some stars for a minute. That old bugger sure packs a wallop for a guy his age. I feel like I got kicked by a mule."

"You got no right to hold me, Marshal," Abe hollered with a shallow, raspy voice.

"I got every right, Walker." Marshal Cook walked to the heavy wooden cell door and spoke through the small window. "Let's see now, you attacked an officer of the law, you disturbed the peace, I haven't checked with Henry yet, but I'm sure there was property damaged, and, as far as I'm concerned, you might have been involved in that shooting tonight."

"You're loco, lawman!" Abe responded between coughs. "I was in that saloon all night, and you got my gun. I had nothing to do with that shooting. I got witnesses."

Abe Walker started to cough. He coughed until the marshal finally opened the cell door and handed him a canteen. Abe took a drink and his coughing spell began to subside. Blood dotted the front of the old man's shirt.

"You want me to get Doc Morgan down here?"

"That old sawbones couldn't pull a tick off a dog," Walker tried to hold back his cough. "Besides, he can't do nothing for me. No one can. I'm a lunger. Been one for a couple years now. It just keeps getting worse."

Marshal Cook shook his head and left the canteen with Abe Walker. He closed and locked the cell door and turned to Charlie.

"You hear that?"

"Yeah. That explains the blood I saw on him. I didn't mean to hit him in the chest," Charlie said, "I just wanted him off of me."

"If he's got that affliction, this will probably be his last drive."

"Well, I'm sorry he's sick. But, truth be told, I don't care if the bastard dies tomorrow. It'll save me the trouble of killing him. He's done nothing but make misery for a lot of people his whole life."

"Well, now that I got him, what do I do with him?" the marshal asked.

"Just keep him here," Charlie said. "Those cowboys won't leave here until Abe goes with them. Nobody can sell his cows but him. They may try and come get him out tonight. And maybe Mac will be with them."

Marshal Cook nodded, sat down, and started going through the paperwork scattered across the top of his desk. He looked at Johnson leaning up against the cell wall. "You want to go get some shuteye for a spell? I'll be here."

The deputy thanked the marshal and said he would be back in a few hours. He handed Charlie his shotgun and left. Charlie sat across from the marshal, rubbing the side of his head. After a few minutes of silence Marshal Cook looked at Charlie.

"You look like hell, Charlie. You should get some rest, too. You going back home or you gonna stay somewhere in town?"

"I don't think I'll be able to sleep much. I think I'll go sit with the boy for a while. I've stayed at Morgan's place before. He said I could stay there anytime I wanted to. I may go over there if I need to lie down."

"I'm sure Hanna wouldn't mind if you bunked in with her," the marshal said with a sly grin. Charlie gave the marshal a condescending look and shook his head.

Marshal Cook continued to stare at Charlie as if wanting him to leave. Finally Charlie set Johnson's shotgun down on the marshal's desk, slung his gun belt over his shoulder and walked toward the door.

"I think I'll just stop in next door," Charlie said. "Then I'll go on down to Doc's place. He's got a real comfortable sofa."

The marshal nodded and went back to shuffling paperwork. Charlie opened the door and heard Abe try to holler.

"You go to hell, lawman," Abe rasped. "I'll be out of here in no time."

"You'd better hush up, Abe, or you'll get to coughing again," Marshall Cook hollered back. "You'd better get some rest, cuz you'll probably have some company later on tonight."

"You want me to stay?" Charlie stood in the open doorway.

The marshal shook his head. "You go on. I can handle this. Besides, Johnson will be back in a few hours. Get some rest. I think you'll need it."

13

Jail Break

Charlie walked next door to Hanna's Eatery, still rubbing the side of his head from Abe Walker's punch. He looked through the window of the darkened restaurant and noticed a dim light coming from the kitchen. He tried the door but it was locked. Charlie lightly tapped on the window and waited. Hanna peered around the kitchen doorway, walked through the restaurant, and unlocked the door.

"He still hasn't woken up," Hanna whispered.

Charlie nodded and followed her back to the kitchen. The oil lamp was no longer on the kitchen prep table, but the candle and globe remained. He was a little surprised at how good Russell appeared. He looked back at Hanna.

"I took that old stained shirt off of him and got him cleaned up just like the Doc said," Hanna explained. "I still have a couple of Walter's shirts. It's a little big for him, but it's better to have a nice clean one."

Charlie smiled as he walked closer to Russell. His hair was parted in the middle and combed off to each side. He looked so young, barely a whisker on his face.

"He's breathing steady, now." Hanna smiled.

Charlie nodded and sat down on the stool next to the cot. "I can't thank you enough, Hanna. I'll pay you back for this. I promise."

"Oh, shoot, Charlie. You don't owe me anything at all for this," she said with a slight giggle. "I'll leave you alone for a little while, now."

"You go get some sleep," Charlie ordered. "I'll sit up with him for a while. You're going to need your rest for tomorrow's breakfast crowd."

"Well, maybe I will lie down for just a bit."

Charlie heard Hanna walk through the restaurant and open and close another door that led to her bed chamber. He put his hand on top of Russell's hand and leaned forward close to his ear.

"You listen to me. You have to come back here, you hear me?" Charlie whispered in Russell's ear. "It's not your time. I've got some things I have to tell you before we part ways. But you have to come back here to me. Some things are going to happen real soon and you have to be gone before they do."

Charlie squeezed Russell's hand. "Come back," he whispered again.

He sat on the stool and leaned against the prep table. With his elbow on the table and his head in his hand, the events of the day replayed in his mind. He felt his eyes getting heavy in the dim light and quiet surroundings. He watched Russell sleep, and before long, he dozed off as well.

A couple of hours had passed since Charlie and Deputy Johnson left the marshal's office. Marshal Cook had finished organizing the paperwork on his desk and was looking forward to the deputy returning because he was beginning to get a little tired himself. He put a fresh pot of coffee on the stove. He hung some of the gun belts he collected in the wall cabinet. Some others were hung on the hat pegs along the side wall, and the rest were rolled up and set in a line across his desk. Just as he sat back down, three of Abe's hired hands came into his office. The marshal rose and pulled Johnson's shotgun across the desk closer to him.

"Can I help you boys?" He recognized two of the three as the ones that stood around Abe at the faro table. He hadn't seen the third one before.

"We're heading back to camp. Just came in to pick up our hardware," the first cowboy said.

The hair on the back of Cook's neck stood up. Something didn't seem quite right.

"Kind of early for you all to be calling it a night." Marshal Cook carefully watched the three.

"Well, we're out of money and you got our boss locked up. Kinda took the spirit out of us being here," the first cowboy said, with a hint of disdain in his voice.

The last cowboy smiled at Abe through the cell door window. After a silent pause the marshal dropped his hand onto the stock of the shotgun and looked over the three.

"Mine's right here on the desk," the first cowboy said as he reached over the desk and picked up his holster.

"My rig is the last one on the hook right there." The second cowboy pointed to it. "And you got my Winchester in the cabinet there."

Finally the third cowboy said, "Mine's the third from the right on that hook."

The marshal gave them each back their guns and told them they could put them on outside of town. If they strapped them on in town he would arrest them. They agreed and slowly left the office. As they left, each one cast a glance back to the cell where Abe Walker stood watching through the small window in the cell door. When they closed the door, Marshal Cook picked up Deputy Johnson's shotgun, cocked both hammers, and moved back against the side wall. He didn't have to wait long.

Suddenly, the door to his office was kicked open and those same three cowboys quickly charged in with their guns drawn. Marshal Cook fired both shotgun barrels as the first two cowboys came through the door together. He immediately dropped the shotgun and pulled his pistol.

The shotgun blasts killed the first cowboy and knocked the second one down. It forced the third cowboy back out onto the sidewalk. From the open doorway the third cowboy fired two shots at Cook but his bullets hit the desk and the wall behind the marshal. Marshal Cook returned fire and his second shot struck a solid blow in the cowboy's chest. He fell backward off the sidewalk and onto the street. The marshal turned his attention to the cowboy writhing in pain on his office floor.

Charlie woke up when he heard Hanna's chamber door open and close. He listened to her walk across the restaurant toward the kitchen. Russell was still asleep. As Hanna re-entered the kitchen, Charlie noticed that she had washed her face, combed her hair, and changed out of her stained blouse. Charlie smiled at her.

"You look real nice, Hanna."

She returned the smile and even in the dim candle light Charlie noticed a slight blush fill her face. Hanna told him to leave Russell to her and go get some rest. Charlie agreed and said he would head down to Doc's place.

Just as he was about to leave he was startled by two shotgun blasts from next door at the marshal's office. Charlie pulled his gun belt off the prep table and drew his gun from the holster. He ran toward the front door and on the way he heard the exchange of handgun fire. He opened the door of the restaurant in time to see a cowboy fall off the sidewalk onto the street. Charlie slowly approached the marshal's office and peered through the glass window.

"Amos? You all right?" Charlie hollered to identify himself so as not to get shot.

"Yeah. Come on in."

Charlie entered the small office and helped the marshal get the wounded cowboy up off the floor. His wounds from the shotgun pellets didn't appear to be life threatening. Charlie checked the other cowboy on the floor but he was dead.

Deputy Johnson was making his way back to the office when the gunfire began. At the first sound, he started running up the street toward the office. He stopped and checked the cowboy lying in the street. He told Marshal Cook that the cowboy in the street was dead.

"Go get Morgan," the marshal said to the deputy. "Tell him we got two dead and one wounded." The deputy left.

"You fired first. You're a killer, Marshal," Abe hollered. "This ain't over, lawman. This is just the beginning."

Charlie stared at Walker through the door and then moved the wounded cowboy to a stool by the stone wall.

"Sit down here against this wall and try not to bleed on the marshal's floor," Charlie said. Then he moved to the cell door and stared at Walker through the small window. "Let's see now. That coward you got for a foreman shot an unarmed boy tonight and run off and left you all alone. You're locked up in jail with a few thousand head of beef wandering around; you got two of your boys dead here and this fella shot to pieces. Did I miss anything? Doesn't look to be going your way, Abe."

Abe Walker spat bloody saliva through the small window, which Charlie dodged.

"My boys will burn this town to the ground to get me out of here! You hear me? You wanna save yourself and this town; you'd better let us go!"

During his boss's tirade, the wounded cowboy lowered his head and looked away. Charlie nodded. There wouldn't be any more trouble from him.

A bleary-eyed Doc Morgan showed up along with Deputy Johnson. The doctor wore the same white shirt and black trousers he wore earlier in the day. His hair was mussed and he wasn't wearing his hat or his coat.

"You look like you just got out of bed, Doc," Charlie said.

"Damn right I did. What happened here?"

"That one in the street and these two here tried to bust their boss out of jail. They didn't quite make it."

"Their boss?" Morgan asked.

"Amos has Walker locked up in jail," Charlie said, and after a moment added, "He's got tuberculosis, Doc."

Doc Morgan shook his head. "That's bad. It's a death sentence. Is he coughing up blood?"

Charlie nodded.

"Well, it's just a matter of time, then." Doc Morgan handed his house key to the deputy. "Get someone to help you get these fellows out of here and take them down to my back room. I'll tend to them later." Doc Morgan looked at the wounded cowboy sitting on the stool against the stone cell wall. "Let's get that shirt off and see where all that shot ended up."

"I'll help Johnson with the bodies." Charlie turned to Marshal Cook. "You need me here anymore tonight?"

"Naw, you go ahead. I think I'll be okay for a while."

"I may lay down on your sofa for a bit, Doc," Charlie said.

"Help yourself," the doctor said. "You know where the blanket is."

"Thanks." Charlie walked out to help Deputy Johnson sling the bodies over Johnson's saddle. They walked the horse to the rear of Doc Morgan's place and set the two dead cowboys on the floor next to the large wooden table in his back room. After the deputy left, Charlie lit an oil lamp. He pulled a blanket from a shelf in the back room and walked through to the front parlor where an old overstuffed sofa sat along the front window.

Doc's front parlor was a small room just off the entry door where the doctor greeted patients and clients. The walls were covered in a maroon and grey striped wall paper and accented with dark stained wood trim. The large grey fabric sofa sat under the front window and a matching winged back chair sat off to the left side. Charlie couldn't ever remember hearing a note from the old pump organ on the opposite wall next to the door leading to the doc's back room. A round dinette-sized wooden table sat in the middle of the room covered with a lace cloth and an oil lamp in the middle of the table. A small secretary desk containing his paper, ink, and quill, sat next to the door leading to the entry. A large thick patterned rug covered most of the dark hardwood floor planks, tying together all the colors in room. It was a very pleasant and comfortable setting.

Charlie took off his jacket, his shirt, and his boots, and turned the lamp down to a dim glow. He lay down on his right side on the sofa, covered himself with the blanket and tried to sleep. He focused on the flickering of the flame as it danced across the cotton wick in the oil lamp, trying to ignore the steady pounding in his head, and soon he drifted into sleep.

14

Future Facts

Charlie woke from another dream. Sleep came to him in only brief periods this night. He would wake, fully alert from some insignificant dream, then take what seemed like forever to drift off to sleep again. He was startled awake when the doctor came back home and went right upstairs to his bedroom. The pounding in his head from Walker's punch had diminished a bit, replaced with a steady dull ache.

The muggy June night added to his discomfort. He sat up on the edge of the sofa and looked out the front window which faced the stockyard corrals across the street. It was still dark with no sign of a sunrise. He couldn't turn off the thoughts that kept swirling around in his head. In his anger he wanted Mac Sherman and Abe Walker out of the way forever. With Abe's illness, it looked like he would soon be dead. Mac, on the other hand, had to be dealt with.

How to deal with Mac was going to be a challenge. Charlie never claimed to be much of a gun hand. He knew he would lose a one-on-one gun battle with Mac. He had to out think him.

With the incessant thoughts and dreams running through his mind and the pain in his head, it was useless to try and go back to sleep. He turned up the oil lamp and sat for a minute looking around at a blurry aura surrounding Doc's parlor room. That's when he noticed his vision was a little fuzzy. *Probably from the lack of sleep.* He felt gritty and he smelled of horses and a week's worth of sweat and trail dust. He needed a bath, a shave, and a change of clothes, but all that would have to wait until he got back to his cabin.

Charlie got up, put on his shirt, boots, and jacket and quietly left Doc Morgan's home. The streets were dark and deserted. He walked up Polk Street heading for the livery to get Gus when he noticed a dim light coming from Marshal Cook's office. Charlie peered through the only window in the marshal's office and saw Deputy Johnson sound asleep in his chair behind the desk. The marshal was nowhere to be seen. Charlie figured he was probably off finally getting some rest.

By the time Charlie reached the livery, the sky in the east was beginning to show a faint grey light. Gus saw Charlie as soon as he opened one of the barn doors, and he gave a loud neigh in happy recognition, nodding his head.

"How you doing, old boy?" Charlie put his arm around his neck and stroked the side of his face. Gus nuzzled his neck across Charlie's shoulder.

Charlie saddled Gus in the stall, untied the halter rope and led him outside. He closed the barn door, climbed into the saddle and they quietly walked out of town. When they reached his cabin, Charlie left Gus saddled, but loosened the saddle cinch, as he put him in the makeshift corral. He gave him a helping of grain and filled his water bucket.

Charlie got a fresh bucket of water from the stream, stripped down and bathed himself outside by the old stump. He then put on some clean clothes and finally shaved his weeks' worth of whiskers. He stared at himself in the broken mirror above his washstand. He felt like a new man, but all this cleaning still didn't help his state of mind regarding Russell, Abe and Mac.

The last thirty years flashed through Charlie's brain like lightening. He remembered the day that he arrived in 1862 from the later part of the twenty-third century. His unintentional time jump gave him a new reprieve on life. Circumstances presented themselves to Charlie that led to his decision to stay and live in the past. Maybe someday he would go back. But that "someday" never came.

Charlie opened the trunk by his bed and removed the canvas bag that contained his time belt. It wasn't very impressive, nothing more than a black synthetic strap that had small silver and gold cylinders attached in an alternating pattern all around the belt. It resembled a cartridge belt one might have for a rifle. In the front of the belt, where both ends clasped together, was a small square black plastic frame that contained a sensor screen and a single switch.

Charlie sat on the edge of his bed holding the belt, still thinking about Mac. He'd been living in a world where he wasn't supposed to be. Since he arrived here he had always tried to live by the simple rule that he could not affect any life or events in this era. There was no way he could just out and out kill someone. He tried hard to follow this rule, but sometimes circumstances dictated otherwise. Sometimes, he had no choice. Facing Mac might be one of those times.

Then there was Russell. Charlie worried about Russell surviving so he could get back to his own time era. If Russell Hicks was the same Russell Hicks he met when he was a boy, then he would have to make sure Russell got back to fulfill a destiny that he knew nothing about. He couldn't tell Russell what an important role he would eventually play in the future development of time travel and teleportation. He would have to find that out on his own. He kept running different scenarios through his mind of what could happen to the future if a time traveler disappeared in the past. Then it dawned on him; he was a time traveler that disappeared in the past, over thirty years ago.

Charlie was sure that Russell didn't just happen here by mistake. In spite of what the boy said, it was not possible. The dimensional matrix, that makes time travel possible, knew exactly and precisely where and when space/time is altered. There couldn't have been any error. The matrix does not make mistakes, it's mathematically impossible. Russell either came here by his own choice or someone sent him here for a reason. Maybe that someone was trying to get rid of Russell and thought the middle of the desolate Texas panhandle in 1892 was the way to do it.

Charlie could see no other course. The solution to getting rid of Russell, he decided, was simple. As soon as Russell could move on his own, Charlie would send Russell home with the time belt. That was the mechanism he used 30 years earlier to come here. But he knew that, one way or another, he would have to deal with Abe and Mac. And it wouldn't be as easy as sending someone home.

Charlie stood with the belt in his hand and let out a long sigh. He didn't like time jumping. However, being who he was, he really had no choice. He had to find out what history had been recorded so he could act accordingly in this time.

"You've done this before," Charlie said to himself out loud, trying to work up the courage for the jump. "One more trip and then you're done, forever."

Charlie set his pocket pistol and his gun belt on the table, and strapped the belt around his waist. He turned on the switch, took a deep breath, and placed his index finger on the sensor screen. Immediately, a haze of blue-green light surrounded Charlie and formed a transparent cocoon-like appearance around him. A virtual display appeared in front of his eyes where he could determine settings for his destination. Charlie punched in the coordinates for Austin, Texas, June, 1895, three years in the future. He watched the counter step down, closed his eyes, heard a familiar snap, and then blacked out.

When Charlie opened his eyes, he was laying in the middle of a rancher's field just outside the city limits of Austin Texas. His heart jumped when he opened his eyes and saw a number of longhorn cows standing over him. He stood up, shooed the cattle away and began walking to the Austin City Hall. Judging by the sun's position in the eastern sky, Charlie guessed it to be mid-morning. As he walked into town, he pulled his shirt out over top of the time belt so no one would see it.

When Charlie reached the City Hall, he greeted the guard and the two exchanged some small talk. Charlie had been there a number of times before and the guard was familiar with him. After a brief conversation, Charlie went into the records room where he could look up the records of anyone who was born, lived in, or died in Texas. He was having a harder time than usual focusing on the pages. Again he brushed it off as not having enough rest.

He found that there were no records at all for Mac Sherman. That would mean that three years in the future, Mac was either still alive, or he left Texas altogether, or his body had never been found. He wondered if Mac Sherman was his real name, or just an alias that he picked up when he left Missouri.

He found that Abe Walker died in Amarillo, Texas in June of 1892. The certificate, signed by Doctor Walter Morgan, stated he died of consumption. This was good news for Charlie. He got his answer about Abe, but he'd have to take his chances with Mac.

Lastly, Charlie looked for any records of himself. He found a death notice for Charles Turlock who died from a fire in June, 1892. A cold sweat broke out across his body. A strange fear overtook him as he stared at his own death certificate. It too was signed by Doc Morgan. "We'll see about that." He ripped the page from the file and folded it up and stuck it in his pocket. "Fire. I doubt it."

He then looked up the land records for Walker's ranch and found that between the years of 1892 and 1895 various sections of Walker's property had been homesteaded or sold at auction to various ranchers and farmers. Charlie thought it was strange that Mac didn't claim Walker's estate. As close as those two had become, and no heirs, Charlie was certain that Mac would have gotten everything; either by decree or by force.

Charlie left the City Hall and walked a long way out of the city until he came to an area where he didn't see anyone around. In a flash of a pale blue light and a loud snap, Charlie was back at his cabin again.

After Charlie woke up, he took off the belt and returned it to the canvas bag and set it back in the trunk. He stared at it for a little while holding the trunk lid open. He thought that once Russell leaves with his belt, he would never have the opportunity to return to the future ever again. A coldness surged through him. That's when he realized that all these years he had been holding on to that one comforting thought of being able to return anytime he wanted. It was his crutch. He knew he could run away from anything with that belt. Something he's been doing his whole life.

"The hell with it." Charlie let the trunk lid slam closed.

Charlie strapped on his gun belt, slid his .32 pistol in his belt behind his back and walked out to Gus. He pulled his '73 Winchester from the saddle scabbard, checked to make sure it was fully loaded, and reinserted it back into the casing. He stroked Gus's nose and watched him finish the few remaining oats in his bin.

His trip to Austin created more questions than answers. The only thing he was sure of was that Abe Walker never left Amarillo alive. But what happened to Mac? Why wasn't Walker's estate claimed by Sherman? ... Or anyone? Why did it get split up? And what about that fire?

"I've got a feeling we've got a tough time ahead of us," Charlie said. Gus's ears perked up and he looked intently at him. Charlie tightened up the saddle straps, climbed into the saddle and in the morning light headed down the trail back toward town.

15

Awakening

Charlie rode Gus to the hitch rail just outside Marshal Cook's office. Before he could dismount, Marshal Cook came out.

"The boy's awake," the marshal said. "Doc's with him now at Hanna's."

Charlie jumped off Gus and ran through the restaurant into the small kitchen. Russell lay on his side while Doc Morgan removed the bandage he put on the day before and looked at the stitching.

Hanna stood next to Doc Morgan peering over his shoulder. When Russell saw Charlie he managed a slight smile. A warm feeling flushed through Charlie to see Russell awake and smiling at him.

"How's it looking, Doc?" Charlie asked.

"Not bad," Doc Morgan smiled, seeming rather pleased with his own handiwork.

"What happened, Charlie?" Russell asked.

"You were shot. Mac Sherman thought you were me and tried to kill you," Charlie said.

"Why would he think I was you?"

"It was dark. You were walking my horse, wearing my hat and my old vest. You were lucky."

"Lucky!" Russell repeated. "Apparently you're the lucky one. I don't feel so damn lucky!"

"The bullet hit your rib and bounced out. If it hadn't, Doc here would be putting you in a box right about now."

"Charlie's right, son," Doc Morgan said. "It's a shame you were shot, but you really are lucky to be alive."

Russell shook his head. "This has got to be the worst two days of my life."

Doc asked Russell if he could sit up which he did with some obvious discomfort. The doctor placed a new linen pad, soaked with chemicals, over the wound and Russell grimaced when the wet pad hit his wound. Doc retied the linen strip around his torso.

Russell appeared a little pale. "I'm feeling pretty dizzy. I think I have to lie back down."

"That's expected," Doc said. "You lost a lot of blood. You feel sick?"

"No, just a little dizzy."

"You need to eat something." Doc Morgan turned and nodded to Hanna. "Hanna will fix you some food. Eat as much of it as you can. You need to get your strength back."

Hanna smiled. "I got some nice soup for ya', Hicks." She added wood to the stove and pulled the soup pot over to the iron plate above the fire box.

"Can he be moved?" Charlie asked.

"He shouldn't be; at least not at this time," the doctor said. "Where you want to take him, Charlie?"

"I was just thinking he might be a little more comfortable in a bed at the hotel."

"Well, you might be right. But I'd wait and see how he feels after he eats something." Doc packed up his instruments. "Try not to move around too much. You got a hell of a hole in your side. We don't want it to start bleeding again."

Charlie followed Doc Morgan out of the kitchen. Hanna stayed near Russell while the soup warmed up.

Marshal Cook joined Charlie and the doctor when they came out of the restaurant. "How's the boy doing?"

"He'll be fine. He just needs some time to heal up," Doc Morgan said. "I'd better get back to my office. I got a couple bodies to bury."

Doc Morgan walked up Polk Street to his home near the stockyards, and Charlie followed the marshal back to his office. When they entered, Charlie looked at the marshal's empty desk.

"A lot of the guns are missing," Charlie said.

"Yeah, after the shooting, it got pretty quiet here. Most of those cowboys came back in, picked up their hardware, and left without a problem. I still have that other one in the cell with Walker. And neither one of them are very happy about it."

The marshal looked through the small window of the large wooden cell door. Walker was sitting on the only cot in the cell. There were streaks of blood on his shirt from his coughing spells. He looked like he hadn't slept all night. The other cowboy sat on the floor leaning against the stone wall.

"What am I going to do with Walker, Charlie?" Marshal Cook paused, looked at Charlie, and let out a sigh. "I don't like it." He sat down on the corner of his desk. "They tried to break out Abe last night. Sherman may bring that whole camp in here to get his boss. If that happens, there's no tellin' how many people will get hurt. You think they'd be trying that again?"

"I doubt it," Charlie said. "Doc said Abe is so bad off he wouldn't make it back to the Pecos from here. He may not even make it out of Amarillo." He paused. "It might be best to just let nature take its course. The problem might solve itself."

"What are you getting at?" The marshal stood and starred at Charlie. "If that ol' bastard dies here without unloading his herd, we'll have a whole new set of problems to deal with."

"That's my point," Charlie answered. "Let Walker out. Tell him he did his time."

"What? You mean just let him go?"

"The first thing he'll do is round up his boys and get his cattle sold," Charlie said. "Once he pays off his hands, most of those transient cowboys will scatter, heading off to their next job. The few hands that work directly for Walker will most likely head back to the Pecos with the wagons and the leads."

"And that will leave just Walker and Sherman," the marshal interjected.

115

"Right," Charlie agreed. As a second thought he added, "But what about that other fella you got in jail?"

"He stays. He tried a jail break and tried to kill me. I think I'll keep him around until the circuit judge gets here."

"When's that?"

"A couple of weeks. Give him a chance to heal up for his trial."

The two chuckled, and the marshal offered to buy Charlie some breakfast at Hanna's. He tossed the cell key to Deputy Johnson and told him they'd be next door.

The two lawmen ate a leisurely breakfast of Hanna's biscuits, eggs and bacon. Marshal Cook did all the talking during the meal. Charlie just listened and nodded while he ate and occasionally got up to check on Russell in the back room. But his mind continued running.

He thought about Abe's impending death and his eventual final meeting with Mac. He thought about Russell and getting him back to the twenty-third century where he belonged. While he listened to Marshal Cook and ate his breakfast, a course of action began to formulate in Charlie's mind. All he needed now was a miracle.

16

Cowboy's Camp

Hanna refilled the coffee cups for the lawmen and picked up their empty plates. "Hicks ate some soup, Charlie," she said, apparently anticipating Charlie's question.

"That's good, Hanna. Thank you." Charlie chuckled. It felt good to laugh. He couldn't remember the last time he did. How sad that his life was in so much turmoil that he had nothing to laugh about. He knew he could always count on Hanna to bring a smile to his face. Somehow, just being around her brought a little comfort to him and made his day a bit brighter, even if it was only momentary. He sipped his coffee and thought about the upcoming day and the things he had planned.

Marshal Cook finished his coffee, picked up his wide brimmed hat, and settled the costs with Hanna. "I'm riding out to Walker's camp to see about Sherman. You wanna come along?"

"Mac's a regular curly-wolf, Amos. Those cowboys just might shoot us down before we get there."

"You got a better idea?" the marshal asked.

Charlie sipped his coffee. "I guess not. Just doesn't seem like a right healthy plan of action, that's all."

"Well, it's my job, Charlie. I have to go and you know it. You're welcome to come along if you're that worried about me." The marshal shut the door behind him and headed back to his office.

Charlie sat alone at the table near the front window, sipping his coffee and watching people walk by outside. When the few remaining patrons left the restaurant, Hanna sat down at his table.

"Hicks really ate good, Charlie. Soup and biscuits," she said again, seemingly pleased with herself. "He fell asleep again after he ate."

"You did fine, Hanna," Charlie said. "I'm going down to talk with Henry and get a room at the hotel for him. He'll be more comfortable there and he'll have a staff of people watching out for him."

Hanna nodded. "You want more coffee, Charlie?"

"No thanks, Hanna. I have to go."

Hanna stood up to leave but Charlie lightly grabbed her hand. "I want you to know that I really appreciate you watching over the boy back there. I know it's a burden on you that you really don't need."

"Oh, Charlie, it's no trouble at all." Hanna smiled. "You needed help, I was glad to do it. Besides, it gives me someone to look after. I haven't had anyone since Walter passed." A frown appeared on her forehead as she lowered her head and paused. Charlie could see that she was lost in a solemn memory. After a moment she said "You go on, now, and do what you got to do." Hanna carried Charlie's coffee mug to the back room.

Charlie left the restaurant and walked over to the marshal's office. He shared the same feelings of responsibility that Marshal Cook had about going out in search of Mac Sherman. He knew he couldn't let the marshal go out there alone. He saw Marshal Cook seated at his desk as he walked by the window. Charlie opened the door. "I've got a couple of things I need to do first. Then I'll be back. Don't go out there without me." He shut the door before the marshal could reply.

Charlie walked a few blocks to the Amarillo Hotel. He spoke with Henry, the proprietor of the hotel, and arranged a room for Russell. Since there were no first-floor rooms, he reserved a room closest to the top of the stairs on the second floor overlooking the street. The problem was getting Russell out of Hanna's and upstairs to a second floor bed. Russell was certainly not in any condition to get there on his own. Henry assured Charlie that it would not be a problem. He had a solution.

Three of the staff of the Amarillo Hotel accompanied Charlie back to Hanna's, carrying an old cavalry stretcher they kept for emergencies. They set the stretcher on the floor next to Russell's cot and Charlie helped them move the boy. Russell let out a cry of pain as the four men transferred him from the cot to the litter. He grimaced and groaned as he was set down on the thin canvas stretcher. The three men and Charlie easily carried Russell from the eatery to the hotel and up the stairs to Russell's new room. After Russell got transferred from the stretcher to the bed, Charlie raised the shade and opened the curtains to let in the sunlight.

"Thanks for your help, men." Charlie handed each one of them a silver dollar. The men nodded their thanks and disappeared into the hallway and down the stairs.

"You okay?" Charlie asked.

Russell nodded while he settled into a comfortable position. "That was horrible, but I'll live. The bed feels better than that cot."

Charlie looked at Russell. He wanted to talk to him about his life. Instead he simply looked away and stared out the window. He didn't know how to begin a story that he never told another living soul. He decided that it would be better to postpone his talk until later, after he got back.

"Look, Russell, there are some things I need to talk to you about," Charlie began, "but, I've got to go with Cook right now. I'll be back later on this afternoon to look in on you. We'll be able to talk better then. You get some rest."

Charlie put on his hat and walked out of Russell's room without looking back at him. He walked over to Solomon's and picked up his order from the previous day. While he was there he picked out a blanket and some new sheets for Hanna to replace the ones Doc Morgan ripped up. He loaded his supplies onto Gus and carried his bundles to the marshal's office and set them on the table.

"I've got to see Hanna for a minute. I got her some things for her."

Marshal Cook just smiled and looked down at his desk. "New bed linens, huh? I don't know, Charlie, seems like it's getting pretty serious," the marshal quipped.

"Just do your paperwork," Charlie shot back. "I'll be back in a minute." Not enjoying the marshal's wit, he gave Marshal Cook an irritated look as he left the office.

Hanna was at the back counter when Charlie came in. All the tables and chairs were filled with people eating their midday meal. He walked to the back carrying his bundle of new sheets wrapped in brown paper. "I got these here for you. I figured you could use a new set. Now, don't say anything or make a fuss. It's the least I can do."

"Oh, my!" She opened the string and the brown paper wrapping. "Thank you, Charlie, thank you! They're just wonderful! I can really use these. You really didn't have to do this!" Hanna gave Charlie a big hug.

"Well, I'd better be off, now." Charlie moved toward the door. "Thanks again for watching over the boy. I'll see you soon."

Hanna flashed Charlie another thankful smile as he left the restaurant. He walked over to the marshal's office and the two looked at each other for a moment.

"That didn't take long," the marshal said.

"Hobble your lip."

"You sure you want to join me, Charlie? You didn't seem too keen on the idea a little while ago."

"I'm not keen on it at all, and I really don't want to join you," Charlie said. Then he smiled, "But I just can't let you go out there and have all this fun by yourself."

It was early afternoon when Marshal Cook and Charlie mounted their horses and headed out of town toward the cowboy's camp. It wasn't long before they arrived in the midst of the thousands of cattle roaming the valley. The dust hung thick in the air as the cows moved around stirring up the earth.

Marshal Cook looked all around. "I don't like this. There ain't a single herd rider here."

"Maybe they saw us coming and headed back to the campsite," Charlie said. "I'm sure they weren't expecting us to come to them. I think they're camped about a mile down the valley. How do you want to do this?"

"I don't think we'll be able to sneak up on them." The marshal grinned. "So we might as well make an entrance." With that, he tapped the sides of his horse with his spurs and took off at a fast gallop down the valley toward the cattle drive's encampment.

Charlie shook his head. "Hell! Here we go, Gus!" Charlie lightly spurred Gus and took off behind the marshal.

The cowboys were all busy somewhat packing up their gear in anticipation of their boss's eventual return when Charlie and the marshal rode into their camp.

The group stopped what they were doing and encircled the two lawmen. Charlie recognized the one cowboy who took a few steps forward.

The cowboy shook his head "I gotta hand it to you boys. You got a lotta sand coming in here like this."

"I remember you," Charlie said. "You were at the ranch. You're Bonnam."

"That's right. I watched you gun down Jeremiah and Mac."

"As I recollect, you never pulled your gun." Charlie tried to bait him into a mistake. It was plain to see by the expression on Bonnam's face that Charlie struck a nerve. The cowboy, nicknamed "Crabtree", ranked second in command behind Mac. Charlie moved the reins to his left hand and lowered his right hand closer to his gun, all the while staring at him. Crabtree nervously looked around at the other cowboys. They were all watching him.

Breaking the silent standoff, Marshal Cook demanded, "Where's Sherman?"

"I ain't seen him." Bonnam shifted his attention from Charlie to the marshal. "Where's Abe?"

"You'll get Walker when I get Sherman," the marshal countered. "I know he came back here last night. Now where'd he go?"

"Gone," said a different cowboy standing behind Charlie.

"Gone where?" Charlie said.

"Pecos, I guess. Don't rightly know," another cowboy behind the Marshal said. "Packed his gear last night and lit out at first light.

121

Just like that. He's only got a half day head start on you boys if you want to try an' catch him."

All the cowboys laughed. Crabtree Bonnam took a few slow steps toward Marshal Cook. Charlie unstrapped his hammer guard and put his hand on his gun.

"Just to let you know, Marshal. We ain't too happy with this situation," Bonnam said. "We spent three long hard months on a tough drive getting here and you got our pay locked up in jail. Then you killed two of our crew and shot up and locked away another."

"They shouldn't have tried to kill me," the marshal replied.

"Just the same, it don't set well with us. Now you come out here wantin' our help? When Abe gets back, your life won't be worth spit. Like I said, you got a lotta sand. You'll get nothing here."

Marshal Cook looked at Charlie and the cowboys surrounding him. It was obvious to both of them that it was pointless to press any further conversation. Marshal Cook turned and headed out of the cowboy's campsite. Charlie followed close behind. Once they got out of sight of the campsite, Marshal Cook stopped his horse and Charlie did the same.

"You think he's really gone?" the marshal asked.

Charlie shook his head. "I don't think he would go all the way back to Walker's ranch with so many loose ends unsettled. His boss and ranch hand are locked up, the herd ain't sold, and then there's me. My guess is he'll find a place to hide out for a while, somewhere close by, like maybe Tascosa. He could blend in and disappear there pretty easily. I figure he'll swing back around Amarillo in due time and set things straight. He won't leave until Walker's out and his boys are paid."

The marshal looked at Charlie. "You got any suggestions?"

"Let Walker out so he can pay his boys."

"That could be risky," the marshal replied.

"We could try to go after Mac. But, with his horse and his head start, we'd be hard pressed to even follow him, much less catch up with him," Charlie said. "That's assuming we know where he went."

The marshal shook his head. The expression on his face showed how upset he was.

"What do you want to do?" Charlie asked.

"Well, it looks like we wait and play it your way." Marshal Cook nudged his horse forward and started walking back toward town. The two rode their horses at a slow pace in silence. The stern look on Marshal Cook's face showed his frustration and disappointment. After a while the marshal shook his head. "This is twice that two-bit cow puncher got away from me. It won't happen again."

Charlie kept silent. He wanted to tell the marshal that Mac Sherman was anything but a two-bit cowboy. Mac was a cool-headed and calculated killer, but telling that to the marshal at this point wouldn't affect his mood at all. So it was best to let it go. They rode back toward town silently.

Charlie began thinking of what he needed to tell Russell. He was a little nervous about the speech he was preparing in his mind. He hadn't mentioned his story to anyone in thirty years and he wasn't sure how Russell would respond, but he was getting himself ready to find out.

17

Release

On the ride back to town from the cowboy's encampment Charlie told the marshal he had some tasks he needed to attend to and that he would meet the marshal back in town. Charlie left the marshal north of town and headed to his cabin with his supplies. Marshal Cook returned to his office.

The marshal was still riled over a wasted trip to the cowboy's encampment and letting Mac Sherman slip through his grasp once again. He pulled the key from his desk, unlocked, and swung open the cell's heavy wooden door. Like a caged animal, unsure of the open door, a dirty, unshaven, and tired Abe Walker slowly emerged from the stone cell followed by the other wounded cowboy. The marshal blocked the path of the cowboy. "You stay put." He closed the door and locked it again.

Walker looked at Marshal Cook, apparently a little confused.

"You're free. You served your time. Get out of here," Cook growled.

He opened the bottom drawer of his desk and removed Walker's hand tooled leather gun belt and holster. From it he pulled Walker's nickel plated Colt .45 with the hand carved ivory grips.

"So you made yourself judge and jury now, too," Abe Walker said. "You made a big mistake, Marshal."

"Yeah, I did." Marshal Cook emptied the cartridges from Abe's gun. "But locking you up wasn't one of them."

"What about my man in there?" Walker pointed to the cell.

"You can have him back when the circuit judge gets through with him." Marshal Cook shoved the holster and the empty gun into Walker's hands and stepped up close to him. "Now get out of my town and stay out. Take your crew and your cows and get your business done. The next time you drive cattle, you take them North to Dodge or East to the Chisholm. But you stay clear of Amarillo. Now get out of here!"

"I'll go where I damn well please," Walker shot back, "And you, or any army like you, won't ever keep me from it!"

Marshal Cook took another step forward, which forced Abe to take a step back. Abe put his hand on Cook's chest to halt his advance, but the marshal slapped it away and took another step forward. Abe backed up until his back was against the front door.

Walker opened the door with the marshal standing right next to him. He stopped in the doorway, glaring at the marshal, and, in defiance of the law, strapped his gun belt around his waist.

"The next time we meet …" Abe began.

"The next time we meet," the marshal interrupted, "you'd better have your guns out because if I see you within rifle distance, I'm gonna kill you."

Then the marshal gave Walker a final shove out of his office and slammed the door shut. He kicked one of the wooden chairs as a release of his anger, but it didn't help. *Turlock had better be right about this.* He took a deep breath and tried to compose himself.

After retrieving his palomino from the livery, Abe Walker rode out to his encampment where his crew gathered around and welcomed him as he rode into camp.

"Is Mac here?" he asked in a painful raspy voice.

Crabtree Bonnam stepped forward. "He packed his gear and lit out of here first light."

"Send someone to Tascosa and tell him to get back here right away," Abe ordered.

"Tascosa? How do you know he's in Tascosa?"

"Because that's where I told him to go," Abe growled. "Now you gonna stand there asking questions all day or you gonna do what I tell you?"

Crabtree grabbed the first cowboy he saw, a saddle bum named Bart Chaney hired only for this drive, and ordered him to cut a fresh horse from the stock and head out to retrieve Mac. He helped Abe off his horse and handed the reins of the big palomino to another cowboy. He guided Abe over to a seat by the chuck wagon.

"That marshal and that ranger came out here this morning looking for Mac. But Mac was already long gone," Crabtree said.

Abe sat straight up and his face reddened with anger. "Those two were here? And you didn't kill them?" he roared.

"They just kind of busted in here. We didn't have a chance to do much of anything, Mr. Walker." Crabtree hung his head.

Abe Walker took a swing at the cowboy but missed and lost his balance and almost fell over. Crabtree backed away and then stepped forward to help Walker regain his balance. "Damn you bunch of cowards! There were fifteen guns here and you were held at bay by an old broke down ranger and one marshal!" Walker roared, trying desperately to contain his need to cough. "You're all yella!"

Abe surveyed his crew who all stood with their heads lowered. He desperately wanted to assemble his men and ride his small army back into Amarillo and deal with Marshal Cook and Ranger Turlock, but he knew he needed to get his herd sold. He was already behind schedule.

"Get on your horses!" Abe ordered.

"We going back after those lawmen?" Crabtree asked.

"No. Not now. We'll take care of them later. Right now, you're going to do your job. I want every cow rounded up. We're moving them to the stocks." Walker turned to Bonnam and pointed his finger in his face. "You will pay for every missing head. So you'd better be thorough."

Bonnam nodded and walked away shouting orders to the other cowboys and before long all were mounted and out rounding up every stray and driving them back to the centralized herd.

Abe pulled his jacket a little tighter around his chest and let out the cough he had been holding in.

"Coffee's hot, Mr. Walker," the cook said. "I was just about to toss it and start packing."

"No coffee," Abe said with a wheeze in his chest. He rose and slowly and unsteadily staggered toward his wagon. "Get me a blanket and a bottle of my medicine."

Charlie straightened up his cabin and stored the supplies he purchased at Solomon's. He gathered up all the dirty clothes he wore on his trip to and from Cañon City and stuffed them into a canvas bag to take to the laundry in town. He rolled up Russell's clothes and shoes and hid them in a drawer in the washstand. While Charlie was cleaning he took inventory of the clothes and items he had acquired over the past thirty years. He set out bare necessity items he would take with him and stowed the things he would leave behind.

Charlie was thinking about coffee and a can of peaches, but he needed to check on Russell. He thought he might just stop in and have some coffee and something to eat at Hanna's. Not that he was looking for an excuse to see her.

He heard Gus neigh loudly and went to the front window to see what the horse was warning about. He picked up the Remington 1883 shotgun he kept by the door, and slowly pushed open the window shutter. He couldn't see anything, but he heard someone or something moving through the trees down the hill below his cabin. He walked outside and carefully moved toward the sound, slipping from behind one tree to the next.

Then Charlie saw one of Walker's cowboys riding his horse through the trees. He recognized this cowboy from his trip to their encampment earlier today. Charlie raised his shotgun as the cowboy drew near.

"What's your business?" Charlie yelled out.

Charlie's sudden question seemed to startle him. It was obvious that the cowboy wasn't expecting anyone among the trees. He immediately stopped his horse, keeping his hands in plain sight.

"No trouble, mister," the cowboy answered, "just looking for strays."

"Hadn't seen any up this far. You'd better head back down." Charlie kept his shotgun aimed.

"Much obliged." The cowboy turned and headed back down the hill.

Charlie lowered the shotgun and walked back up the hill. He saddled Gus, tied on his saddle bags, and tied the canvas clothes bag to the saddle horn.

"I hope that fella didn't recognize me." Charlie patted Gus on his neck. "You ready to take another ride? How you feel about pulling one of Tuck's buckboards later?" Gus gave a snort.

18

Infection

Russell was having problems with his chamber pot at the hotel. The first problem was that he hated using it, since he was only introduced to one the day before. The second problem was that his wound was hurting him a lot more today than yesterday. Any movement at all brought on a burning and stinging pain around the wound. He was tired and weak and was covered in sweat. He was struggling to get back into bed when there was a knock on the door.

"Come in," Russell hollered.

Doc Morgan pushed open the door and rushed in to help.

"Thanks," Russell said after settling into a comfortable position.

"How you feeling today?"

"I feel horrible. It seems to be hurting a lot worse. It's starting to burn."

"Let's take a look."

Doc Morgan helped Russell remove his shirt and then unwrapped the bandage he had tied around him. The injury was swollen and red around the sutures. The slightest touch brought on a twinge of pain. The doctor went to the door and called down for one of the hotel staff. Shortly after, a young boy appeared at the door.

"Go down and tell the cook to pour some boiling hot water in a bowl. Bring that bowl up here along with a few clean towels," the doctor ordered.

The boy ran off with his orders and the doctor closed the door.

"What is it?" Russell asked.

"That wound is infected," the doctor said. "I'm gonna have to open it back up and drain it."

Russell could feel the blood drain from his face. The fear of cutting open that wound again caused his nerves to quiver. "The wound is infected?"

"Appears so." Doc Morgan opened his bag and pulled out a couple of instruments and two glass vials with liquid in them. One vial contained a clear liquid, and the other looked like weak tea.

"What are those?" Russell asked.

"This one is pure alcohol." The doc pointed to the clear liquid, "and the other one is a mixture of carbolic acid and camphor. It's a pretty good antiseptic." Just then there was a soft knock on the door. Doc Morgan answered it, and a young man came in carrying a tray with a steaming bowl of hot water and a stack of fresh towels.

"Set that next to the bed," the doctor ordered.

The servant did as the doctor asked and left the room. Doc Morgan set the instruments he removed from his bag into the bowl of water and poured a little of the antiseptic mixture into it as well.

"I'm going to cut just the end of the sutures here and see what I can get drained out of there," the doctor said.

"Will it hurt?" Russell heard a tinge of fear in his own voice.

Doc Morgan paused and gave Russell a sympathetic look. "Like blazes. You'd better hold on to something."

Russell didn't want to look. With nervous apprehension, he grabbed hold of each side of his pillow and buried his face in it. The first incision was not very painful, just a tug on a couple of the stitches. However the second incision went considerably deeper into the tissue. Russell clenched his fists around the pillow and let out a painful scream that he tried to muffle into his pillow. Russell could feel a warm liquid running down his torso from the wound. Doc Morgan shoved one of the towels next to Russell to absorb the pus that was draining from the wound.

130

"That wasn't too bad," Doc Morgan said.

"Maybe not for you," Russell retorted.

Doc Morgan smiled and removed a stack of clean cotton pads from his bag. Each cloth was neatly folded into a square pad. He set the stack of cloth pads on the tray next to the bowl of water.

"I made these pads for you," the doctor said. He dipped one of the pads in the hot water and carbolic acid mixture, and placed it over the wound. Russell jumped and let out a painful sigh initially, but he got used to it as it cooled.

"Keep a pad on the wound just like this and keep it wet with the water from the bowl. It will help draw out some of that infection."

Russell looked at the wet cloth pad covering his wound, and nodded to acknowledge his instructions.

"I'll have a boy check on you. If the water gets too cool or runs out, have him get another bowl of hot water and pour a little of that carbolic acid mixture in it. You have to keep it wet and as hot as you can stand it. Change the towel when it gets too wet. And change that pad every couple of hours or so."

"I guess I'm stuck in this place another day," Russell muttered.

"Well, you won't be doing any dancing for a while, that's for sure." Doc Morgan cleaned and packed his instruments. "I'll be back to check on you this evening. Just stay lying down and tend to that pad."

Russell let his head drop back down to the pillow and he let out a loud sigh of disappointment.

The doctor smiled at Russell as he opened the door. "Don't worry. It'll be better in a day or so." The doctor stepped out and closed the door behind him.

Russell relaxed in bed, keeping his hand on the wet pad to keep it from falling off. He was looking forward to going back to Charlie's cabin with him. He had had enough of Amarillo. He was not used to being alone. Even though this was America, to Russell, four hundred years in the past was a strange land in a strange time with strange customs.

Charlie rode Gus to Old Town, and went to the window of the telegraph office next to Doc Morgan's house. He jotted a quick note and handed it to the telegraph operator. The operator studied the note.

"Where's this going?" the operator asked through the window.

"Trinidad, in the Colorado territory," Charlie replied. "A Mister Frank McCrudy."

The operator made some scribbles on the side of the note and checked a chart on the wall. "That'll be two bits." Charlie tossed him a coin, thanked him, and led Gus across the street.

Just opposite the telegraph office was the Wah-Sam's Chinese Laundry. Smoke rose from the fires in the back of the laundry that heated the three huge kettles they used to clean the clothes. Charlie walked in, carrying his canvas sack of dirty clothes, and a dusty wool blanket.

"Ahh, Chayee! Wecom. Wecom." The old proprietor shuffled to the counter and bowed.

Charlie nodded his greeting and set his bundle on the counter.

"Ahways good business fom you." The old laundryman smiled.

"Yeah, Sam, I bring you a lot of business," Charlie said.

"Many tings now." The laundryman sorted through Charlie's laundry. "You gone long time?"

"No, but I will be. I need to pack more clothes. Wrap these twice. I'll need to keep them as clean as I can for a while. And clean that blanket, too."

The old laundryman acknowledged Charlie's instructions and took the bundle of clothes along with the blanket to the back room.

"I'll pick them up tomorrow," Charlie yelled after the old Chinaman.

"No! Two day!" came the answer from behind the curtain separating the front of the store from the laundry area.

"What's that you say?" Charlie growled.

"Two day. You come back two day." The Chinaman came back to the front of the store.

"One day!" Charlie demanded. "I need these tomorrow!"

The Chinaman shook his head and half-heartedly bowed to Charlie and muttered in his native language as he once again disappeared behind the curtain.

"Tomorrow!" Charlie called after him. There was no response.

"One of these days I'm gonna figure out what the hell you're saying to me, you old bastard!" Charlie shouted at the curtain. Again, no response. Charlie shook his head and left, knowing it was useless to continue this one-sided argument.

Charlie and Gus made their way up Polk Street past the Amarillo Hotel, and stopped in front of Hanna's eatery. Charlie needed to see a friendly smile right about now. When he entered the restaurant, he noticed Marshal Cook sitting at the front table by himself looking out the window. Charlie sat down at his table, and neither said a word for a moment.

"I'll be right there, Charlie," Hanna hollered from across the room.

Charlie looked at Hanna, and took in all the warmth from her broad smile. Life was good for another moment.

"I turned that diseased bag of bones loose today," Marshal Cook finally said, still looking out the front window. "No sense keeping Walker here anymore."

"It's probably for the best," Charlie said.

"That poor bastard didn't eat a thing," the marshal continued. "All he did was cough and drink water most of the night. He looked like hell this morning."

Charlie nodded.

"I'm gonna have to burn everything in that cell, you know." Marshal Cook looked at Charlie.

"I'd be glad to help you."

Hanna came over and set a cup of hot coffee in front of Charlie and placed a friendly hand on his shoulder. Her touch sent a warm relaxing sensation throughout his body.

"You want something to eat?" Hanna asked.

Charlie glanced at the marshal.

"I already ate. You go ahead," he said.

"I got some nice ham steaks today. You'll like it," Hanna said.

"That'll be fine," Charlie replied.

Hanna left Charlie's side and headed back to the kitchen to prepare his meal. Charlie and Marshal Cook sat in silence for a minute.

"Something on your mind, Charlie?" the marshal asked.

Charlie took a sip of his coffee before answering. "You remember a fella named Frank McCrudy?"

"McCrudy, McCrudy ..." the marshal said, obviously rolling the name over in his mind. "Sounds familiar, but I can't quite place it."

"About five years ago he got caught up in a bank heist in Tascosa that went bad."

"Oh I remember," Marshal Cook said. "You swore he was innocent. You even testified for him."

"Yeah, that's him," Charlie said. "He got five years for something he didn't do. Just happened to be walking by when it all went down. Anyway, every time I took some prisoners to Cañon City I'd stop in and pay him a visit."

"What brought him up now?" the marshal asked.

"I got a telegram from him yesterday. He got out a couple of months ago and settled in Trinidad. Wants me to come visit."

"Trinidad? Ain't that up in the Colorado Territory? Is he a miner?"

"I guess he is now," Charlie answered. "Ain't much else there 'cept coal mining."

"You going?" the marshal asked. "What's he want to see you for?"

"Don't know. I guess he'll either thank me or kill me." Charlie smiled. "Maybe I'll stop in and see him with the next prisoner trip to Cañon City."

After another silent moment, Marshal Cook looked at Charlie. "I need to know what you're planning to do, Charlie. I mean about Abe and Sherman."

"How about deputizing me as a Deputy City Marshal for Amarillo, Amos?" Charlie replied. "If I'm goin' after Sherman, I need to do it legally."

Marshal Cook raised his eyebrows. "Can't you do it as a Texas Ranger?"

"We don't have any papers on him and he's not in the Book of Knaves, so I can't touch him without orders." Charlie said. "I guess I could wire Missouri and see if there are any warrants on him. But that could take days, even weeks. Besides, if they don't officially request our help, there's nothing much I can do."

"That damn book." Marshal Cook sounded a little disgruntled. "Pretty much gives you cause to do whatever you want, don't it? That book of hard-cases you got from the governor opens any doors. Way I hear it, that book and that badge give you the right to do whatever you need to do."

Charlie set his mug back on the table and leaned his chair back and gave Marshal Cook a disturbed look. He glanced out the window for a moment and turned back to the marshal. "Well, some men just need killing." Charlie picked up his mug and sipped his coffee.

"Yup, I s'pose they do. You Rangers always seem to work on the fringe of the law anyway. Most people you bring in are tied over their saddle rather than sitting in it."

After a moment Charlie sarcastically said, "You're in a fine mood today. Are you gonna deputize me or not?"

The marshal looked at Charlie and shook his head. "Don't see much point in it, but if that's what you want, I'll get ya' a badge." Marshal Cook smiled. "So, now you'll be working for me? I think I'll like that."

"Don't go getting any ideas, Amos. This is just temporary." Charlie returned his smile. Hanna brought Charlie his meal. Charlie thanked her and began to eat.

Marshal Cook stood up and finished what little coffee was left in his cup. "I'm gonna let you eat in peace. Come see me when you're finished and I'll get you sworn in proper."

"I'm gonna go see the boy first," Charlie replied. "Afterwards, I'll be by to see you."

"Don't wait too long. I may just change my mind. I gotta think about your qualifications for the job." The marshal laughed as he left the eatery.

Charlie ignored the marshal's remarks. He ate in silence, thinking of the speech he was going to make to Russell. How was he going to tell him? There's no easy way to break that kind of news to someone.

19

Confession

It was late afternoon when Charlie entered the Amarillo Hotel. The lobby was filled with people, as it was every day. Some were there to sit and relax, while others were engaged in conversations and business. The Amarillo Hotel had become the place to see people and to be seen by people.

Charlie had been inside the hotel lobby on numerous occasions but the opulence of the décor never ceased to amaze him. He stood for a moment and marveled at the large gold and crystal chandelier and matching oil sconces along the walls and staircase. The white wainscoting and the red and grey striped wallpaper that lined the walls in the lobby gave the hotel an elegant feel and appearance. Charlie looked down as he walked toward the staircase and could see his reflection in the dark stained, highly polished, hardwood floor. He remembered that Henry originally had a large embroidered carpet made for the lobby. However, with the spurs, saloon traffic, dust, mud and manure, the carpet became stained and terribly worn in just a short time. So Henry had it removed and refinished the hardwood flooring. Charlie continued up the stairs to Russell's room and knocked on the door.

"It's open," Russell shouted.

When Charlie opened the door he saw Russell lying shirtless on his side holding a wet cloth patch on his wound with a stained towel folded up along his side.

"How you feeling?" Charlie asked.

"Not very good," Russell said. "It hurts like hell." After a pause, he added, "Doc said the wound's infected. He cut it open this morning to drain it."

Charlie didn't expect this. He'd assumed Russell would be a little better today. He tried to hide the concerned look on his face. Charlie pulled the only chair over to the side of the bed and sat down. Russell struggled to a sitting position, still holding the wet pad against the wound.

"Did you get him?" Russell asked.

"Get who?"

"The guy who shot me," Russell said. "Isn't that where you and the marshal went?"

"Yeah, but he lit out before we got there. Not sure where he run off to. And those cowboys weren't any help."

"You going after him?" Russell asked.

"Yeah, but not now," Charlie said. "We'll get him in due time."

Russell lowered his head and looked away. Charlie could see the disappointment and anger in Russell's frown.

"I want to be there," Russell said.

"That won't happen. But don't worry. I promise you that Mac Sherman will answer for this."

Russell nodded. There was a marked silence as Charlie struggled to start the conversation he had been practicing in his head. He looked at Russell's eyes and then turned away. He let out a heavy sigh and turned back to face Russell.

"I need to talk to you," Charlie finally blurted out.

"I know. You said that before you left. What do you want to talk to me about?"

"Getting you back home."

"You mean *my* home? Or your cabin?" Russell asked.

Charlie walked over to the window and opened it. A warm breeze fluffed the lace curtains to the side. He stood for a minute looking out onto Polk Street as the people moved about in the late afternoon. Then he sat back down and leaned in a little closer to Russell.

"I can get you back to where you came from," Charlie said.

"You kidding me? How can you do that?"

"As you may have already guessed, like you, I'm not originally from this time era."

"I knew it! I had a feeling! You're a jumper!" Russell's eyes widened and he let out a laugh. In his excitement he stammered. "When ... when did you come here? How did you ... how did you travel?"

"Settle down. I'll get to all that." Charlie paused as he collected his thoughts. "I never really wanted to time jump at all. It puts a strain on the body that just seems to get worse with age. Still don't like it. I was really just trying to run away. I picked a hell of a place to hide, didn't I?"

"You time jumped to run away? Run away from what?"

Charlie lowered his head. "When I was a lot younger, about your age, I accidentally killed a man. I didn't intend to, it just happened. It was an accident. Alarms sounded and I panicked. I took my father's time belt and just left."

"Whoa, Whoa! Whoa! A time belt?"

"Yeah. My father made it as a prototype. As far as I know, it's the only one in existence. At least it was when I left."

Charlie stood and walked back over to the window. The memory of that night, thirty years ago, rolled over in his mind. Russell asked another question or two, but Charlie ignored them. He stared out the window not looking at anything in particular while the flashback of that night replayed in his mind. After a moment, Charlie returned to the present, looked over at Russell and smiled away his nightmarish memory. "I actually jumped quite a few years after you."

"After me? How?" Russell questioned.

"By the time I jumped, time travel and teleportation was a precise science and the technology was pretty wide spread," Charlie said. "It was all strictly controlled by the government, but it was a regular occurrence. It was becoming a lot easier and quicker to teleport from one place to another than to take conventional transportation."

"When did you jump?"

"Let's see, it was August, 2275."

"2275! That's over 50 years after I jumped."

"Like I said, I jumped after you."

"But what about this belt?" Russell asked.

"Don't worry. You'll see it soon enough. When I jumped, I just turned it on and disappeared. I didn't know much about it. I didn't know where or when I would end up. I just wanted to get away. That was a long time ago. I was just twenty-one years old. I jumped back to August of 1862."

"You came here in 1862?" Russell said. "That was thirty years ago. That must have been a shock."

"I didn't exactly come here to Amarillo. Amarillo didn't exist thirty years ago," Charlie said. "I ended up on top of Mr. Slaughter's mountain in Culpepper County, Virginia, looking down on the Civil War battle of Cedar Mountain. I was scared to death. I was a very young and naive twenty-one year old."

"You fought in the Civil War?"

"I wouldn't call it fought. I sort of watched from atop that mountain," Charlie said. "I never saw anything so barbaric in my life. The smoke and fire, the mass killings and brutality was beyond description. People standing out in the open getting shot at, and lines of men blindly charging into certain death. It was lunacy."

Charlie paused, stood up and walked back over to the window. He let out a heavy sigh.

"How did you kill someone?" Russell asked.

"It was a mistake; a stupid mistake. The government, and the rest of the world leaders for that matter, agreed that time travel and teleportation had to be strictly controlled and regulated. They wanted to keep it out of the hands of the commercial market and potential criminal abuses. So they set up specific, designated, government controlled travel ports."

"Travel ports?" Russell asked.

"They're like the old airport terminals or train depots. If someone wanted to travel, they had to go through a travel port. My father ended up being in charge of a number of these ports throughout the northeast." Charlie paused, removed his hat and wiped his brow with his sleeve. "Most people used the ports to travel from one place to another. Very few ever used it for time jumping. Time travelling was a lot more controlled and monitored."

"And you worked with your father?" Russell guessed.

"I reluctantly worked for my father, not with him," Charlie said. "He was a brilliant man, one of the top scientists involved in space/time alteration. Not much of a father, but a great scientist and administrator."

"Sounds like you didn't like him very much." Russell said.

"Let's just say we saw things differently. He wanted me to follow in his footsteps. I had other ideas. He thought that if I worked in a teleport station maybe I would come to like it as much as he did."

"But you didn't," Russell interjected.

Charlie smiled. "Actually, I did like it. It was really fascinating. I learned a lot. But I wouldn't give my father the satisfaction of knowing that."

Charlie stopped and sat back down, he repositioned his hat back on his head. The memory of that night was as clear as yesterday. "One night, I showed up to work a little late. I was out celebrating my engagement with some friends and we had dinner and a few drinks. I wasn't drunk, but I wasn't a hundred percent. I was working the night shift at my usual teleport station. I had no one scheduled to go out the entire night, which was a blessing. However, I was scheduled to receive three people during my shift. I set up the station to receive."

Russell leaned forward with eyes widened, hanging on every one of Charlie's words. "Did all three come together? Or one at a time?"

"They traveled separately. They had to. They were all scheduled at different times," Charlie answered. "The first traveler was a woman who came in without any problems. I reset the station for the next traveler, who wasn't due for another couple of hours. I put the station back online, ready to receive." Charlie paused. "Usually I read, watched vids, listened to music, or filled out reports, anything to pass the time. But this night I was tired and thought I would catch a quick nap." Charlie lowered his head.

"During my nap, there was a problem," Charlie continued. "An airlock seal failed and I didn't catch it. When the next teleport transmission happened, the jumper was destroyed at the receiving station. My station. Had I woke up sooner, I would have caught the error and took it offline or shut it down."

Russell sat with his mouth agape. He looked like he wanted to say something, but couldn't find the right words. He finally broke the awkward silence. "All this experimenting and I never considered the danger of all this. What'd you do?"

Charlie nodded an understanding. "It's not a game. You remember that. Anyway, alarms were going off all over. Lights were flashing, systems were shutting down, and I didn't know what to do. I panicked. I was scared and ran into my father's office to hide. I was afraid of the Enforcers. If they found me I'd be taken away or maybe even eliminated. I was hiding in my father's office trying to think of a way out of there when I noticed his time belt on the shelf behind his desk. I strapped it on and hit the switch and here I am."

"Didn't they look for you?" Russell asked.

"Zealously," Charlie said. "When I got to the top of Slaughter's Mountain, I hid the belt under a rock by a tree. It must have taken them a while to figure out what happened to me. I'm sure my father was involved. He's the only one who would have noticed his belt was missing. I think they tracked me to the time and to the general area but couldn't pinpoint me personally."

"What do you mean, couldn't pinpoint you?" Russell asked.

"It would have taken days or even weeks for them to figure out the exact path I took through the matrix. So they just guessed where I was, probably based on my father's last trip. He was a fanatic about history. He would take trips to the past, recording his findings. He was writing his own history book. You'd be amazed at how much history has been inaccurately recorded." Charlie stood and began a slow pace around the room. "I was mesmerized by watching the battle go on below me. The Union had the advantage over the Confederates. Then the strangest thing started happening. Union soldiers started to disappear in a blue flash of light. One here, three over there, two over there."

"A blue light?" Russell asked.

"Yeah. Similar to the one you came here in," Charlie answered. "I was wondering about the light and it suddenly dawned on me. The enforcers were locking in on any warm body they could pick up, thinking it might be me and they were transporting them to 2275. It was awful."

"Whatever happened to them? Didn't they send them back?"

"I don't know," Charlie said. "Hundreds of troops just vanished. In the Civil War records of the Battle of Cedar Mountain, they are all still listed as missing. I don't know what happened to them. After a while, I guess they gave up looking for me."

"Troops just vanished?" Russell exclaimed. "That's unbelievable."

"The soldiers on both sides saw this happening, and the battle sort of stalled with everyone just watching. I can't imagine what must have been going through their minds."

"That must have been horrible for those guys!" Russell tried to sit up straighter in bed but let out a groan of pain. Charlie helped Russell get into a comfortable position. "You okay?"

Russell nodded and placed a new wet pad on his wound.

"After the vanishing stopped," Charlie said. "The Union army was in disarray. They had to have been psychologically destroyed. They just witnessed a good part of their army disappear right before their eyes."

"I imagine so," Russell said.

"The Rebels counterattacked and some officer on a white horse swinging his sword in the air brought his troops around the Union's flank and the momentum of the battle shifted to the Confederates. They ended up overpowering the Union and driving them north and back across the creek."

The two sat for a moment in silence. Charlie was about to say something and continue his story when there was a knock at the door. He opened the door, and one of the hotel's staff brought in a pewter pitcher of water and two glasses and set them on the bedside table.

"Will you be wanting dinner this evening, sir?" the man asked.

"Yes, he will. Not for me," Charlie answered for Russell.

The servant bowed slightly and left the room closing the door behind him.

Charlie filled the two glasses with water and handed one to Russell. Charlie took a long drink. "You doing okay?"

"Yeah. Fine. What happened after the battle?" Russell asked.

"Later that evening, just as the sun was setting and the battle died down, I walked down the hill. I came across the body of a confederate soldier who'd been shot in the head. His uniform was intact. I pulled his body and his rifle back up the hill and put on his shirt and his uniform jacket. I could tell without trying that his pants and boots would be way too small for me."

"Who was he? Did you know the soldier's name?" Russell asked.

"Not at first. I found out his name later. But that doesn't matter now." Charlie walked over to the window again and just stood there watching the town while sipping his water. "I should have gone back," he said under his breath, "it would have saved so much turmoil."

"How about you? Are you all right?" Russell asked after a long pause.

Charlie nodded and turned back and looked at Russell. "I slept up on top of that mountain that night. The next day I picked up the time belt, a few of the soldier's belongings, including his pistol, and started heading west. For the next five years I just worked and clawed my way across the country until I got to Texas. I met some good people and some bad people. I learned something from all of them. There were some hard lessons and some tough scraps, but through it all I learned how to stay alive in this time." Charlie stopped and thought about his conversation. "This isn't exactly what I wanted to talk to you about. How and why I got here really isn't important. What I wanted to talk to you about is you."

"Me?" Russell asked. "What about me?"

"Believe it or not, you play an important role later on."

"In what?"

"Well, the problem is that I can't tell you anything about it."

Russell shook his head appearing confused. "I play an important role in something and you can't tell me what it is?" Russell tilted his head and scowled at Charlie. The young man's eyes pleaded for more information.

Charlie wanted to tell him all about the role Russell would play in the future development of time travel and teleportation. But, just like he was trying not to affect life in the past, he knew he could not influence life in the future either.

Charlie sat next to Russell on the bed. "Listen. I can't tell you certain things because that knowledge may affect your actions in the future and I can't have that happen. The less you know the better."

"I can't believe this." Russell put his hand to his forehead and looked down at the floor. After a moment he looked up. "Why are you telling me this?"

"What I can tell you is that the work you and your team are doing now with time travel is pivotal in its future development. Keep doing what you're doing. I want you to remember this conversation when you get back. And that's all I'm going to say about it."

"That can't be. There has to be some mistake."

"No mistake," Charlie answered. "You have to get back home so you can continue doing what you do."

Russell's face turned pale.

"You don't look so good," Charlie said.

"I think I'm going to be sick."

Charlie helped Russell lie back down and get comfortable. He then pulled the chair a little closer to the bed and sat down. He thought it best not to burden Russell with any more information because he appeared troubled and overwhelmed by all that was said.

"Charlie. Why didn't you ever go back? Why did you stay here?" Russell asked.

"I should have. It would have been a lot easier on everyone."

"On everyone except you," Russell added.

"At first, I was afraid to go back," Charlie said. "I wanted to go back. I really did. I missed my friends, my coworkers, my fiancé, and, believe it or not, even my father. Every time I considered it, I got scared. I kept telling myself I'd go back tomorrow or the next day. After thirty years of tomorrows I just sort of felt like I belonged here. Even now, after all this time, I'm still afraid to go back." He paused and snickered. "Doesn't make any sense, does it? But, it doesn't matter anymore because you're going back instead."

"When?"

"As soon as possible. Tomorrow, maybe. It all depends on you being able to move around on your own or not."

144

"Tomorrow," Russell muttered to himself. He turned his head away from Charlie and stared up at the ceiling.

Charlie wanted to talk to him about how Russell got here and the problems he might face when he got back, but he wanted Russell to digest what he had told him so far. "Are you going to be all right?"

"I'm a little overwhelmed, but I'll be okay. Tomorrow, huh?" Russell seemed happy over the prospect of going back home.

Charlie stood and moved the chair back against the wall.

"You leaving?" Russell asked.

"It's getting late. Gus had a rough day today. I thought I'd get him back to the cabin; give him a chance to rest."

"But we have dinner coming,"

"You have dinner coming," Charlie countered. "It ain't as good as Hanna's, but it's still good food. And you'd better eat all of it. You'll need your strength." He backed toward the door. "I'll swing by in the morning to check on you. See how you're feeling."

"Charlie ..." Russell said just before Charlie closed the door. Charlie stuck his head back inside. "Thanks for telling me all this. I know it was hard for you."

Charlie nodded and closed the door. He had never told anyone his story before, carrying that secret around inside him for over thirty years. It gave Charlie a therapeutic relief that he had not expected. His shoulders relaxed as if a great burden had been lifted from him. He felt so good that he decided to treat himself to a drink before he went back to his cabin.

He walked through the lobby and entered the saloon. It was a little quiet for this late in the afternoon. Charlie knew it would start filling up as the evening drew closer. He crossed to the bar.

"What'll it be?" the bartender asked.

"You got any real whiskey back there?" Charlie asked, "Or is all you got that rotgut you get from Ethyl?"

The bartender leaned forward and whispered. "I got a little whiskey left that came all the way from Kentucky. But it's a dollar a drink."

Charlie pulled some coins from his vest pocket and did a quick tally.

"Well, give me one of those Kentucky whiskeys, and a glass of beer." Charlie laid his coins on the bar.

The bartender set a small whiskey glass on the bar, selected a bottle he kept hidden, and poured Charlie a generous shot of Kentucky bourbon. He returned a minute later with a glass of warm beer. Charlie sipped the whiskey and let the soothing oak flavor slide down his throat and warm his chest. He felt good and relaxed for the first time in days.

Charlie noticed a couple of Abe's riders staring at him from the other end of the bar. The light-hearted euphoria that Charlie was feeling evaporated as he recalled the events of the past couple of days. Marshal Cook was stewing over twice losing Mac and letting Abe out of jail. He also didn't seem very pleased with the idea of having Charlie as a deputy. Russell was lying upstairs with a hole in his side that was meant for him. Charlie was worn out from being up all day after a horrible night's sleep on Doc Morgan's sofa.

He shot back the remaining whiskey and then took a few drinks from his glass of beer. All of a sudden he didn't want to be there anymore. He thought it best to get deputized and go home. Without finishing his beer, he left the saloon through the hotel lobby and walked to the marshal's office.

"Okay, I'm here, swear me in," Charlie said as he entered.

"Well, hello to you too," the marshal said. "How's the boy doing?"

"Doc says his wound is infected. But he's going to be fine. Should be up on his feet in a day or so."

"I feel bad for the boy." Marshal Cook pulled a badge from a drawer in his desk. "Here he stops for a visit and almost gets himself killed."

"Yeah. He's a little anxious to get out of here," Charlie said. "Let's get this done so I can get back up the hill and get some rest."

The marshal went about swearing Charlie in as a Deputy City Marshal for the town of Amarillo and put him on a special duty to track down the wanted fugitive Mac Sherman. Charlie thanked the marshal and walked outside to Gus, who was still tied at the hitch rail in front of Hanna's.

146

"Okay, boy, you're leading," Charlie said. "Let's go home. Tomorrow is shaping up to be one hell of a day."

20

Cattle

It was dusk when Chaney, dispatched to find Mac, reached Tascosa. The backwater cattle town of Tascosa was about 35 miles from where Abe Walker set up his camp and grazed his herd. For a seasoned rider with a fresh horse, it was a little over a half day's ride. Most of the businesses were primarily one-story adobe structures that lined both sides of Main Street which paralleled the Canadian River.

The railroads had bypassed Tascosa and it was slowly being squeezed into obscurity. However, it was still a town with viable businesses. It was still a local watering hole for the residents, ranch hands, travelers, and drifters.

The town was just beginning to get lively. Chaney stopped at Scotty Wilson's restaurant and got a bite to eat. While there, he asked if anyone knew of a new cowboy who may have come into town the previous day. No one knew of any or if they did, they weren't saying. He went to the Equity Saloon and then to the Jenkins & Dunn Saloon and asked the same questions and got the same response. Wherever he went and whoever he asked, nobody knew anything about Mac. The town, in general, seemed to be collectively protecting the anonymity of its inhabitants.

Unable to find the slightest trace of Mac, he decided to change his tactics. He thought if he could find Mac's horse, he would at least

know whether the foreman was in Tascosa or not. He walked up Main
Street and looked around McCormick's livery. Mac's horse wasn't
there. He went over to Court Street where he looked into the County
Livery. That's where he saw the red roan. The cowboy stepped in to
make sure it was definitely Mac's horse. As he got close to the roan, a
voice came out of the darkness.

"You lookin' for something?"

Will Chaney was startled, but right away recognized the voice.
"Mac!"

Mac Sherman stood up in the horse stall next to his roan.
"What are you doing here, Chaney?"

"Abe sent me to fetch ya'." Chaney paused. "I gotta tell ya'
though, he don't look too good, kinda sickly."

"Why? What happened to him?"

"He and that ranger got in a scrap. Abe had the better of him
'till the marshal broke it up and hauled Abe off to the jail."

"Turlock. Damn him!" Mac said. He paused, then turned back
to Chaney. "Never mind about the sickness. Abe will be fine. He's out
now?"

"Got out this morning. He sent everyone out to collect strays
and then he climbed into his wagon."

"It's too late to head back now. We'll get a start at first light.
Where's your horse?"

"Tied at the Russell Hotel."

"Bring him here," Mac ordered. "We'll bunk in the barn here
and head back first thing in the morning."

Abe woke the next morning inside his wagon with his blanket
wrapped around him. He felt a crushing pain in his head and his body
was shaking uncontrollably. His clothes were damp from sweat. He
could hear the commotion of a busy camp and smell the aroma of
campfire biscuits outside his wagon. As he moved he heard the sound
of glass clinking. An empty whisky bottle and a near-empty bottle of
laudanum lay next to him on his blanket. That would explain the pain
and the shakes, he thought. He ached all over. He quickly downed
what was left of the laudanum. The previous sleepless night in that

cold stone cell had left him sore and stiff. It took a lot of medicine and a lot of "liquid comfort" to get him to fall asleep.

He moved slowly to a sitting position and could already feel the tightness and irritation building in his chest. Any movement at all was a chore. It took every bit of his energy to pull himself up and climb out of his wagon. When Abe appeared, most of the camp stopped what it was doing and watched him as he moved along, bracing himself against the wagon.

"Coffee," Abe said softly as he walked to the chuck wagon and sat down. The cook brought him a tin cup of hot coffee. "How you doin', Abe?"

"I feel like hell." Walker looked over at his men. "What the hell you lookin' at? Get on with it!" The crew of cowboys returned to packing up and getting ready to move the herd.

"Crabtree got the boys started breaking down the camp. Can I get ya' anything? You feel like eatin'? I got ham-'n-beans and biscuits."

"Not now. Not hungry." Abe savored that first sip of hot coffee. "Is Mac back here yet?"

"Nope."

"Damn. I got to go into town. I wanted Mac with me," Abe said almost to himself. He sat sipping his coffee and staring into the cup.

After a moment, the cook said, "Mac's wanted, Abe. He can't go to town with ya'."

Abe looked at the cook and then remembered that he was right. He downed his coffee and stood up. "I need to get cleaned up. Bring me some hot water and get my suit." Abe threw off his blanket and walked back to his wagon. "And more coffee!"

By the time Abe had washed, put on his suit, and took a few more slugs of his medicine, the pain had diminished and the shakes had subsided. He was starting to feel alive again. He walked around the campsite and inspected the packing. It was late morning and Abe was getting restless. He walked to where a group of cowboys were congregating around Crabtree Bonnam.

"Any word from Sherman?" Abe asked Bonnam.

"Not yet, Mr. Walker. Even if they left Tascosa at dawn, it will be a couple more hours before they get here."

"I can't wait that long," Abe Walker said. "Get the crew mounted and get those cattle moved to White Horse Lake. We'll have to hold them there in a tight herd until they get enough pens opened for them. By that time I should have them sold. Get our horses. You and I are going to town."

"Yes sir, Mr. Walker." Crabtree turned to the cowboys standing around and laid out instructions as Walker ordered. Before long, the crew was assembled and they began to move the herd to the lake below the stockyards. Crabtree saddled his horse and Abe's palomino and walked them over to where Abe was standing.

Abe Walker climbed up into the saddle on his palomino and stowed his gun belt in his saddlebags. "Don't want any more trouble."

Crabtree Bonnam climbed up into his saddle and did the same with his gun belt.

With the chants and whistles of the cowboys driving the herd in the background, Abe and Crabtree began their ride into Amarillo.

Amarillo's livestock brokerage office was at one end of a row of three small buildings near the stockyards. Doc Morgan had the office on the other end, and a telegraph and post office occupied the middle office. It was just after noon when Abe Walker and Crabtree Bonnam reached the livestock brokerage office of J.J. Billingsly, the local representative of the Jacob McCoy Trading Company out of Chicago. But he wasn't in his office. In fact, no one was in his office. The door was locked.

"Today Sunday?" Abe asked.

"No, sir. I know it ain't Sunday. Where you suppose he is?" Crabtree asked.

Abe looked around the stockyards and the Old Town area and off in the distance he saw the magnificent Amarillo Hotel. There were always a lot of businessmen in the lobby. "Let's try the hotel."

The two cattlemen rode through town and reined in at the Amarillo Hotel. They tied their horses to the hitch rail and went inside.

As usual, the hotel was bustling with people. Abe searched the lobby and saw Billingsly seated on a maroon crushed velvet sofa chatting with two other gentlemen sitting in matching armchairs directly across from him. The two gentlemen were both smoking cigars. Billingsly held a lit cigar in one hand and sipped on a glass of whiskey. Abe walked up and stood between the trio and looked directly at J.J. Billingsly.

"I'm looking for you, Billingsly. We got business to discuss."

"Hello, Walker," the broker said. "I heard you were around. I was expecting you earlier."

"I got a little tied up."

"I heard that, too. Well, I'm in the middle of something right now with these gentlemen. I'll be happy to meet with you in about an hour or so when I'm finished here," Billingsly offered.

"We'll meet now. Your business with them can wait."

One of the men to Abe's right stood up. "Now see here ..." he began but Crabtree put his hand on the man's shoulder and pushed him back down in his chair without saying a word. Billingsly glared at Walker. He crushed out his cigar and swallowed what was left in his whiskey glass. He let out a deep sigh and then smiled to his companions.

"Would you gentlemen mind excusing us for a bit while I meet with Mr. Walker?" Billingsly asked. "It's obviously an urgent matter." The two men mumbled their displeasure over the situation as they slowly left the area and headed for the hotel's saloon. Abe sat down in one of the now vacant armchairs.

"I got over three thousand head of good Texas longhorn out by White Horse Lake. What are you paying?"

"First of all, Walker, there's no such thing as a 'good' Texas longhorn. They're scrawny and their beef is tough. The demand these days is for those beefier cows out of Montana and Wyoming."

"I'll ask you again. What are you paying?" Abe repeated.

"Three thousand head, huh? I'll give you three dollars a head." Billingsly sat back and puffed out his chest. He smiled and waited for Walker's reaction to such a low offer.

"You bastard!" Abe bellowed as he stood up. "I can get six dollars in Wichita!"

"You can't get six dollars anywhere. I know what every broker is paying from San Antonio to Dodge, and nobody's giving six dollars for longhorns."

"You really don't want to cheat me, Billingsly," Abe threatened. "I know they're selling beef back east for thirty and forty dollars a head."

"That's right, they are." Billingsly stood. "But we're not back East and you can't get them there. I can. It costs a lot of money to move three thousand head of beef."

Abe was furious and wanted to thrash this low-life wheeler-dealer. But he knew he didn't have much choice. He needed Billingsly and he needed to make a deal. He didn't have the time or the strength to move his cows to Dodge City or Abilene or Wichita looking for a better deal; a deal that he may not get. Abe swallowed his ire and his pride and sat back down.

"I can't take three," Abe said. "That wouldn't even cover my costs. But I'll take five." Billingsly lit a new cigar, took a long puff, and sat back down on the sofa. Abe knew he was over a barrel and he knew Billingsly knew it too. He was just wondering how far Billingsly would push him.

"Five is out of the question." Billingsly leaned back and thought a moment. "I'll tell you what, Abe. I'll give you four. That's the going rate for longhorns, now. You won't find a better price anywhere else. Trust me."

Abe thought about it. He could take four and make a profit, but he wanted more. He needed more. Abe smiled back at Billingsly and then whispered something into Crabtree's ear. Crabtree nodded and then left, heading for the saloon. The smile on J.J.'s face faded as he watched Abe's sidekick walk to the bar.

Finally, Abe spoke. "You know, four might be your going rate for average cattle, but I think my cattle are better than average. Now my man over there can go out right now and find a dozen or so people who would agree with me. If that happened, I might get the idea that you're trying to cheat me. I don't think I'd like that. And I guarantee you wouldn't like that either."

J.J. Billingsly sat motionless. He removed a handkerchief from his breast pocket and dabbed a bit of sweat from his forehead. "What do you want, Walker?"

"I told you. I think my cows are worth five. And I can parade a group of educated gentlemen through here who would agree with me."

"You can parade whoever you want through here. You can parade President Cleveland through here and your cattle still won't be worth five. To me or to anybody," Billingsly said.

Abe stood up, his fists clenched and his chest tightening. He was angry that Billingsly didn't buy his bluff.

"But, I'll tell you what I'll do to save time and all this unnecessary bickering and threatening." Billingsly stood to look Walker in the eye. He had Abe's attention. "Let's say I'd offer you four-ten, which is a better than fair offer. You would naturally balk at that, and would probably come back with an offer around four-fifty. I'd laugh and then we'd bicker and negotiate and threaten each other a little more and finally I'd offer you my top price of four an' two bits per head, because I will not go any higher and you will take no less. What do you say?" Billingsly smiled while he thrust out his hand for Abe to shake to consummate the deal.

Abe did a quick tally in his head of what this fast-talking broker just offered. He knew Billingsly wasn't easily intimidated and that the offer on the table for four dollars and twenty-five cents a head was a decent payday for him. After a moment, Abe shook the broker's hand. The deal was done.

"That's fine." Billingsly called over to a short thin man with wire glasses wearing a dark suit and a bowler. He gave instructions to the small man who nodded and left the hotel. Crabtree, standing by the front door, watched the man leave and then looked at Billingsly and Abe.

"He's going down to the yards to get your cattle into pens so we can get an accurate count. When we have a count, we'll pay you. I assume you want cash so you can pay your boys?"

Walker nodded and then gave a nod to Crabtree who left the hotel to follow the small well-dressed man to the stockyards.

Walker left Billingsly, agreeing to meet him at his office later that afternoon. He went to the front desk of the hotel and reserved a room for himself. Once he got his key he left the hotel to go to the stockyards and watch the transfer.

By late afternoon, the tally was complete: 3208 head. The cattle were sorted, penned and being readied for the next train. Walker left the broker's office with a satchel full of cash. He and Crabtree went to the hotel and up to Abe's hotel room, number twenty-one. Crabtree carried Abe's saddlebags to his room and set a small table in front of his chair. Abe set the satchel of money on the table and pulled his record book from the saddle bags so he could record the payments to his crew. Abe also pulled his gun from the saddlebags and placed it on the table next to the money.

"Take the crew and head back to camp. Finish packing up and get everyone to come here to this room for their pay. And tell them to keep their guns handy, but out of sight," Abe said. "And if Mac is back, tell him to meet me here tonight, after dark. I've got a job for him."

21

End of Drive

Charlie rose early in the morning, got dressed, and took his time getting Gus fed, watered and groomed. He went back in the cabin and ate a simple breakfast of canned peaches, some jerky, and coffee. While he ate, he looked around the cabin, double-checking what he set aside to take with him and what he would leave behind.

Charlie pulled Russell's jeans, tee-shirt, and gym shoes from the drawer in the washstand and laid them out on the bed. He'd need these to go back home. Charlie took off his Texas Ranger badge and put it inside his trunk. Then he pinned on his new Deputy City Marshal badge. It didn't look much different or weigh any different than his old badge, but somehow it felt different; almost felt like a demotion. He and Amos had been working together for a couple of years now. The badge shouldn't make any difference, he thought. Looking at his reflection in the cracked mirror piece hanging above his washstand, he shook his head and shrugged off those feelings. It was time to go back to town. With Abe out of jail, he knew this would be the day Abe would move his cows. He needed to be there. Charlie picked up his jacket and the old hat that Russell wore and went out to saddle Gus.

Charlie rode straight to Tuck Cornelius's Livery at the end of town and left Gus there for the day. He pulled his Winchester from the scabbard on Gus's saddle and walked straight to the marshal's office. Marshal Cook was sitting at his desk.

"I see Abe brought his cows to town," Charlie said as he entered.

"Yeah, Johnson saw him a little while ago at the hotel with Billingsly. I figure everybody's gonna get paid off today. That could mean trouble later on."

"Usually does, Amos." Charlie sat down across from the marshal.

"You're wearing my badge, now. Why don't you go down to the hotel and keep an eye on everybody for a while?"

Charlie smiled. "You givin' me an order, Amos?"

"Just a suggestion, Charlie," the marshal replied, returning the smile.

"Well, to be honest with ya' I was heading down there myself. I need to check on Russell, anyway."

Charlie left the marshal's office and walked toward the hotel. As he got close, he saw the broker's well-dressed assistant hurry from the hotel and head toward the stock yards in Old Town. A few minutes later he saw Crabtree exit and follow the little man. Charlie slowed his pace as he watched both men until they were out of sight. Then he continued on to the hotel.

When Charlie entered the lobby he caught a glimpse of Abe Walker signing the register and picking up his room key. Charlie stepped to a corner of the lobby behind some other patrons to avoid being seen. When Walker left the hotel, Charlie went to the desk and found out that Abe took room twenty-one. That room was at the far end of the hall, just down from Russell's room. It was the last room next to the back stairway that led to the side alley. Charlie told the clerk that no one was to know that Russell was in the hotel.

Charlie quietly climbed the steps and went into Russell's room without knocking. The sudden intrusion startled Russell. "Charlie!"

"Sorry for bustin' in on ya'. Walker took a room down the hall and I didn't want him or any of his crew to see me. We don't want them to know you're here."

"Why not?"

"They think you're dead. That's why not. It's better if they keep thinking that way." Charlie pulled back the curtain and looked out onto the street for a moment. Then turned back to Russell. "How you feeling today?"

"It doesn't hurt as bad as it did yesterday. Doc came in last night and said it was looking pretty good. He put some more of that stuff on it and a new pad and then bandaged it again."

"Can you move around much?" Charlie asked.

"Some. But not all that well, yet. I imagine I probably could if I really had to, though."

"Well, you have to."

"Why? What's happening, Charlie?" Russell sat up and had a concerned look on his face.

"Abe's selling his cows today. That means this place will soon be crawling with hungry, tired, thirsty and rich cowboys. None of that is good. We gotta get you out of here."

"Where am I going?" Russell asked. "Am I going back home?"

"Not yet," Charlie answered. "But we got to let them cowboys keep thinking you're dead."

Russell had a puzzled look on his face.

"If anybody finds out you're still alive, word will get back to Mac and he'll come here to finish you. I can protect you better at my place." Charlie handed him his old hat and his jacket. "I need you to get cleaned up and dressed. Take your time. I don't want you bustin' that wound open. Then just stay in here and I'll be back later today for you. Right now I gotta keep an eye on some cowboys."

"Why does he want to kill me?"

"He'd worry that you'd testify at a trial against him. If there's no witnesses, no trial," Charlie explained.

"I never saw his face," Russell protested. "I wouldn't know Mac Sherman if he came up and stood right next to me."

Charlie sighed and put his hand on Russell's shoulder.

"Mac doesn't know that. Furthermore, he don't care. He wouldn't believe you, anyway. As far as he's concerned, you stand between freedom and the gallows for him. If he finds you, there won't be any talkin' with him. You won't have the time."

158

Russell sat on the edge of the bed holding the jacket and hat. He looked away from Charlie and began to turn a little pale.

"Like I said, you'll be safer at my cabin. Now get yourself ready." Charlie opened the door, stopped in the open doorway and turned around to look at Russell. He could see the fear in the young boy's eyes. "Everything is going to be fine. Don't worry," Charlie said reassuringly. "Tomorrow you'll be back home where you belong. I promise you."

It was mid-afternoon when Mac Sherman and Chaney returned to the campsite from Tascosa. Everyone was gone except for the cook and his two helpers.

"Abe took the herd to town. He's doin' business," the cook said. "You'd better lie low for a spell. The law was out here yesterday looking for you."

"I got to get to town. I need to get my pay!" Chaney said to Mac.

"You'll stay here," Mac said. "Don't worry. You'll get your pay. After the cows are sold, everyone will be back here to bust camp. Then you'll all go in to see Abe together."

"So we wait?"

"Yup. We just wait," Mac said. "Finish packing your gear."

It took all afternoon to round up and pen Abe Walker's cattle, and it was late in the day before the crew of cowboys got back to their campsite. They were all glad to see Mac. As tired as they were, they hurriedly finished their packing and, along with the wagons and the leads, headed back into town as one group.

Charlie sat on a wooden chair on the sidewalk outside the hotel entrance with his Winchester across his lap, waiting for the parade of cowboys to come and get their pay. He wanted to make sure they saw him as they entered and left the hotel. As the caravan of cowboys and wagons came down Polk Street and filled the area around the hotel, Marshal Cook walked over and joined Charlie. The cowboys and crew all went in as one group to meet Abe and collect their pay. They acknowledged the two lawmen as they passed them on their way in and on their way out.

In the controlled area of his hotel room, Walker paid each cowboy and then offered each a bonus if they would stay and help settle things with the marshal and the ranger. The regular ranch employees didn't want any part of Abe's feud with the lawmen, but they felt they didn't have a choice if they wanted to keep their job. They took their pay and their bonus and went downstairs to the saloon to wait further instructions. The transient cowboys, hired just for the drive, declined the bonus offering and just collected their pay and left town right away. They knew there was going to be trouble and they wanted to get as far away from it as they could. The bonus was a nice tempting incentive, but it wouldn't be any good if they weren't around to spend it. They didn't want to get caught up in any of Walker's personal feuds. The two lawmen that they had encountered had already proved they would be plenty of trouble.

Abe paid the cook and the cook's helpers, and sent them and the wagons on their way back to the Pecos ranch. When all were paid he took the remaining cash and put it back in the money bag and stuffed the bag into his saddlebags. He had some pay left over. Out of the twenty cowboys that made the drive, one transient cowboy and one regular ranch employee were dead, and another ranch employee was wounded and in jail.

He instructed Crabtree to go and wait downstairs in the saloon with the rest of his crew. He would wait in the room for Mac. Four regular ranch hands, including Crabtree Bonnam, were in the bar sipping liquid courage and waiting for Mac to join them. They appeared a little nervous about their upcoming assignment.

Once the wagons were gone and the transient cowboys scattered, Charlie and Cook went back to the marshal's office. Deputy Johnson decided it was a good time to take a break and get something to eat before he started his evening rounds. Paydays for cattlemen were always trouble for Johnson. He hated dealing with drunken, rowdy cowboys. Usually, the just-paid cowboys would bathe, eat, and start spreading their money around town. By evening's end there was always a lot of trouble.

As this evening began to unfold, something was already different. Johnson watched the majority of the cowboys get their pay and quickly ride out of town. Yet some of Abe's ranch hands were simply hanging around inside the hotel. Usually by this time they would be out and about town. Something wasn't right.

22

Night Moves

At dusk, Charlie told Marshal Cook he had some errands to run and left his office. He picked up his laundry and then walked back to the livery and borrowed a buckboard from Tuck, promising to return it later that evening. Charlie knew that Gus didn't like being harnessed to a wagon, but he didn't have much choice. Charlie left his saddle and tack at the livery, set his bundles in the back of the buckboard, and drove the wagon to the side entrance of the hotel along the side street that crossed Polk.

Charlie tied Gus to the hitch rail and went inside the side door and up the back stairs to the second floor. He slipped past Walker's room and lightly knocked on Russell's door.

"Who's there?" Russell asked.

Charlie opened the door and quickly stepped inside, closing the door behind him. Russell sat on the bed wearing the white shirt that Hanna gave him, those old ill-fitting boots, Charlie's jacket and his old hat. He still had on the blood-stained pants and suspenders, but the jacket covered most of the stains.

"How you doing?" Charlie asked.

"Not bad. I think I can move around okay. But I can't move very quickly."

Charlie pulled the heavy blanket off of the bed and roughly bunched it up in his arms. "We're going down the back stairs and out onto the side street. We have to walk past Walker's room so try not to make any noise. I got a wagon downstairs. You get in the back and I'll wrap this blanket around you. You ready?"

"Do I have a choice?" Russell asked.

Charlie smiled. "I s'pose not."

Russell stood and took a few seconds to get his balance. Charlie opened the door and peeked out to make sure the hallway was empty.

"It's clear, let's go." He held the door open for Russell and then helped him along the hallway to the narrow stairway. The stairs proved to be a slow and painful experience for Russell. He had to step down with a straightened right leg and pull the left leg down to join it, one step at a time. There were no handrails along the back stairs so he had to lean on Charlie for support.

When they reached the bottom landing, Charlie looked through the glass of the side door. It was getting darker by the minute. No one was around the immediate vicinity so Charlie opened the door and helped Russell to the buckboard. He unfolded the blanket and laid it across the bed of the wagon and helped Russell lie down. The blanket provided little relief from the hard surface, but it was better than nothing. Russell grimaced as he shuffled his body to a somewhat comfortable position.

"You all right?" Charlie asked.

"No, but I'll make it," Russell answered.

Charlie took the wrapped laundry bundles and placed one under Russell's head and loosely packed the other bundles around Russell's side to help cushion the ride.

"These ain't the most comfortable things to travel in. The road's pretty rough, so just hold on." Then, as an afterthought, "It'll still be better for you than riding atop Gus."

Russell pulled the blanket across him and Charlie climbed in and drove the buckboard behind the buildings until he got north of town where he finally got onto the trail that led to his cabin. Even though Charlie was driving Gus at a slow walk, he couldn't make the ride smooth. With every bump or stone they encountered the buckboard jostled up or sideways drawing a groan from Russell.

Charlie talked back over his shoulder and asked Russell how he was doing. There was no answer. He looked in the bed and saw Russell staring up at him. "You all right? Something bothering you, boy?"

"I just got some second thoughts, that's all," Russell answered. "I mean, what if I stayed here with you?"

"That's impossible. You can't stay here. Too much of the future rides on you getting back to your right time."

"But why? What difference would it make?" Russell argued.

"I don't have an answer for you. I wish I did," Charlie said. "All I can tell you is you have to go back and continue your work. You'll see later on that I'm right."

"Well, explain to me how someone like you can come here from the future and stay and someone like me can't," Russell protested.

"I can't," Charlie said. "I don't exactly know why. But, what I do know is that for some reason I don't have a future timeline after my age of twenty one. I know that because I checked on it. It was like I died or ceased to exist back then. It just proves to me that I never left here. But, you do have a timeline, and it's an important one. Maybe someday you'll be able to figure it all out and explain it to me."

Charlie pulled Tuck's buckboard up to his cabin. By this time it was dark. Charlie climbed off and helped Russell out of the wagon and into the cabin.

"I think I would have been better off riding up front with you," Russell said, holding onto his side. "That was a horrible way to travel."

"Just take it easy. We don't want you to start bleeding." Charlie helped Russell sit down on the bed. Charlie lit the lantern and told Russell to lie down and relax. He started a fire in the stove and then walked to the trunk by his bed.

Charlie retrieved the canvas bag from his trunk. He pulled the chair close to Russell and in his hands he held the time belt that brought him to the nineteenth century.

"You hurting?" Charlie asked.

164

"It hurts like hell," Russell replied. "You ever been shot?"

"Twice. I didn't like either one." Charlie smiled. "But I do believe yours is worse than either of mine."

"That's comforting," Russell said sarcastically, still holding on to his side.

Charlie held the belt for Russell to see. "This is the time belt I talked to you about. It's going to take you home, Russell. But you have to pay attention. This is very important. You hear me?"

"Yeah, I'm listening." Russell sat up and studied the gold and silver cylinders alternately attached around the belt in Charlie's hand.

"I need to know precisely where you came from, and exactly what time it was when you jumped here," Charlie said.

"It was one of the labs in a complex where I work. I work at the National Lab in Upton, New York. They set the switch at nine thirty on the evening of June 27, 2220."

"Upton, huh." Charlie recognized the name.

"You know it?" Russell asked.

"My father was lead physicist there for a number of years. Of course he brought me there with him. You were gone by the time we got there."

"You didn't like it, I suppose."

"I didn't like being moved around. Especially if it was associated with my father," Charlie answered. "Looking back, though, I was a spoiled, stupid kid."

Charlie put on the time belt, turned on the switch and placed his finger on the small screen. Immediately a blue-green transparent cocoon engulfed Charlie. Russell scooted back away from the glow, apparently surprised by the sudden light. He watched while Charlie punched settings into the virtual display in front of his face. Then, Charlie turned the switch off on the belt and the hypnotic glow vanished. Russell sat on the bed, leaning against the wall with his mouth gaping open.

"You've seen this light before?" Charlie asked.

"Not like that," Russell said. "When they sent me here, I stood in-between two large metal disks, one was silver and one was gold. When they turned it on, there was a bright flash of bluish light that filled the entire room."

"Well, Dad refined it a bit," Charlie began. "I put in the settings for just outside the Upton National Laboratory. I'm sending you back there thirty minutes before your operators send you here. It'll be dark, so you shouldn't have any trouble. It's critical you stay hidden until after you jump."

"But ..." Russell began, but Charlie interrupted him.

"I need you to tell me the absolute truth, here, all right?" Charlie looked into Russell's eyes. Russell nodded. "I need you to tell me if you came to 1892 on purpose or not."

"What do you mean ... on purpose?"

"Did you come to 1892 for a reason? Or were you really going to 1992?" Charlie repeated.

"I swear, Charlie. I really thought I was going to 1992."

"Then someone back there, probably one of your operators, messed up for some reason."

Russell frowned. He looked at Charlie with a questioning look then shook his head. "No, that can't be right," Russell said. "Everything is checked and double checked." After a pause he added, "at least I thought it was."

"The time system is too perfect. You'll find out why later on," Charlie said, "The matrix cannot make a mistake. The space/time target of the matrix is pinpoint accurate. The target has to be physically set. One of your operators had to have reset the year right before you jumped."

"I can't believe it!" Russell looked away. "Why would they do that?"

"Now I don't know whether it was intentional or not. I guess it's possible that it could have been reset by mistake. But if it wasn't a mistake, then someone back there tried to get rid of you for some reason."

Russell stared past Charlie at the lantern on the table. It was clear to Charlie that the boy was running the memory of that night over in his head, trying to remember the slightest details. Russell held his head in his hands for a moment and then looked up at Charlie.

"If I hadn't met you, then I would have been stuck out in that desert forever. I'd probably be dead by now!" Russell lowered his head. "I can't believe this. Who could have done this? Why would they do this?"

"Russell, I need you to think. Try and remember the night you left. Was there anything different? Anything out of the ordinary?" Charlie asked.

Russell automatically started to shake his head but then stopped. Suddenly, he looked up at Charlie.

"There was a suit."

"A suit?"

"Yeah, a guy in a suit. I remember," Russell said, wide-eyed. "We were getting ready for the jump and I saw a man in a dark suit walk in and talk briefly to one of the operators. I didn't pay any attention to it because I'd seen this guy in there before so I didn't think anything of it. He was a corporate representative for one of our suppliers. It was a little strange because they usually come in the daytime, rarely at night."

"That's your man," Charlie said. "You need to find out who he is, and what he said to the operators. You think you can do that?"

"Why don't you come back with me?" Russell asked.

"Impossible. Only one can travel at a time. We would both be destroyed if we tried to travel together," Charlie said matter-of-factly. "You'll have an advantage because they won't be expecting you to ever come back. Just be careful. Stay out of sight for as long as you can."

Charlie slipped the time belt back into its canvas enclosure and handed it to Russell. They exchanged looks silently. Russell held it for a moment.

"Charlie, what if I don't want to go?" Russell said.

"It's not that simple. You don't have a choice, here. You have to trust me and believe me. You have to go back."

"But what about you?" Russell asked.

"I'll be fine. I've been here for thirty years. I figure it's my punishment for what I caused to happen to that traveler that died on my watch. I kind of belong here now." Charlie looked away in deep thought. "Maybe it's why I don't have a time line after 2275. Maybe I'm supposed to be here. Either way, it's too late for me to go back now, anyway."

Russell appeared a little shaken at Charlie's revelation. "What do I do?" Russell asked.

"First thing you do when you get back is get that wound looked at. Tell them you fell on something; maybe a broken glass or something like that. "

"I mean what about now … tonight?"

"Nothing, right now. I have to get Tuck's wagon back to him. Then I have a few things to do in town. You'll be fine here. You stay put. I'll be back in a little while."

"But …" Russell began, but stopped when Charlie came close to him.

"Look. All you have to do is strap that thing around your waist, turn on the switch and place your finger on that little screen. It'll take a few minutes for the system to analyze you and your genetic structural makeup for conversion to energy, but once it gets you, that bluish light and the display will appear. At that point the counter will start rolling. When the number gets down to one, close your eyes. The flash gets pretty bright inside. When you wake up, you'll be home."

"Won't you be here when I go?" Russell asked.

"Yeah, yeah, I'll be here," Charlie said reassuringly. "But, just in case I'm not back by morning, you strap that thing on and get out of here. You savvy?"

Russell nodded.

Charlie opened the front door and turned to Russell with a smile. "Get some rest. And relax. You're as good as home." With that, Charlie closed the door and in a minute Russell heard the buckboard drive away toward town.

"But I don't want to go home," Russell said under his breath to himself as he closed his eyes and pulled the blanket over him.

23

Last Rites

Mac Sherman sat on a rise outside Amarillo and watched the silhouettes of the buildings fade into darkness as the sun set. Once he saw lights start to show in various windows, he mounted his horse and rode into town using the cover of darkness to conceal him. He approached the Amarillo Hotel from one of the back streets and tied his horse to a drain spout in the rear of the building. He took a few steps toward the side entrance of the hotel but as soon as he turned the corner, he saw a buckboard wagon pull away. He jumped back behind the hotel and waited until the wagon was out of sight. Mac then made his way to the side entrance and up the back steps to Abe's room. He tapped on the door.

"Come," Abe said.

Mac walked in and closed the door behind him. Although they were both happy to see each other, neither one said so. Abe managed a brief smile and pulled a few folded papers from his suit pocket. He took a drink from a newer bottle of laudanum and coughed a little.

"You look good in a suit," Mac said sarcastically. Abe did not appear amused. He ignored the comment as he handed Mac the papers.

"I drew this up for you," Abe said with a raspy voice.

Mac opened the paper and saw that it was Abe's last will, leaving everything he owned to Mac. Mac scanned over the papers and

looked up at his boss. He didn't know what to say. Abe held up his
hand to quell any questions.

"I got no kin," Abe said. He took another sip of his medicine.
"Indians took my wife, and that god-damned ranger killed my boy.
After Turlock killed Jeremiah, I've counted on you for everything.
You've been like a son to me. It's no secret I'm dying, and my time's
close. If I don't name an heir, it'll all be taken away and lost.
Everything I built my whole life will be gone. You're the only one I
can count on to run the place and keep it together."

"Mr. Walker, I … I don't know what to say."

"You don't say nothin'. It's all legal and signed. When I'm
gone you take that paper to the circuit judge in Pecos. He knows all
about it. It's done."

Mac nodded and folded the papers and tucked it away in his
pocket. Abe walked over and sat in the chair behind the small table
that held his saddlebags and his gun.

"We got one more thing to do," Abe said. "Bonnam is
downstairs with the boys, waiting for us. Did anybody see you come in
here?"

"No. I came up the back." Mac walked closer to the old man.

"Good. It'll be easier if no one knows you're here."

There was a hurried knock on the door. Mac and Abe looked at
each other.

"Who's there?" Abe managed to say. Mac pulled his gun and
moved against the wall behind the door.

"It's me, Mr. Walker. Crabtree."

"Come in."

Crabtree Bonnam entered the room and walked over to where
Abe was sitting. Mac closed the door and walked out from behind it,
gun in hand. The sound of the door closing startled Crabtree who
turned toward him. "Mac!"

"Well?" Abe said.

"I overheard some fellas downstairs talking about that boy that
Mac shot."

"What about him?" Mac asked.

"He ain't dead."

Abe and Mac flashed a surprised look at each other.

"What do you mean he ain't dead?" Mac grabbed Crabtree by his arm and stared into his eyes. "I put a hole in that boy big enough to pull a mule though. What are you talking about?"

"I'm just telling you what I heard. And to beat all, they got that boy right here in this hotel. Just down the hall."

"So what," Abe said. "That boy don't concern me. We've got that ranger and the marshal to deal with. I want to get my man out of jail, get our business done, and get out of here."

"Well that boy concerns me!" Mac said defiantly. "He looked up at me and saw my face. If he lives, he could put a rope around my neck. I got to finish this. Where's he at?"

"Leave it be," Abe Walker ordered. "That boy ain't going nowhere with a wound like that. We can deal with him after the lawmen get what's coming to them."

Mac felt a rush of anger as blood surged through his body. He hated loose ends and wanted to end this now.

"First things first," Abe said trying to calm Mac down. The three sat down to plan their assault on Marshal Cook's office to free their jailed ranch hand.

At Tuck's Livery, Charlie unharnessed Gus from the buckboard, saddled him, and then he led him to an empty stall. "I'll be back to get you in a little while." Charlie stroked Gus's neck. He pulled his Winchester from the saddle scabbard and left the livery. Just as he was leaving, Tuck Cornelius came out of his office.

Charlie thanked him for the use of the wagon. "So what do I owe ya'?"

"Just a dollar," Tuck said.

Charlie gave Tuck a silver dollar, smiled and started to walk away. He stopped, had a second thought, and walked back to Tuck.

"Listen, Tuck, if anything should happen to me, make sure Gus gets taken care of, will ya'?" Tuck had a surprised and concerned look on his face. "He knows you and trusts you. I'd appreciate it."

Tuck opened his mouth to say something, but then just nodded. He agreed to take care of Gus, as Charlie requested. The two shook hands and Charlie walked off heading for the hotel to settle things with Walker once and for all.

Deputy F.G. Johnson walked up the sidewalk along Polk Street checking closed businesses and looking in on the saloons and brothels for any trouble. It was the same routine he did every night, but tonight he was a little more vigilant with the cowboys in town. He kept glancing back to the hotel to watch for Abe and his ranch hands. He was on the opposite side of the street, directly across from the Amarillo Hotel, when he saw four men exit the lobby. He didn't think much of it until he realized they weren't going anywhere. The group of four stayed in front of the hotel on the corner of the sidewalk. The deputy backed against a doorway in the night shadows to watch these boys.

One cowboy left the group and walked off the sidewalk and up the street and stopped in front of the marshal's office. From the street, he looked into the marshal's window. The other three cowboys intently watched him from their position in front of the hotel. After peering into the marshal's office window, the cowboy walked back down the street and fell back in with the other three. This seemed a little strange to the deputy.

Johnson couldn't recognize these men in the darkness at such a distance. He wanted to get a closer look. Just as he was about to step off the sidewalk, a fifth cowboy walked from the side of the hotel and joined the other four. Deputy Johnson stopped in his tracks. Even at this distance he could see the last cowboy was wearing a gun. When the fifth man showed, the other four cowboys went to their horses and pulled their gun belts from their saddle bags and strapped them on.

This looks like trouble. Staying in the darkness as best as he could, Deputy Johnson hurried up the street toward the marshal's office. The marshal had better know about these boys.

24

Shootout

As Charlie walked down Polk Street on his way to the hotel for a final meeting with Abe Walker, he noticed the deputy running up the other side of the street. The deputy beckoned him to come to the marshal's office. Charlie quickened his pace and got to the office just as the deputy finished telling the marshal about the cowboys.

"What's wrong?" Charlie asked.

Marshal Cook tied down his holster around his thigh, and walked out of the office into the moonlit street. Charlie and Deputy Johnson followed the marshal outside and closed the door behind them, leaving the lamp burning bright. Charlie looked at the night sky. It was clear with a crescent moon, not very bright but light enough to distinguish figures.

"Amos, what's going on?" Charlie repeated.

"I think we got another jail break brewing," Marshal Cook said. "Johnson, get across the street to Portwood's and keep out of sight." The deputy ran across the street and hid behind two barrels sitting on the sidewalk in front of the Portwood Drugstore. The marshal turned to Charlie. "You're a part of this whether you like it or not."

"A part of what?" Charlie asked again, still a little confused.

"Johnson saw Abe's cowboys at the hotel." The marshal pulled his sidearm and checked the loads. "They all pulled their guns from their saddlebags and put them on. I think they're heading this way. We got a little moonlight tonight. I think we'll have a better time of it out here in the open." Cook re-holstered his gun and looked at Charlie. "It looks like Mac is with them this time."

Charlie clenched his jaw as the thought of putting a bullet in Mac Sherman formed in his mind. He had already made up his mind to end this feud with Abe Walker, one way or another. But it looked like Abe would have to wait. Mac was the bigger fish for him right now.

"I'll take cover just down from Johnson." Charlie walked across the street and knelt down alongside a trough. He had a clear view of the street and the marshal's office from where he was. Charlie watched Marshal Cook walk to the mercantile next door to his office and take cover in the recessed doorway. Then the three lawmen waited.

After a few minutes, Charlie noticed the silhouettes of five cowboys slowly making their way up the street toward the marshal's office. With his aging eyesight he couldn't recognize any of them in the dark. The five stopped in front of Hanna's Eatery. Charlie chambered a round and raised his Winchester. He aimed at the center of the group of five cowboys. He cursed under his breath as his shaking hands kept him from drawing a steady bead on any one of them.

The cowboys all pulled their guns and three of them slowly approached the marshal's office from the street. The other two cowboys stepped onto the sidewalk and inched their way along the wall. The first cowboy looked through the window. His face was illuminated in the light. Charlie felt the tension rise within him and he clenched his jaw. *Crabtree Bonnam!* The other cowboy standing alongside Bonnam was Mac.

Marshal Cook partially stepped out from the cover of the doorway with his gun in his hand. "Hold up, there! Drop those …"

Mac Sherman's arm was a blur as he raised his gun and fired a shot at the marshal. In mid-sentence, Marshal Cook jumped back into the doorway and Mac's bullet hit the door jamb right next to where the marshal was standing. Mac fired a second shot at Cook who pressed himself farther back into the recesses of the doorway. The second bullet struck closer than the first.

As soon as Mac fired, Johnson cut loose with his shotgun and sprayed number four buck shot across the cowboys in the street. One of the three stumbled to his knees and fell to the ground. The deputy reloaded his shotgun, but before he could fire again, all the cowboys turned and fired at him. Bullets splintered the wooden barrels and the store front behind the deputy. Johnson ducked behind the barrels. Marshal Cook shot at the cowboys and they returned fire.

From the cover of the trough, Charlie aimed at who he believed to be Mac and pulled the trigger but apparently missed. He cocked his rifle again and fired a second, a third, and then a fourth shot. He wasn't sure who he was aiming at or if he ever hit anything. The cowboys returned fire in his direction, and began to move toward the sidewalk to get off the street. In the melee, a second cowboy fell to the ground and a third took off running down the sidewalk and into the alleyway along the hotel.

Apparently realizing the futility of the gun battle, Crabtree Bonnam tossed his gun down and raised his hands. "I'm done! I'm done! Don't shoot!"

The other cowboy next to Crabtree tossed his gun down as well. The shooting stopped. It was over. Although it seemed longer to Charlie, the whole shootout lasted less than a minute. Marshal Cook stepped out onto the sidewalk with his Peacemaker in his hand and approached the two surrendering cowboys. Deputy Johnson ran across the street, shotgun leveled and checked on the two downed men.

"This one's alive but he's pretty shot up. He won't last the night."

The deputy checked the other cowboy lying in the street. "This one's dead."

Charlie hurried across the street and looked at the two downed cowboys. Neither was Mac. "Damn it!" He turned to Crabtree and put the muzzle of his rifle against Crabtree's chest. "Where's Mac?" he hollered.

Crabtree's eyes widened and he shook his head. "I don't know, I swear!"

Charlie pushed the rifle harder against Crabtree's chest, forcing him back against the wall, and cocked the hammer of the rifle. "Where is he?"

"I don't know. Maybe at the hotel," Crabtree blurted out.

"Hotel?" Charlie repeated.

"He found out your boy was still alive. He wanted to kill him earlier. He may be going back there."

Charlie pulled his rifle back and gave a defiant look to Marshal Cook. "I'm going after Mac." He took off at a run toward the hotel.

Charlie ran through the hotel lobby and up the stairs, stopping at the top of the stairs when he saw that the door to Russell's old room was standing wide open. He cocked his rifle and cautiously approached and entered the room with his rifle leveled. The room was empty. He stood in Russell's empty room trying to think of where Mac would have gone. Then he remembered Abe's room.

Just as he came out of the door, Mac was standing at the end of the hallway outside Abe's door. He fired three quick shots at Charlie who dropped his rifle and quickly dove back into Russell's vacant room. From a reclined position, Charlie pulled his handgun and without looking fired two shots down the hallway. He waited a second for return fire from Mac, but none came. He rolled over and slowly pushed his head through the open doorway to peer down the hall. It was empty. Then he heard the side door of the hotel slam closed.

Charlie got to his feet, picked up his rifle and headed to Abe's room. He kicked open the door and a startled Abe Walker stood holding his bottle of laudanum. He looked at Charlie and at Charlie's rifle through his wide, bloodshot eyes. Abe glanced at the small table where his gun was sitting.

"Go ahead," Charlie said. "Pick it up. I want you to try for your gun. Go ahead. Give me a reason."

Abe Walker didn't move. He swayed a little bit from his drug-induced stupor. He stood in stocking feet with his jacket and tie off and his shirt unbuttoned. It appeared to Charlie that Abe was getting ready for bed.

Charlie took a few steps closer to Abe. "Your plans fell apart, Abe. You lost a lot of good men this trip." He poked the rifle into Abe's chest and Abe backed away. "Is that what you had in mind, you bastard? Pick your gun up. Go ahead." Charlie poked Abe again with the rifle a little harder this time. Abe grunted from the jab of the rifle barrel. "That empire you spent a lifetime building is going to hell. And all because of your hatred. Tell me. Was it worth it, Abe? Was it?" Charlie tried to poke Abe again, but this time Abe slapped the rifle muzzle away and tried to charge Charlie. He was so unstable from the medicine that he lost his balance, dropped his medicine bottle, and stumbled to the floor. He got himself onto his hands and knees, coughing.

"Where's Mac, Abe?" Charlie asked.

Abe shook his head and coughed harder. It was obvious to Charlie that he was having a difficult time trying to catch a breath. Charlie picked up the bottle of laudanum and held it out so Abe could see it.

"Mac. Where'd he go?" Charlie again asked.

Abe was coughing so hard that blood spurted with each hack. He fell back down to the floor unable to hold his weight any longer. Charlie handed him the bottle and Abe took a long gulp. He caught a breath and in between short breaths he said. "You'll … you'll never … stop him … in time." Abe rolled on his back cradling the bottle of opium extract in his arms.

"In time for what, you diseased bastard! In time for what?" Charlie said, his anger rising.

Abe looked up at Charlie and just smiled. In Charlie's rage he brought the butt of his rifle down on Abe's chest and heard bones break. Abe let out a painful cry and cough at the same time. Charlie backed away and watched as blood filled Abe's mouth. Abe struggled to breathe but couldn't clear his air passage. He thrashed about on the floor in an attempt to raise himself, but was too weak and he fell back down. He raised his head but it too fell back hard to the floor. As Abe continued to struggle, Charlie backed to the doorway. Finally Abe rolled on his side and lay still on the floor. Charlie just closed the door and walked down the back stairs and onto the side street next to the hotel.

"Time for what?" Charlie repeated to himself out loud. He kept running the evening over in his mind. *What's Mac going to do?* Abe said "no time". Suddenly his eyes widened as he pulled the pieces together.

"Damn! Russell! He's going after Russell!" Charlie ran up Polk Street as fast as his fifty-year-old, out-of-shape legs would carry him. Marshal Cook called to him as he ran past the shootout scene, but Charlie kept running. *No time! No time!*

When he reached the livery his chest heaved as he sucked air into his lungs. He pulled Gus out of his stall, climbed into the saddle and as fast as Gus could run they headed back to his cabin. *There's time. There's got to be time.*

25

Showdown

Charlie reined in Gus by the stream that flowed at the bottom of the hill near his cabin. The dim light from a crescent moon was no help in trying to see into the cottonwood trees that surrounded the cabin. His heart was racing with fear and anticipation. But he knew better than to make any rash movements. He could be riding into a trap. He sat in his saddle listening and watching in the dark. Other than his own heartbeat pounding in his ears, all he heard was the regular sounds of the breeze and the critters in a north Texas night.

Charlie began to finally think rationally about this. How would Mac know that Russell was out here? No one knew he moved Russell, except maybe a few hotel workers. That's it, the hotel staff, Charlie thought. They were the only ones that knew Russell was still alive and which room he was in. They would be the only ones to know that he was no longer there. Someone on Henry's staff had told Mac what he wanted to know.

There were no signs of Mac or any other visitor. A light tap with his heels urged Gus forward up the hill to the cabin and inside his corral. He left Gus saddled. Lantern light shone through the shutter slats. He went in and found Russell unharmed and sound asleep. Charlie breathed a sigh of relief. *There is time.*

Leaving Russell to his slumber, Charlie went back to the corral and unsaddled Gus and got him some water and grain. After Gus was cared for, Charlie took his saddle inside and set it by the door next to his shotgun. He restarted the fire inside the stove.

Charlie laid his bedroll out on the floor in front of the stove and hung his gun belt over the back of the chair, making sure it was in easy reach of his bedroll. He blew out the lantern and lay down by the stove. Soon, the warmth, the flickering and the crackling sounds of the fire soothed him to sleep.

The sounds of Gus moving around and a low whinny roused Charlie from his sleep. He looked through the slats in the shutter. It wasn't quite light yet, but the dark night had ebbed to a softer gray. He heard a horse whinny again, but this one didn't come from Gus. Charlie slipped his .32 pistol in his trouser belt behind his back, and pulled his Colt from the holster. Russell stirred in the bed and woke up with Charlie holding his hand over his mouth.

"Somebody's outside," Charlie whispered in Russell's ear. "Don't make a sound."

Russell stared wide-eyed at Charlie and nodded. The fear in Russell's eyes was unnerving. Charlie removed his hand from the boy's mouth. He crouched down, cocked his gun, and slowly opened the front door. He peered outside but couldn't see anything in the dim morning light. He slipped outside, closing the door behind him and stayed low and close to the cabin wall as he headed for Gus's stall. Before he turned the corner to the stall he heard a voice.

"Turlock!"

Charlie froze. It was Mac. He'd recognize that voice anywhere.

"Don't do anything you might regret, Ranger."

Charlie stood and slowly turned to see Mac Sherman step out from behind a tree brandishing his black Peacemaker revolver with ivory handgrips.

"What are you doing here, Mac? I thought you'd be on your way back to the Pecos by now," Charlie said.

"I thought about it," Mac said. "But after things died down a bit I went back to town to see Abe. That's when I found out that old coot died last night. Damn shame. I asked around and some folk say you paid him a visit. So I came right out here to thank you."

"Thank me? For what?" Charlie asked. "You got a funny way of thanking people with a gun in your hand."

"Can't be too careful, ya' know." Mac took a step closer to Charlie. "Yep, with Abe dead, and no kin, that ranch is now mine. Everything of his is mine. Abe wrote it all down. I got the paper right here that says so. You did me a big favor."

"You came out here for nothing. What makes you think I killed him?" Charlie said.

"Well, it might just be a hunch, but I'll bet he wouldn't have died if you didn't have words with him."

"What'd you really come here for?" Charlie asked. "If it was to kill me, you could have done that from that tree back there and saved a lot of talk. What do you want?"

"Where's the boy?"

Charlie tried to put on his best blank poker face. "He's dead, Mac." Charlie tried to sound convincing. "You killed him. Shot him down in cold blood. Don't you remember?"

"No. He's alive. I heard that in town. It's funny what a bunch of drunken cow punchers will talk about. Now where is he?" Mac insisted

"You go to hell. I'm getting a little tired of this conversation." As fast as he could, Charlie raised his gun and fired in Mac's direction. Mac jumped back and to the side. Charlie turned and took a quick step hoping to reach the corner of the cabin for some cover. Mac fired back at Charlie, but his aim was off and his slug hit the cabin wall just as Charlie dove around the corner. He rolled to a crouched position and fired a second shot at Mac who had retreated to the cover of the trees. Silence.

With his failing eyesight and bad hearing, Charlie knew he would never be able to find Mac in this dim morning light. He hoped to draw out his location. He peeked around the corner of the cabin at the trees where Mac had withdrawn.

"You hit?" Charlie hollered at the tree line, hoping for a reply. There was no answer. Charlie looked at Gus who was at the coral fence staring at the trees. He could see where Gus was looking and just

181

as he raised his gun he caught a glimpse of a shadow as it moved from one tree to another. Charlie fired at the shadow and then pressed himself against the cabin wall. Two shots rang out from the trees. Charlie heard the one slug whiz by him and the other bullet hit the wall.

"Why don't you let this go, Mac? This is only gonna end bad for one of us. You got everything of Abe's. You can ride out of here and live well."

"Not with that boy alive, Ranger." Another shot sounded from the trees and this bullet hit the wall next to Charlie's face. Mac was moving around the trees for a clear shot. However, Charlie could still not see where he was. He crawled over to where Gus was and tried to focus on where the last shot originated. There was no movement. Then a twig snapped and Gus raised his head and looked at the tree off to his right. Charlie saw a shadowed figure step out from a tree and he fired one shot. He heard a muffled grunt. Charlie ran for the cover of the old stump in front of the cabin.

Mac fired two shots as he ran and one of the slugs struck Charlie in his right arm just above the elbow. The impact knocked Charlie to the ground. He lost all feeling in his right arm, and his gun tumbled to the ground out of his reach. Wincing in pain, Charlie grabbed his right arm with his left. He could feel the wound in the side of the arm, but no exit wound. *The bullet's still inside.* He quickly scooted himself to the cover of the stump.

"I warned you." Mac walked from the cover of the trees closer to Charlie. In the dim light of the dawn, before Mac got close to him, Charlie reached behind him with his left hand and pulled the .32 pistol from his belt. He slid it out of sight behind his back but close enough to grab.

The pre-dawn light was getting a little brighter with each minute. Charlie noticed a slight limp as Mac walked toward him. One of his bullets had grazed Mac's left leg. Charlie propped himself up against the stump. It was all over. He was feeling a little light headed from the loss of blood from his wounded right arm.

When Mac got close, Charlie asked, "What do you want with him? He can't do you any harm."

"He saw my face. I saw him look up at me. He could be the

182

one to put a noose around my neck. I can't let that happen." Mac cocked his gun and aimed it at Charlie's head. "Now, you're gonna tell me where that boy is or I'm gonna kill you. You choose. "

Russell sat perfectly still inside the cabin listening to the exchange of gunfire outside. With each shot he jumped and caught his breath. He wanted to hide, but there was no place to go. He was only able to take quick, shallow breaths from the fear that raced through his body. Then the shooting stopped. Russell sat paralyzed on the bed. Then curiosity got the better of him. Walking slowly and deliberately in the darkened cabin he carefully pulled open the shutter and saw Mac standing holding a gun. He couldn't see Charlie at all, but at least he heard his voice. He moved away from the window and bumped Charlie's shotgun, knocking it over. He caught it before it hit the floor and he stood holding the shotgun looking at Mac through the window.

Russell Hicks had never fired a gun in his life. In fact he had never held any kind of weapon before. All guns were banned in his time. There were still controlled shooting sports for a privileged few, but for the most part, all firearms were in the hands of either the enforcers or the military.

Russell remembered seeing Charlie, the deputy, and the Marshall all handle their guns. He was hoping he could do what they did. *I have to do something.* He couldn't let Mac kill Charlie. He silently slid the barrel of the shotgun through the window and pointed it at Mac. He pulled the trigger and the shotgun roared to life in his hands. The recoil of the blast sent the butt of the gun into Russell's cheek and knocked him backwards. The gun dropped to the floor.

Outside, Charlie was sitting on the ground leaning against the tree stump with his crippled right arm draped across his lap. His left hand hung by his side touching the handle of his hidden pistol. He knew Mac was going kill him and that once he was dead, Mac would go inside and find Russell. He had nothing to lose at this point. He was not afraid to die and in one respect would actually welcome death as a relief from this life of regret. He had to take the chance to try and stop

Mac. Charlie inched his left hand around the handle of the pistol, and just before he pulled it a shotgun blast sounded from the window. That was the break he needed.

Mac jumped at the sound of the blast and stumbled to the side. Charlie quickly pulled the Smith & Wesson double-action with his left hand and fired three shots at Mac. Mac fired once back at Charlie, but his shot was wild. Mac fell, severely wounded.

Mac lay on his back, turned his head, and looked at Charlie. He tried to raise his gun, but his strength was quickly draining away, along with his life.

"You should have headed on to the Pecos, Mac," Charlie said. Mac coughed and blood trickled from the corner of his mouth. "At least … now … you'll carry a scar from me," he said between shallow breaths. He looked into Charlie's eyes. Those were his last words.

"Russell!" Charlie yelled.

Russell limped outside holding his right side, still obviously in pain. "Oh no!" he said, seeing Charlie's wounded arm.

"Bend down here and help me up," Charlie said. Russell did as Charlie asked and the two helped each other back into the cabin. Charlie sat at the table and instructed Russell how to re-light the lantern. He pointed to the washstand. "Bring that bowl over here to the table and pour some of that water in it for me."

Russell filled the wash bowl from the bucket sitting on the floor and brought it and a towel over to the table. Then he helped Charlie pull his shirt off over his head.

"There's a knife on that shelf next to the stove," Charlie said, "bring it over here. Russell retrieved the knife and Charlie told him to cut the sleeve off his undershirt above the shoulder. Russell cut off the sleeve, exposing the wound in Charlie's right arm. Russell sat at the table across from Charlie and watched Charlie clean the wound.

Charlie noticed the swelling and the bruise that was beginning to form on Russell's cheek. He fought back a smile as he knew exactly what had happened. "Remind me to teach you how to shoot."

Russell smiled back and then quickly frowned looking at Charlie's wound.

"That was a dumb thing to do," Charlie said. "Firing that gun you basically told Mac where you were. But, under the circumstances, it was the perfect thing to do … and at the right time. You saved my life as well as your own."

"Did I … did I kill him?" Russell asked in a sheepish voice.

Charlie chuckled. "You know, it's hard to miss something ten feet away with a scatter gun. But I believe you clean missed everything. You sure scared the hell out of him, though. It gave me a chance to pull my gun. No, you didn't kill him. I did."

"What are we going to do?"

"Don't worry. I'll take care of all this," Charlie said. "But we have to get you out of here right away. You can't be anywhere near here after this."

Charlie took a clean neckerchief from the washstand drawer and wrapped it around the wound in his arm. "Here, tie this tight across here for me."

Russell tied a good tight knot and sat back down at the table with Charlie. "Does it hurt?"

"I guess it should," Charlie said, "but right now I can't feel anything in this arm."

"What do we do now?"

"I need your help to clean up this mess and then we'll get you home," Charlie said. "I got your old clothes over there. Change into them. I'm sending you back in the same clothes you came here in. I'm going outside to get a few of Mac's things."

The sun had not risen yet, but it was just light enough to see outside. Charlie found Mac's roan tied to a small tree halfway down the hill. He approached the horse and stroked his neck. He checked the horse's legs and chest.

"You're a fine bit of horseflesh, here. I wonder what you're called." He patted the roan's neck and stroked his nose. "You'll do fine." Charlie saw that Mac carried a rifle scabbard but no rifle. He left the horse tied to the tree and pulled down the two sets of saddle bags Mac had draped across his saddle. He carried the bags back inside the cabin and set them down on the table.

Russell sat on the bed dressed in his jeans, tee-shirt, and gym shoes all ready for his trip back home. He was holding the time belt.

"Give me a hand." Charlie walked back outside. Russell followed. "Take that gun belt off him and bring it inside." Charlie picked up Mac's gun and hat.

"Is this the guy who shot me?" Russell stared at the bloody body of Mac Sherman.

"Yeah, that's him," Charlie said. After a pause, he asked "Are you okay?"

Russell knelt down on one knee next to Mac's body. He didn't answer, he just nodded and began to unbuckle Mac's gun belt.

Charlie walked back inside and set the hat and gun on the table next to the saddle bags. Russell came in a moment later holding the gun belt.

"Here," Charlie said, "strap that belt around me."

"You're going to wear Mac's gun?" Russell asked, a little confused.

"Yup. Just help get it around me."

Russell buckled the belt around Charlie. It was a little tight since Mac was thinner than Charlie. But he did manage to get it buckled. Charlie slid Mac's gun into the holster and turned to look at Russell. He stopped cold as he finally noticed Russell dressed in the 1990's style clothing that he arrived in. Charlie paused for a long moment as the previous five days flashed through his mind. Although he knew there was no choice, he really didn't want him to go.

"What is all that stuff?" Russell broke the awkward silence.

Charlie's mind was brought back to the present by Russell's question. "These? Oh, these are Mac's things. These are Abe's bags and this set is Mac's bags. I'm going to go through them. Help me get his body inside here." He walked back outside.

"Inside? You mean in the cabin?" Russell followed.

Charlie didn't answer. With his left hand he grabbed one of Mac's arms and started to drag the body toward the door. Russell caught up to him and grabbed the other arm and together the two wounded men struggled to pull Mac's dead body into the cabin. Once in the light, Charlie was surprised to see that all three of his shots had hit his target. Mac had a wound in his stomach, one in his left side, and one in his neck, which more than likely was the wound that killed him.

Russell sat down at the table while Charlie went through and emptied Mac's pockets. The only things there were Abe's last will, a pocket watch, a knife, and a few coins, which Charlie tucked away in his pocket.

"What are you doing?" Russell asked.

Charlie realized his scavenging was making Russell a little uneasy. He took Mac's things and placed them on the table and looked over at Russell.

"He won't be needing these things anymore," Charlie said. "Things are different here than where you come from. Usually Doc Morgan gets the spoils, but when I'm through with this, there won't be anything left for him to root through."

"When you're finished with him?" Russell raised his voice a little and sat back in his chair with a concerned look on his face, "What are going to do, Charlie?"

"I'm gonna fake my death using Mac's body. As of today, Charlie Turlock will be dead."

Russell didn't reply. He just sat openmouthed.

"It's better this way. I'll just start over somewhere else."

"What about him?" Russell pointed to Mac's dead body.

"Him? What about him? He's dead!" Charlie said, a little irritated with Russell's line of questioning. "What the hell does it matter? Especially to you? That's the guy who tried to kill you, and he came out here to finish the job. Now you're worried about what will become of him?"

Russell dropped the conversation. He stared down at Mac's body and fiddled a little with the time belt he was holding. Charlie sat down across from Russell. In a calmer voice he answered Russell's question.

"There's no record of Mac Sherman in Texas and there never will be," Charlie said, "it's like he just disappeared. Don't worry. It'll be fine."

Russell nodded and kept silent while Charlie began sorting through the saddle bags.

"Where will you go? What will you do?" Russell finally asked.

"I'm thinking of going to see an old friend in Trinidad," Charlie said. "But that don't concern you. You won't be here."

"But Charlie, what about your name? Who will you be now?"

"Name don't matter. I'll figure something out."

Russell didn't know what to say about this. The two sat silently across the table from each other, both holding on to their respective wounds.

"We're a pair, aren't we?" Charlie said. Russell just smiled.

It was time, and they both knew it.

26

Going Home

Russell listened intently as Charlie explained the workings of the time belt. Since this would be the first time he wore it, the system would need to reset the genetic-to-energy calculations. Russell would need to keep his finger on the sensor screen until the processor began the countdown. Charlie further explained that he had already set the coordinates for the target and Russell wouldn't have to touch a thing. Once the counter began, Russell would have five seconds to turn the switch off and stop the jump.

Russell was a mix of conflicting emotions. He was excited to be going back home, but at the same time, he wanted to stay with Charlie. He had grown fond of this old grizzled lawman.

"What's wrong?" Charlie asked. "You say you're excited, but you don't look too happy about getting out of here."

"I'm a little nervous about going back, Charlie. If people back there are really trying to get rid of me, once they see me, they'll probably try it again. Maybe the next time they won't be so subtle about it."

"You'll be fine," Charlie said and then paused. "Just stay out of sight as long as you can. Find out as much as you can before you contact anyone. Most importantly, when you do contact someone, make sure it's someone you can trust."

"I'm scared. I don't know how to do any of this 'sneaking-around' stuff."

"You just fired a shotgun at a guy," Charlie said. "You've never held a firearm in your life. Yet you picked up a gun and shot it. I think you'll do whatever you need to do. You've got it in you. You'll do fine." Charlie patted Russell's shoulder and repeated, "You'll do fine." He then stepped back, looked at Russell, and smiled. Then his smile disappeared.

Russell didn't like that look. "What's wrong?"

"Is that wound still bleeding?"

"I don't know. Is that a problem?"

"If that bandage has your blood on it, the system may think it's a part of you and try to reattach it permanently during the transformation. You'd better take it off."

Russell hadn't considered the perils of jumping with an open wound. He removed the time belt and unwound the bandage and noticed that most of the swelling and redness had gone. It was replaced with a horrible discoloration from bruising. But it wasn't bleeding or leaking at all.

"Looks like it's healing pretty well," Russell said.

Charlie looked at the ugly wound and grimaced. "Well, if you think so, I guess." After a pause Charlie asked, "You ready?"

"You mean go now?"

"Not much sense in delaying it." Charlie hung his head and mindlessly fingered some of Mac's items on the table. He raised his head. "Look, when you get back, you'll need to get to your home right away. It's very important that you make sure you're not seen. Understand?"

"What if I jump into the middle of a group of people?" Russell asked.

"Well, I tried to find a place out of the way, but close enough to the facility. If people are there, you're on your own." Charlie smiled and winked at Russell. "Now when you get to your home, the first thing you need to do is put on a clean fresh modern bandage. Throw your clothes away and go get some real medical help. Tell them you fell on a broken glass or a sharp stick or something."

Russell acknowledged all of Charlie's instructions.

190

"Before you go, you have to promise me a couple things," Charlie said.

"Sure, what?"

"First, you have to promise me to keep up with the science and technology. It's critical that you stay on top of the newest revelations. You'll eventually understand why."

Russell nodded.

"Next, you have to promise to never come back here, ever! Got it?"

"Never?"

"Never!" Charlie emphasized. "And, last, you have to promise to destroy this belt when you get back."

Russell shook his head. He didn't think he could do that. This belt held the keys to everything he dreamed of concerning time travel. He needed to study this belt. He needed to find out everything he could about it. It would advance his research by decades.

"I ... I don't know, Charlie."

"You have to promise," Charlie demanded. "Time travel ain't what you think. It's dangerous. Not only for you or the jumper, but more so for the people and the lives they interact with. There's no way to measure what harm can be done to future generations just by interacting with the people and events in the past."

"You've been here a lifetime, Charlie. What harm have you caused?"

Charlie lowered his head. "Like I said, there's no way to know. I did my best." He looked Russell in the eyes. "For thirty years I used that belt to jump forward in time and check the historical records of all the people I came in contact with. I did my best to preserve their history, not to interfere with it. It was why I never owned property or took a wife or had a family. I looked at it as my responsibility, or my sentence, to preserve their history as it was before I got here."

"Well what about all the people you arrested or killed over the years?" Russell asked.

"I tried to check on them all. If I knew I was going out after someone, I looked up the people I was going after," Charlie explained. "I found out their fate in the historical records before I left. I did everything I could to fulfill their fate. Usually, if there were more than one of us, I tried to let the other Rangers take action. If there was a gun battle, I shot wild so my bullets weren't the ones that killed anyone. There were some times, however, when I didn't have a choice. I had to hope for the best." Charlie lowered his head again. It was obvious to Russell that Charlie was thinking of some of those past times.

"Like the gun battle at Walker's ranch?" Russell asked to break the silence.

Charlie looked at Russell and gave him a nod. "Yeah. Like Walker's ranch."

Satisfied with Charlie's explanation, Russell stood and turned on the switch. A tiny red light on the small box lit up. Russell placed his finger on the sensor screen and the tiny red light began to blink. Almost thirty seconds passed when suddenly the blue-green translucent light engulfed him. He saw the display in front of him and watched the counter descend. When the counter reached the number two, Russell turned the switch off. The light disappeared and Russell stood looking at Charlie who had a puzzled look on his face.

"I wanted to say thanks. You could have killed me or left me out there in the prairie. You didn't have to take me in, and I wanted to thank you for all you did for me. I won't ever forget you." He offered his hand to Charlie who gladly shook it and smiled broadly. They looked at each other in silence, trying to preserve that one last look. Russell knew they would never see each other again. Finally, Charlie grabbed Russell and pulled him close and gave him a slight hug with his left arm, his wounded right arm hanging limp at his side.

"You'd better go. Remember to close your eyes when the counter reaches one. The flash on the inside is pretty bright," Charlie instructed.

Russell turned on the switch and with a smile placed his finger on the screen. The light engulfed him and he watched the counter. When the counter reached one, Russell closed his eyes and in a flash, he was gone.

A sudden and painful emptiness overtook Charlie and he dropped into the chair. Not only was his new-found companion gone, but so was his only escape. His fate was now sealed. Any return to the future was now impossible.

Charlie slumped forward, leaning on the table. He felt his eyes moisten. He had become fond of Russell. He thought of him as the son he would never have. But he knew there was no alternative. Russell had a destiny to fulfill that he didn't know anything about.

All of the plans he had formulated didn't seem so important anymore. He looked around at his meager home knowing he would soon be leaving it for good. He looked at the blood-stained pants and Hanna's husband's shirt rolled up on the bed.

"It's better this way," Charlie said to himself. "Isn't it?"

27

Disappear

Charlie wasn't sure how long he sat at the table blindly staring at Mac's belongings, as if in another world. All he could think about were the past days he spent with Russell and how much he missed him already. A beam of sunlight shone through the open shutters and reflected off the still lit lantern into his eye, jolting him back to reality. Charlie regained his thoughts. He had a lot to do, and it was going to be more difficult with only one good arm.

Charlie sorted through Mac's belongings and tossed the clothes and most of his personal items aside. Then he came across the satchel that contained Abe's money from the sale of the cattle. Mac must have grabbed it when he found Abe. There was over ten thousand dollars in that bag. He thought about Amos, and Hanna, and Tuck and Doc and how they really could use this money. But he couldn't risk being seen by anyone. That would thwart his whole escape plan.

Anything of Mac's that he felt he could use he put back into Mac's saddle bags. He left the money bag sitting on the table, not sure what he should do with it. Charlie tried on Mac's hat. It was a little small, but it was a close enough fit to work for a while. He'd get a new hat later.

Charlie removed the Deputy City Marshal badge from his vest and pinned it on Mac's body. Then he hung his old hat on the chair next to his holster and gun.

Charlie already knew what he needed to take with him and what he was going to leave. His fresh wrapped clean clothes and personal items were packed in a small canvas valise. The food, ammunition, matches, and other items Charlie set aside, he put in both Abe's and Mac's saddle bags. He rolled his duster and other camp supplies in his bedroll, and looked around the cabin one more time. That was it, except for the money.

Charlie set the valise, the bedroll, and the two saddle bags outside the cabin by the old stump and went back in for one last look. From the trunk he retrieved the Texas Ranger Frontier Battalion badge and tucked the badge in his vest pocket. He realized he had no choice about the money. He had to take it with him. As much as he wanted his friends to have it, he knew he couldn't risk the exposure. He stuck the money bag in his shirt, picked up his Winchester rifle and went back outside.

Charlie fashioned a sling from another neckerchief and placed it around his damaged right arm. Carrying one item at a time, Charlie got all his gear down and tied onto Mac's roan. It was almost too much for the roan to carry. "I'll get you a mule when we get to Tascosa. Help with the load." He patted the roan's neck.

In his final act, Charlie took the can of kerosene he kept for lamp fuel and dumped it all around the inside of the cabin, completely dousing Mac's body and Russell's old clothes in the process. He tossed the lantern and globe onto the floor making sure the globe broke. He stood in the open doorway, struck a match, and tossed the lit match into cabin. With a resounding "whoosh", the inside of the cabin burst into flames. Charlie stepped back and watched for a minute as his history and his life burned away in front of his eyes. He was done. Charlie Turlock no longer existed. He was dead.

Charlie walked over to Gus and pulled the rail away from the corral entrance. He put his arm around Gus's neck and held him for one last moment.

"I know how you hate fire, boy," Charlie said. "You can leave anytime. Tuck will be by soon to get you. He'll take good care of you."

Charlie turned and walked away staying close to the cabin and the flames. Gus bowed his head and began to follow, but the fire spooked him and he walked away from the cabin in the other direction. Charlie climbed into the saddle on Mac's horse and rode away towards Tascosa.

As dark smoke from the cabin fire filled the early morning sky north of Amarillo, Charlie rode a red roan northwest along the rail tracks. The townspeople from Amarillo began riding out to see about the fire.

The ride on a horse he wasn't used to was rough on Charlie, especially with only the use of one arm. When he finally crossed the bridge over the Canadian River, he continued through Tascosa and rode out the Dodge City Trail to Doctor J.M. Shelton's place at the end of McMasters Street. The doctor told Charlie his arm was pretty tore up and that it would be better to take the arm off. Charlie wouldn't hear of it. So the doctor removed the slug, cleaned the wound the best he could, sewed it up, and bandaged it. He said that there was a lot of muscle and tissue damage and that when it healed, his arm would never be the same. He might get some feeling back in it, but not to expect much.

Mac was right, Charlie thought, he would be carrying a mark from him for the rest of his life. Charlie walked the roan down Main Street to McCormick's livery to board him over night. He purchased a burro to take the weight of his packs off the roan. Then he walked two doors down to Jesse Sheet's North Star restaurant and had a nice big dinner.

Charlie took a room for the night at the Russell Hotel. He registered as A.J. Campbell, occupation – miner. He asked the clerk for five envelopes and a piece of paper, which he took to his room. Charlie sat at a table in his room watching the sun get lower in the western sky. He took the piece of stationary and wrote a series of numbers on it and placed the paper in an envelope along with his

Texas Ranger badge. He sealed the envelope and wrote "HICKS" on the outside of the envelope in large letters. Then he wrote "Ranger's Office, Amarillo" below the name.

Charlie pulled the money bag from under his shirt and sorted the cash into five stacks. He put four of the stacks into the four remaining envelopes and addressed one to Doctor Walter Morgan, one to Hanna, one to Amos Cook, and one to Tuck Cornelius. Like the envelope to Hicks, he addressed them to their places of business in Amarillo and set them aside to deliver to the desk clerk for mailing on the next stage.

The next morning, A.J. Campbell's room was empty and the roan and the burro were gone from McCormick's Livery. Two half-eagle coins sat on top of the five envelopes addressed to Amarillo at the clerk's desk. The latest page in the registration book had been torn out. There was no sign that an A.J. Campbell had ever been there.

28

Life After Charlie

The afternoon edition of *The Amarillo Champion* announced that long time Texas Ranger Charles Turlock died in a fire in his cabin early that morning.

The news of Charlie's demise quickly spread around the town. As with all news spread by word of mouth, rumors of the body, murder, suicide, and the fire were widespread and unchecked. Amarillo was mourning the passing of one of its more familiar and likable citizens.

Marshal Cook had the grim task of bringing the body down to Doc Morgan's office. Deputy Johnson remained in town while Marshal Cook and Captain Bill McDonald rode out to Charlie's cabin along with two other rangers in a wagon. The four lawmen went through the burnt rubble. There wasn't much left. Almost everything was burnt beyond recognition, including the body. The stove, and some metal dishes and the remnants of his shotgun and handgun were about the only recognizable objects. Marshal Cook couldn't bring himself to put the body into the wagon. He left that task to the rangers.

The marshal walked around the burnt shell of the cabin and looked through Gus's stall. His emotions overwhelmed him. He walked a little into the trees to hide his tears from the others. That's when he saw Gus at the bottom of the hill standing in the stream. He choked back a sob as he climbed down the hill toward Charlie's horse and took hold of his halter rope. He walked him over to his bay, tied him to his saddle horn.

He patted Gus on his neck. "We'll see if Tuck can find a nice place for you."

Captain McDonald stood at the top of the hill and shouted down. "We're heading back to Morgan's place. You coming along?"

"I'll be there in a bit. You go on ahead." The marshal climbed back up the hill and watched as the wagon carrying what everyone believed to be Charlie's body, drove off to town with Captain McDonald leading the wagon.

Marshal Cook kept looking around the scorched ground and the ashes of what used to be Charlie's cabin. There was a distinct aroma of coal-oil in the air. The scorched and partial remains of the meager furniture and belongings all had the same odor. This whole thing just didn't seem right to him, but he couldn't put his finger on exactly what it was. He had a strange feeling about this. Charlie would have gotten out if it was just a fire, unless he was unable to move. There had to be something else. Something he was missing. Maybe it was wishful thinking, but he just didn't want to believe Charlie was dead. There was something about that body that just didn't seem right to him, but he couldn't get past his grief to focus on it. But if it wasn't Charlie, then whose body was it? And the question that was burning in the marshal's mind that no one else seemed to be asking was "what happened to Hicks?"

That afternoon, after dropping Gus off at Tuck's livery, the marshal delivered the sad news to Hanna. The initial shock caused her to faint into his arms. He set her in a chair and revived her with some cold water. The two sat side-by-side at a table while the marshal held her. She wept uncontrollably for quite a while. After her crying subsided, Marshal Cook released his hold on her and patted her shoulder.

"I have to go see Doc Morgan, Hanna. I'll be back later to check on you. Are you gonna be all right?"

Hanna didn't answer. She gave the marshal a brief nod and slowly got up from the table seemingly in a trance. After the marshal left, Hanna closed her restaurant and locked herself away in her room. She was so distraught that she could not face a single person. Later that evening, Marshal Cook tried to talk to her, but she didn't want to see anyone. She wouldn't answer the door.

Doc Morgan was normally not a drinking man, but today he sat with a bottle of whiskey and a glass, trying to drink away his grief. He was so overwrought he couldn't bring himself to go into the back room of his house to see the body, much less work on it. His work room was already filled. He had Abe Walker's body back there on the large wooden table, and the bodies of the two cowboys shot down in the street the previous night. Now, there was Charlie's body lying on a wooden plank on the floor. He sat in his parlor on the sofa where Charlie laid just a few nights before. Charlie was a good friend. He would certainly be missed.

Marshal Cook rode his bay to the rear of Doc's place and went in. He was expecting to see Doc Morgan there busy working on Charlie's body. Instead, the back room was dark and deserted, except for the bodies. The stench from the three corpses and Charlie's burnt remains was overpowering. The marshal propped the back door open to let in some fresh air.

"Doc? Doc, you here?" Marshal Cook walked through the back room into the parlor and found Doc Morgan sprawled out on his sofa. A bottle of whiskey sat on the parlor table half empty. A glass lay overturned on the carpet next to the sofa. The marshal sympathized with Doc, but he had to get him awake and coherent. He pulled the doctor up into a sitting position.

"Doc! Doc! Come on now, wake up."

Doc Morgan's head rolled from one side to the other. He opened one eye and tried to focus on the marshal. "Go away. Leave me be." He waved a hand at the marshal as if dismissing him.

"Come on, Doc. You got to look at that body."

"Go away!" the doc shouted. His eyes moistened.

"Doc! Damn it! You got to look at that body. I don't think its Charlie!"

The doc looked at Marshal Cook through blurry, bloodshot eyes. He put both hands up to his head. He wrinkled his forehead, shook his head, and looked back at Marshal Cook. "What? What was that you said?" The doc reached out and grabbed the marshal's arm.

"There's something that's been bothering me about that body." The marshal sat on the sofa next to Doc Morgan. "But I was so upset over the thought of Charlie being dead that I missed it. The more I thought about it, I realized the body is all wrong. It's too short and too thin to be Charlie. I also think the boots are wrong. But I need you to look at it."

Doc Morgan sat on the edge of the sofa. He ran his hands through his mussed hair. He again looked at the marshal with a puzzled look on his face.

"Are you all right?" the marshal asked. "Can I get you something?"

"Water. There's some water in that pitcher on the stand," the doc said. Cook poured some water in a glass and handed it to Morgan. The doc took a long drink and then stood up and steadied himself. Marshal Cook stood by to catch him if he wobbled too much.

"Not Charlie?" the doc asked again.

"I don't think so. But you're the one who can tell me that."

"If it's not Charlie, who is it?" the doctor asked.

Marshal Cook shook his head.

Doc Morgan walked through the parlor to his back room. He stopped at the first table and poured water from a bucket into a large metal bowl. He splashed water into his face a few times and then wiped his hands and face on a nearby towel.

"Light that lamp there," he said.

Marshal Cook complied and brought it to Morgan. The two moved Abe's body to the floor and lifted the wooden plank carrying the burnt body and set it on the table. Doc grabbed a long pointed instrument from his box and along with the lamp, slowly walked around the charred corpse looking at every detail. He looked at the charred remains of the head and the few strands of hair that remained, the tiny bits of clothing seared to the flesh, the remains of the leather boots blistered to the feet. He measured the length and width of the body at different points. After the walk-around examination, the doc went back to the bowl and washed his hands.

The marshal stood by anxiously waiting for the doc to say something. "Well?"

"You might be right. At first look, it don't look to be Charlie," the doc said.

"I knew it!" the marshal said.

"Now hold on there. It still might be Charlie. Fire has a way of shrinking down and distorting a body. Burns away skin, fat and muscle in nothing flat. The only thing that makes me doubt it being Charlie is the length. That usually doesn't change very much. I'll need to look at it a little closer. At this point, if I had to make a guess, I'd have to say it ain't Charlie."

"Is that Hicks?"

"No. I thought that too, for a moment," the doc said. "But Hicks was a couple inches taller than Charlie. This body is shorter than Charlie. Fire wouldn't cause that much shrinkage in their height." The doc stood quietly for a moment and then looked at Marshal Cook. "Something else, this fella has a couple of gunshot wounds. He may have more. I won't know until I look at it some more."

"I don't understand," the marshal said as he and the doctor walked back into the parlor. "If that ain't Charlie, then where is he? And who's back there on the table?" They both sat down and remained quiet, trying to digest this latest revelation.

"You think Charlie did this on purpose?" Doc Morgan poured another glass of water.

"Why would Charlie want everyone to think he's dead?" the marshal asked.

"Maybe he and Hicks just wanted to get away and start over somewhere else. Maybe Charlie went to California with Hicks. We both know he was going to leave the Rangers soon," the doc said.

"It couldn't be that simple. It doesn't make any sense. Charlie wouldn't go like that."

"Why not? He's done with the Rangers. He don't have Abe Walker's threat hanging over him anymore," the doc said. "Hicks would have a tough time traveling with that wound in his side. Charlie probably decided to leave with him to take care of him. It's the perfect time to leave."

"But why leave? And why leave like this? He has a lot of friends here. His life was here. Just don't make no sense," the marshal said. "And who the hell is back there on that table? There's got to be something else. I can't imagine him doing something like this. I smell foul play here."

"Why do you think something bad happened to him?"

"Cuz his horse and everything he owned was there. Nothing's missing – his guns, his clothes, his saddle. Charlie wouldn't have left all that."

"Gus was there?"

"Yeah. That's what I mean. None of it makes sense."

The two sat quietly for a few minutes evaluating all the information they had. Doc Morgan got up and poured another tall glass of water and drank it all down at once.

"Wait a minute." The marshal stood up and looked at Doc Morgan. "Charlie said he was going after Mac Sherman." He paused while he fitted together the puzzle pieces in his mind. "That's it," he exclaimed. "That has to be it."

"What? What has to be it? What are you talking about?"

"Mac Sherman. That has to be Sherman on that table." Marshal Cook began to pace a bit. "The last thing Charlie said last night was that he was going after Sherman. The next time I saw him he was running to the livery and he and Gus lit out like the devil himself was after him." Doc Morgan sat down on the sofa, listening intently to Cook's theory.

"I've never seen Mac Sherman," the doctor said. "Was he short?"

"I only saw him close-up once a few days ago when Hicks got shot. But I remember him from a few years back when they came through here. He was a short, wiry fella with a fierce scar across his forehead. Mean as a box of snakes."

"If that's the case, then you might be right. That could be him lying back there on the table. But then again, where's Charlie and Russell?"

Marshal Cook shook his head and sat down in the easy chair next to the sofa. Doc Morgan looked down at the empty water glass he was still holding. Both were in deep thought trying to piece together what they've learned so far.

"Charlie had to have started that fire." The marshal broke the silence. "That's the only explanation. But why? There has to be a reason."

Doc Morgan looked over at the marshal. "He wanted everyone to think it was him."

"But why, Doc?" the marshal asked.

"I don't know." Doc Morgan stood and looked out the window at the stockyards across the street. "I don't know." He turned back to the marshal. "You know, Charlie seems to have gone to a lot of trouble to make people think he's dead. Maybe we should stop wondering about it and just let it be."

Marshal Cook had a disapproving look on his face. "I don't like to leave unanswered questions."

"Well, what good would it do, Amos?" the doc replied. "Charlie's gone. If you wanna go running around the country lookin' for him, then you go ahead. But you know Charlie, if he don't want to be found, you're never gonna find him. If he's alive and if he wants us to know where he is, he'll let us know. He'll more-n-likely get settled in somewhere and send us a telegram. I say we let it go. Let Charlie go out the way he wants."

"What if he didn't want it?" the marshal countered. "What if this was all set up by … by … someone else?"

"Who? Who else is left? Walker's dead, half his crew is either dead or you got 'em locked up, and now Sherman's dead. Who else would want to harm Charlie?"

The marshal looked at Doc Morgan as if he was just bested in a game of wits. He shook his head and sat back down. "It just doesn't make sense. Charlie burned down everything he owned and then left without Gus. Even if he just lit out, he would have taken something with him. And he wouldn't have just abandoned Gus."

"Maybe you're right," doc said. "But until we have his body or we hear from him, we'll never know for sure." Doc Morgan paused and then added. "I'll look at that body some more. See what else I can find out. In the meantime, let's just keep this between us. It won't do no good to get everyone all riled up with no answers."

Doc Morgan stood up and held his hand out to Marshal Cook. The marshal took Doc's hand and shook it.

"This is just between you and me then," the doc said. "No one else is to know. Until we get some answers!"

"Agreed," the marshal said. They shook hands again and the marshal went out the back door and rode his bay back to his office.

Doc Morgan went back and did a more thorough inspection of the burnt corpse. There was very little left to identify the body. The only thing he found was the partially melted City Marshal badge. All Doc knew was that the body was a man who was a little shorter than Charlie. He turned the body over and discovered some small patches of clothing on the back of the body that were spared from the intense fire. He never saw Charlie in a shirt with that pattern and color.

Everything he found out about this corpse pointed to it being someone other than Charlie. Doc Morgan was now certain that this burnt body was not Charlie. Probably Mac Sherman, like the marshal said. He was also fairly certain that Charlie set this all up. He remembered the oath he and Marshal Cook shook hands over. *No one will know until Charlie lets us know.*

The doctor knew he couldn't embalm or prepare the body at all. He just wrapped it in linen and put it in one of the pine boxes he built earlier that week. He roughly chiseled the name TURLOCK into the wooden lid and nailed it shut. He'd work on the other three corpses later.

The next day, most of the town and all of the rangers turned out for a brief ceremony and prayer service held at the grave site. Everyone believed the pine casket contained the body of Charlie, everyone except the marshal and the doctor. During the prayer service, Hanna stood dressed in black leaning against Marshal Cook and holding onto his arm. Cook wanted desperately to tell her about Charlie, just to ease her grief, but he knew in his heart she would be the worst person to tell. It would be best to let her grieve and then move on with her life. Doc Morgan and the marshal were true to their oath and never spoke of the burnt body again.

With the service done, the casket was lowered into the grave and everyone went back to town to restart their daily lives. The grave was filled in with dirt and a simple wooden marker was placed on the grave with Charlie's name on it, nothing more. For a long while, every Sunday, a small bouquet of Amarillo wildflowers appeared on the grave with Charlie's marker on it. Eventually, the bouquets stopped appearing. But no one really noticed.

Life in Amarillo eventually returned to normal. The stories about Charlie got fewer and farther between. As the old timers who knew Charlie moved on and went away, the stories of Ranger Turlock went with them. Eventually Charlie was nothing more than an old embellished story that got shared in a saloon over a drink. He was finally lost to the time.

29

Upton

June, 2220

When he opened his eyes, Russell was unsure what had happened. He found himself lying on the lawn in the dark, completely confused. He pulled himself up to a sitting position. He tried to remember where he was and why he was sitting outside on the ground behind the maintenance building. For some reason, his short term memory was a scrambled mess. His eyesight was hazy and everything appeared cast in various oscillating hues, switching from one color to another. He tried to focus on the side of a building wondering what was happening to him. His nerves felt like they were on fire. Random images and thoughts popped into his mind for a fleeting moment and then vanished as quickly as they came. Nothing made sense.

He tried to stand up, but a piercing pain shot through his right side and he fell back to the ground. He grabbed his side and placed his hand on the sutured gunshot wound. He vaguely remembered he had a wound, but could not remember how he got it. He noticed the jeans and tee-shirt he was wearing, and then the time belt.

"What is all this? What does all this mean?" Russell said. "It all seems kind of familiar, but I don't understand." The burning pain from his nerve endings began to subside. Favoring his right side, he managed to get to his feet and stand up. He felt dizzy and nauseous.

Something was wrong. Everything seemed somewhat familiar, but he could not tie it all together. His eyesight finally returned to normal.

"My name. What's my name?" he said to himself. He concentrated and tried to remember. "Russ? Charlie? Doc? Where are these names coming from? Why are they in my head?" He kept trying to tie the memory fragments together. The harder he tried the more fragments surfaced and confused his mind even more. Finally, as he concentrated, certain thought patterns began to fall into place. Then, as if someone sneaked up behind him and tightened up some loose bolts, everything started to come together. He finally began to feel he was intact. He must have regained consciousness before his transformation was complete.

"Charlie!" he said aloud. "Damn, he did it. I'm back." He remembered it all, now. Amarillo, getting shot, Doc, Marshal Cook, it was all coming back to him in waves. Then he remembered his botched time jump. He remembered what he needed to do.

Staying in the shadows of the buildings and hiding behind the shrubbery and stacks of cargo in the yards, Russell limped to his living quarters on the other side of the complex. On the way he contemplated the transformation problem he just experienced. He would have to study this belt.

When he reached his quarters, his facial image was scanned at the door panel of the apartment building and the door swung open. Entering the hallway, he made his way to one of the many individual transport tubes. His wound was beginning to bleed again. He unstrapped the time belt and held it rolled up tightly in his hand. At this time of night, the halls were normally deserted. Before he stepped into the tube he checked the clock in the hallway; it read 9:10 PM. It had taken him ten minutes to revive and walk to his living quarters.

The transporter scanned him and flashed his picture and identity on a display in the tube, showing his apartment on the fourth floor. In a matter of seconds he was shot upward to his floor. When the tube's door slid open, Russell stuck his head out and saw the empty hallway. He walked to his apartment door, and placed his hand on the sensor screen on his door panel. A light scanned his palm, and a mechanical voice said "ACCESS VOICE RECOGNITION." Russell answered in as clear a voice as he could muster: "Hicks, Russell. ID code is *49920*."

He heard a slight click and the door panel quickly slid open. As soon as Russell went inside, the door panel slid closed behind him. Pre-set lights came on in his apartment and pre-programmed music began to play. He was immediately engulfed in red and green laser lights that scanned his body from head to toe.

"GOOD EVENING MR. HICKS. YOU APPEAR TO BE INJURED. I WILL NOTIFY MEDICAL," a mechanical voice announced.

"No," Russell replied. "Cancel medical."

"CANCEL CONFIRMED."

Russell moved into the bedroom and removed his clothes. He hid the time belt in his dresser. He'd find a more secure place for it later. Then he stepped into the bathroom and stood in the middle of the shower chamber.

"Shower," Russell commanded and steady streams of warm soft water began spraying him from the nozzles strategically placed in various locations on all the marble and stainless walls, floor, and ceiling. His wound burned as the chemically treated cleansing water poured over it. He cleaned himself thoroughly and commanded "Stop." The water jets ceased. Warm soft air began blowing on him slowly at first and steadily increased in velocity until he was completely dry.

"Stop," Russell commanded again and the fans stopped. He combed his hair, and on the medical panel in his bathroom, selected four-by-four antibiotic bandages. He pressed the button three times and the panel dispensed three bandages which Russell put on over his wound. He dressed in his blue employee overalls and looked around his room for his encoded employee chip. Then he remembered, *the lockbox*!

"Time!" Russell said aloud.

"9:25 PM, JUNE 27th, 2220," the mechanical voice announced.

Five more minutes until he jumped to Amarillo, he thought. He had to hurry.

209

As quickly as a wounded man could move, and at the same time trying not to attract attention to himself, Russell made his way to the building where his time jump was in process. Before he went in, he saw a man in a suit leave the lab building and walk right past him directly to a waiting personal vehicle in front of the lab. The man was preoccupied on his data cell and didn't pay any attention to Russell. The man climbed into the seat, barked a destination command and sat back while the computer controlled vehicle sped away. All Russell could do was watch as the vehicle disappeared in the dark. The suit! *That's the guy I saw in the lab!* "What the hell was Paul Camber doing here this time of night?" Russell murmured.

Russell didn't like Paul Camber and he certainly didn't trust him. An account representative for an international electronics conglomerate that supplied a few electronic components shouldn't be here this time of night. Something wasn't right, Russell thought. But he didn't have time to worry about that now.

Russell let himself into the non-descript grey concrete building that housed a number of DARPA's ultra-secret black projects. There was no trace of these projects. They weren't on anyone's books, so they didn't officially exist. These were the type of projects where a person could be entirely erased and no one would know anything about it. Russell had to be careful.

Although there were a few people around, no one paid any attention to him as he walked to the door of his lab. After a palm scan, the door clicked open and Russell went in. As soon as he entered, there was a bright flash of a blue light that filled the entire room. He looked over at the large silver and gold disks housed in a separate glass enclosure, and watched himself disappear in the light. A chill ran through his body at the vision of his body dematerializing in-between the two disks. He froze for a second, startled by the sight. After the flash disappeared, he regained his composure and ducked behind a power panel and watched the two operators at their stations.

Michael O'Riley sat at his console with his back to the glass enclosure. Steven Marcohen, was standing at his station watching the data roll across the glass top display of his desk. With their backs to him, Russell made his way to the lockbox and retrieved his data cell and employee chip. He quickly scampered back to the cover of the power panels.

"I lost him!" Steven yelled. He appeared to be quite agitated as he looked over at Michael.

"What do you mean lost him?" Michael jumped to his feet.

"He was there, and then, all of a sudden, his genetic ID just vanished! My God! He's lost. We lost him, Mike! What do we do?"

"Settle down, Steve. We couldn't have lost him. Run diagnostics. Make sure the equipment didn't fail." Michael turned to go to Steven's station when he suddenly stopped. A blinking red light on the panel of his console was flashing the destination date. "Oh my God!" Michael froze.

"What?"

"He's not lost. He's in another dimension."

"What are you talking about?" Steven asked. "He can't be in another dimension."

"The destination," Michael said. "It's set wrong. Instead of 1992, it was set to 1892."

"How could that happen?" Steven asked.

"I don't know! Somebody had to have changed it, or … or … somehow I accidentally reset it. I don't know! I don't know!" Michael replied.

"Well get him back!"

"We can't just get him back, Steve! It's not that simple. The entire system is programmed for 1992 but with the matrix set to 1892, God knows where he ended up. We'd have to reprogram the whole system just to find him!" Michael said. He dropped back down in his chair and stared at the blank screens at his station, in what appeared to be deep thought.

"What'll we do?" Steven asked.

"Quiet. I'm thinking. Go get Zeller. Hopefully I'll have this figured out when you get back."

Russell ducked farther back behind the power panels as Steven rushed past him on his way out of the lab. He was relieved to find out that he wasn't sent to 1892 on purpose. Russell decided to make himself known, but just as he was about to step out, Michael leaned back in his chair and laughed. It wasn't an accident.

211

EDWARD L GATES

30

Doctor Zeller

Russell struggled with the notion that Michael was the one that sabotaged his time jump. A cold sweat broke out all over his body and he trembled with fear. He sank lower behind the power units and watched Michael sit motionless behind his station. He was now certain his being sent to 1892 was deliberate. Michael just kept staring at the blank tracking screen as if expecting something to happen.

Russell wasn't sure what to do. Fear gripped him and he couldn't move. He thought about Charlie and wished he was there. He thought about confronting Michael when Steven returned with Doctor Melissa Zeller.

Doctor Zeller was the physicist in charge of the teleportation program and Russell's boss. She was a tall slender lady and quite attractive for her age. Not that the mid-fifties was old, but most people of that age group show certain signs of aging. With her, however, any signs of her age were non-existent. Her short red hair bounced as she walked, or rather marched. She always moved as if she had a deliberate purpose to her gait, as if she was bearing down on a target. Russell froze as Steven and Doctor Zeller passed by in a hurry.

"Report!" Doctor Zeller demanded as she got within earshot of Michael.

Michael, apparently startled by her abrupt arrival, rose and quickly turned to face his boss. He didn't, or couldn't speak at all. He just stood staring at Doctor Zeller with his mouth open.

"Michael?" Doctor Zeller said again. "I'm waiting."

Michael stammered a bit as he began. "We ... we ... we programmed the destination mark for an area just north of Amarillo, Texas on this date in 1992. Everything seemed to go exactly as before. No problems at all." Michael looked over at Steven, who still had a bewildered look about him.

"Go on," Doctor Zeller urged.

"Well, after a few minutes, Steve just said he lost track of Hicks. Gone, just like that."

Doctor Zeller walked over to Steven and stood close to him. "How did this happen, Steven?" She asked in a stern managerial voice. Steven couldn't look her in the face. He kept looking down. "I'm waiting, Mr. Marcohen. You need to tell me what happened."

Russell fought back the urge to jump out and tell what he knew. He stayed in the shadows and watched Steven briefly raise his head and look at Doctor Zeller.

"It was my fault," Michael said interrupting Doctor Zeller's interrogation of Steven.

"Your fault?" Doctor Zeller turned now to Michael.

But then Steven finally spoke up. "Well, it ... it was crazy! I was tracking him. We had good data on him. It appeared he transformed fine. Then ..." He again looked at Doctor Zeller and then over at Michael.

"Then what?" Doctor Zeller demanded.

"Then ... then he just wasn't there anymore. I thought the tracking system failed but the diagnostics I ran proved everything was functioning correctly. He just disappeared."

Doctor Zeller stepped back from Steven. "They don't just disappear, Steven. Get him back." She turned to Michael "You two get Russell back here. I don't care how you do it and I don't care how long it takes. You get him back here!"

"He's in another dimension," Michael said. "It's not that easy. It's going to take some time."

"Another dimension? What dimension?"

214

"We're not sure." Michael lowered his head.

"What do you mean you're not sure?" Doctor Zeller raised her voice. "How in the world did he miss a programmed dimension?"

"Like I said, it's my fault." Michael said. "Somehow the matrix year was off by one digit. It got switched to 1892 instead of 1992. The programming is set for 1992 but the matrix was set to 1892. I didn't catch it until Steve said he lost him."

"Then find him in 1892 and get him back here." She turned and stormed out of the lab.

Russell knew the problems Michael and Steven would face. They would have to trace the exact path Russell took through the matrix to 1892, mathematically rebuild that same path, and then try to retrieve him. He knew they would both be busy for quite some time. He also knew they would never succeed. This would be a good time to make his way out of the lab and pay Doctor Zeller a visit.

31

Revelation

Russell watched the two operators. They were busy running trace sequences through the time matrix trying to locate the exact path Russell followed. Michael moved the setting back to 1892 and began to run a new set of scans. He appeared surprised that the scan didn't locate Russell in 1892. He stood and with a bewildered expression on his face, watched the negative returns coming to his station from the scan.

"Got something?" Steven asked.

"No," Michael said. "No, but there should have at least been ... No. I mean I got nothing. Not a thing. There's no trace of him." He sat back down at his station. He looked over at Steven to ensure Steven was busy and not paying any attention to him. Then Michael went back to running meaningless traces just to appear busy. It was obvious to Russell that Michael had no intention of bringing him back at all.

With both operators feverishly working at their respective stations, Russell slipped unnoticed out of the lab. He moved outside and into the night shadows of the grey concrete building housing top secret DARPA black projects. Russell kept rolling the revelations he had just uncovered over in his mind trying to digest it all.

First there was Mr. Camber. As an outside sales rep, he had limited access to the buildings and was restricted from the labs. Any

216

visits to the various labs in the building were usually controlled and escorted by an employee or a guarad. Russell wondered how he was able to get unfettered access.

Paul Camber's corporation was well connected in the government and had deep pockets. Through some corporate and government espionage, they found out about the time-travel project. The value of this project to their corporation, both commercially and criminally, would be immeasurable and have global implications. They were determined to do whatever it took to acquire the technology for their own private use, regardless of consequences and cost.

A few weeks ago, Mr. Camber asked Russell to supply him with certain information and documents about the project. Camber told him that he could "… make it worth his while" if he cooperated. Russell refused his offer and Paul Camber told him he'd made a big mistake. At the time Russell didn't know what he meant by that. Now he did.

Camber either changed the date himself while Michael was busy, or successfully bribed Michael to do it. He must have convinced Michael that they had to get rid of Russell and supply technical project information to him. Russell was sure Michael was getting well paid for his betrayal. He had to talk to Doctor Zeller.

Russell walked out of the building's shadows and across the courtyard to the administration building. It was one of the most secure buildings in the complex. There's only one way in and one way out. Aside from the massive steel door that was virtually impregnable when closed, the entrance was controlled by a very large, heavily armed guard whose job is to find any reason to deny entry. The guard's station is a small enclosure of steel, concrete, and two inch-thick shatterproof glass plates.

"I want to see Doctor Zeller," Russell announced as he approached the scanners on the front of the booth.

"Pretty late. I don't think the doctor is here."

"She's here," Russell said. "She just came back from the lab. Tell her Russell Hicks needs to speak with her. She'll see me."

The guard stared at Russell for a moment. Russell could tell by his demeanor that he was not very happy to see him. "Hicks?" He asked.

"Yeah, Russell Hicks." He placed his ID chip on the sensor by the gate.

"Scan." The guard said and Russell put his right hand on a palm scanner. The guard watched a screen inside his office for the results of Russell's palm scan. Seemingly satisfied that Russell was who he said he was, he pressed his data cell and announced to Doctor Zeller that Russell was here to see her. It was a short conversation.

A steel gate next to the guard booth swung open. Russell walked through the gate and stopped as the guard approached. "Through the second door."

Russell looked down the hallway of a series of large thick metal doors, resembling bank vaults. The second door slowly opened for him. He thanked the guard and entered into a small entry room. The large door closed behind him and he heard the bolts engage to lock him in. Once the door was secure, a second smaller door on the opposite side of the room opened to reveal a small staircase that led to Doctor Zeller's office.

Russell found it difficult climbing the stairs with the wound in his side. He looked up at the top of the stairs and there to greet him was Doctor Zeller. She watched him struggle to climb the steps.

"I'm glad they got you back, Hicks. Are you hurt?"

"Yes. I'm hurt. But they didn't get me back." Russell paused at the top of the stairs. "They're still looking for me. They don't know I'm back here yet." He kept walking past her into her office and sat down. Doctor Zeller, frozen in place by his last remarks, didn't reply. She stared at him with a confused and concerned look on her face as he passed her. She followed him into the office and closed the door.

"What are you talking about?" she asked in an authoritative tone.

"We need to talk about a lot of things I learned. And you're not going to believe half of it," Russell said.

Doctor Zeller sat down behind her desk and leaned forward to her desk console. "Does this involve the project?"

"Most definitely."

"Then I'd better get Mike and Steve over here." She reached for her communication switches.

"No!" Russell reached forward and stopped her hand. "Let them keep searching. They'll be busy for hours. You need to know some things first."

Doctor Zeller leaned back in her chair. Russell told her the whole story about his encounter with Charlie and the old west. He told her about Charlie's time travel and how he got back using Charlie's device, which was decades ahead of anything he and Doctor Zeller could ever imagine at this stage of their project. He spoke about his wound and what happened to him afterwards. Russell paused in his story and sat quietly for a moment gathering his thoughts of the past week with Charlie. Eventually the story rolled around to his encounter with Paul Camber and the suspicion he had about Michael. He was certain that the "mistake" Michael supposedly made was not a mistake at all, but a deliberate attempt to get rid of him.

"I would have been lost for good if it hadn't been for Charlie," he finally said.

Doctor Zeller didn't answer at first. It was as if she was transfixed by Russell's story. Finally she shook her head. "I don't know what to say." She leaned back in her chair and folded her hands behind her head. "Some of this is just too unbelievable! What are the odds of you travelling to an arbitrary time dimension and running into another traveler? This is just too much."

Russell leaned forward and supported himself on Doctor Zeller's desk, "Charlie was no fool. He had some very stern warnings about how dangerous time travel could be; not only to the past and the future, but also for the traveler. He lived it for thirty years. He saw himself as a caretaker of that era. He's been right about everything he's said. I believed him. I think we need to re-evaluate not only what we're doing here, but why we're doing it." Their discussion went on for hours.

Russell was pale and in pain. He felt as if he would faint at any time. Doctor Zeller summoned a medical team to her office. The medical techs wanted to take him to their facility but Doctor Zeller and Russell both refused and made them swear to keep this treatment secret for now. Doctor Zeller told them Russell would be brought to the medical facility the next day and they could report their late night call then.

Hours had passed. In utter frustration Steven crumpled up his empty paper coffee cup and threw it at the console of his station. "That's it!" he yelled. "I'm done. I don't know what else to do. I can't think anymore."

Michael turned toward Steven and appeared just as frustrated. "I don't know either, Steve. I'm with you. I've checked 100 years on either side of that target in the matrix and got nothing. It's like he just disappeared."

Steven walked over and sat on the corner of Michael's station desk. "What'll we do? We've only been able to rebuild a third of his path. I don't even know if we'll be able to find any further trace, much less rebuild it." He leaned forward and put his head in his hands. "If this gets out, we're done. This project is over."

"This project is not over," Michael said. "Everyone knew the hazards with this game. Even Hicks. He above all knew the risks involved. Hell, he's the one who told us about the possible problems." Michael stood and walked a few steps away. "No, this project isn't done. They need this to keep going. They need us to keep going. They need us to work out the kinks." He paused and stood looking back and forth between Steven and the humming equipment. Steven sat motionless with his head still in his hands. "I'm going to get some coffee. You want any?"

Steven shook his head and Michael headed for the lab door and stopped abruptly. "Oh my God!"

Steven joined Michael and stood staring at the doorway. Coming through the door was Doctor Zeller and Russell Hicks. Russell was limping a bit and holding onto Doctor Zeller's arm as they walked. Behind them walked four well-armed enforcers.

"Gentlemen," Doctor Zeller said, "I have a few announcements to make. As you can see, Mr. Hicks has rejoined us. He has quite a story to tell that I think you two need to hear. I think we should go into the conference room for a while. Shut everything down. As of right now, this project is going to take a different turn."

Steven was quick to welcome Russell back with a smile, a handshake, and a pat on the back. "No wonder we couldn't find you.

You're already here!" The joy of seeing Russell again was evident with Steven's smile. Michael, a little pale, didn't move. His expression was one of fear and confusion. Russell looked at Michael. As their eyes met Russell shook his head and Michael turned away. Doctor Zeller helped Russell into the conference room while Michael and Steven shut down the system under the watchful eyes of the four security enforcers. When all was shut down they went into the conference room and closed the door behind them. Two of the enforcers entered the conference room while the other two stood outside the closed door.

It was almost dawn when they all emerged from the conference room. They were tired and worn out, both physically and emotionally. With his head bowed and tears rolling down his cheeks, Michael was led away in handcuffs by two guards. Doctor Zeller had the guard captain issue orders to apprehend Paul Camber and immediately pull all contracts from his corporation and put everything involving that company on hold pending investigations. Steven walked out alongside Russell and Dr. Zeller.

"What's going to happen to Mike?" Steven asked.

Doctor Zeller turned to face Steven. "Hopefully he'll cooperate and tell us what information, if any, he leaked out. He could go away for a long time for espionage. We'll just have to see how bad we've been hurt."

"What about Camber?" Russell asked.

"He was the instigator behind all of this," Doctor Zeller replied. "He tried to have you eliminated. I'm sure he was just following orders. There has to be someone higher up pulling his strings. Their government contracts will most likely be cancelled and a full investigation launched. It won't go very far because they own half the politicians, but at least the investigation will appease the other half. Camber won't see the light of day for a long time. He'll probably end up as the fall guy for all this. You were lucky, Russell."

"Yeah, I guess I was. It's mind boggling. Here a person who hasn't been born yet saved my life four centuries ago. Makes you wonder what the hell we're doing."

221

Doctor Zeller turned and looked at Steven. "Go home for the remainder of this week. Get some rest. Get out of this complex for a while. Go away and think. When we get back together next week, we will be heading in a new direction." She turned to Russell. "You promised the medical team to go to their clinic this morning and have that wound taken care of properly. After that, you need to take some time and get some rest as well. I want both you and Steve to start fresh when you get back. So think about what we discussed."

Steven double checked the equipment and made sure everything was shut down and the documents were all locked up. He then left the building leaving Russell and Doctor Zeller in the lab with two security enforcers. They began a slow walk through the now quiet lab toward the front door.

"I want to see that belt as soon as you get back from medical," Doctor Zeller ordered. Russell stopped. After a long pause he shook his head. Doctor Zeller stopped and looked at him with a quizzical look about her.

"That can't happen," Russell said. "That belt is destroyed. I made a promise to Charlie that I would destroy it as soon as I got back."

"You didn't!" Doctor Zeller said, shocked.

Russell nodded. "Charlie knew firsthand the dangers and problems with time travel. He couldn't let his equipment contribute to any further time jumps. He made me promise to destroy it and that's what I did." It was a lie. Russell knew that Doctor Zeller would have it analyzed and quickly duplicated. She would do it with all the best intentions for the good of the project, but the possibility and probability of it being misused or falling into the wrong hands was too great. Russell couldn't let that happen. If anybody was going to analyze that belt, it was going to be him.

Doctor Zeller shook her head. "How could you do that?" Her disappointment was plainly visible. She walked to the lab door in silence and stood looking out at the early morning sunlight. "Are you going to be all right?" Doctor Zeller asked.

"In what sense?" Russell replied with a smile. "The wound is already feeling better. I'm sure it will heal fine. I'm not sure about the rest of me. But, I think our new direction of only working on

222

teleportation, and scratching the time-travel portion, is the right way to go."

"Russell, I want you to head this project," Doctor Zeller said. "I'll get it squared away later. When you come back you'll be the tech director for this. Is that okay with you?"

Russell's eyes widened and he felt his jaw drop open. He heard Charlie's voice echoing in his mind telling him he would someday be important. He smiled at the recollection and thanked Doctor Zeller for the opportunity and promotion. "I'll do my best," he said. "But, I got to be honest with you. Once this project gets moved along I'll most likely be leaving."

Doctor Zeller was a little surprised by his statement. "Why? Where will you go? What will you do?"

"I have quite a few education credits that I've earned that I have to spend. I think I'll head back to school for some brush-up classes. I made a promise to an old friend about continuing my studies. I've always wanted to teach, so I'll be heading in that direction. Once this project goes public, and it will eventually, it will open up an entire new industry. There will be a huge demand for educators in that field. I want to be there at the beginning."

Doctor Zeller smiled. "A great idea. That's why you're so valuable. You're always thinking ahead. You seem to be able to see the future. You sure you're okay?" she asked.

Russell smiled and nodded. Then he looked at her and asked "How 'bout you? Are you going to be all right?"

Doctor Zeller chuckled. "I think I can sell this project change. It would be a lot easier to sell it with that belt in hand, though." Russell smiled and looked away for a moment. "Anyway, if I can't sell it, we all may be going back to school. Go get some rest. You're going to need it. Get that wound taken care of. I'll take care of the bosses. Good night or I guess it's now good morning, Russell."

Doctor Zeller turned and headed toward the admin building, escorted by the two security enforcers. She stopped and turned. "It's good to have you back."

Russell stood alone at the door of the now quiet lab. He looked around and felt at home. Charlie was right. He had to come back. He had a smile on his face as he recalled his brief time with Charlie.

Maybe I'll take some American History courses this time. And then chuckled as he shut off the last light switch plunging the lab into darkness.

32

Epilogue
June, 2245

The systems in Doctor Hicks's office had been running all day and all night. Various three-dimensional virtual displays hung suspended in mid-air around the room. Russell, now 46 years old, watched the search results with increasing frustration. He couldn't believe there were no historical records anywhere regarding a Texas Ranger named Charlie Turlock. Russell could not shake the feeling that something was wrong and that it had to do with Charlie. He hadn't thought much about that old ranger in the past twenty years. Now, he couldn't get him off his mind.

Apparently, Charlie had done a good job of covering his tracks. The computers had been hacking into every historical record and archive data bank it could find. So far the only historical record it found was regarding a *C. Turlock* who served with the 4th Virginia Infantry in the Northern Virginia Campaign during the Civil War. He was one of the many men listed as missing during the Battle of Slaughter Mountain near Cedar Creek.

While the scans continued, Doctor Hicks was busy packing up his personal belongings in his office. He had been teaching astrophysics and fundamental principles of teleportation since his graduation. He recently resigned his teaching position and accepted a

225

new position with the government overseeing the development of teleportation hubs for the private sector. His work and research had been groundbreaking in every aspect and he had become the recognized authority on teleportation. A feat he secretly attributed to the existence of Charlie's time belt.

Lately, Doctor Hicks had been experimenting with remote viewing and telepathic transmissions, and had some pretty impressive results with some of his students. With these feelings about Charlie, he was wondering if telepathic thought transmissions could happen across space/time.

It had been twenty-five years since Charlie sent Russell back from Amarillo. Russell continued to work for Doctor Zeller for a few more years before he left and returned to school. As he promised, he dove into his studies and advanced to the top of his field. He also promised Charlie that he would never return. But now, he had to find out about that old ranger and going back to the nineteenth century may be the only answer.

The computers couldn't find any trace of him after the Civil War. He tried having a few of his best remote viewers find Charlie via psychic and telepathic means. But they all came up empty. He had to go back. If for no other reason than to settle the feelings of gloom he had for the past few days.

Since Russell had returned to his home in New York in 2220, he had become an avid collector of old west artifacts. He collected period clothing, some furniture, coins, old tools, household objects, etc. He became fascinated with the "Old West", since he had actually been there. Russell changed into one of his vintage 19th century vested suits, placed a dark brown derby on his head, pocketed as many antique coins as he could carry, and pulled Charlie's time belt from a locked safe he kept hidden in his closet. He had promised Charlie he would destroy the belt once he returned to his own time, but he just couldn't bring himself to do it. He felt bad about lying to Doctor Zeller about its destruction, but it was too valuable to his work and it had to be kept a secret.

Russell stepped into the shower compartment of his bathroom, strapped on the belt and initiated the sequence. He was engulfed in the familiar blue-green light and the virtual display appeared before him.

Russell adjusted the settings on the display, entered the coordinates for Amarillo, Texas and set the date for June 27, 1912 - twenty years after Charlie sent him home. Russell watched the timer count down. He closed his eyes when the counter reached one, heard a snap and he blacked out.

When Russell opened his eyes, he was lying in a field a few yards from the road that led into Amarillo. He lay still for a few moments taking stock of his condition. No nerve pains, no crazy vision issues, no jumbled memory or thought patterns. He woke completely intact and fully aware of his senses. It was dawn and he could see the outline of the city off in the distance. Russell was surprised to see how much Amarillo had grown over the past twenty years.

He dusted himself off and walked around the outskirts of the town until he came to the train depot. He stayed hidden among the stock corral, cargo crates, and storage bins until a train pulled into the station. When the train stopped, he blended in with the disembarking passengers. No one paid any attention to middle-aged Russell Hicks as he made his way out of the depot and walked down Polk Street.

He stopped and surveyed the city. He couldn't believe his eyes. The city was now a large metropolis. Russell noticed that the intersecting side streets had all been named or numbered. The back alleyway that paralleled Polk Street was now called Tyler Street and was a thriving business and residential district on its own. On the other side of Polk was Taylor Street which began the residential area. The Amarillo Hotel was still there, but now had a three story brick annex next to it where the saloon was. A lot of the old wooden structures had been replaced with brick and stone buildings. Polk Street was still the central business area of Amarillo and now featured a trolley motoring up and down tracks in the center of the street. A number of motorcars were parked where horses were once tied. Russell chuckled at seeing horses and wagons standing alongside cars.

He continued walking down Polk Street past the hotel trying to get his bearings. Everything was different. He stopped and stood outside a large two-story brick and stone building which housed a hardware store on the street level and a law office and real estate office on the second floor. He kept staring at what he believed should be Hanna's Eatery and Marshall Cook's office. Russell looked around trying to decide if this was the right spot or not. He was sure this was where the marshal's office used to be. A clerk from the store saw Russell staring at the building and walked out onto the sidewalk.

"You lost, mister?" the clerk asked.

"No, at least I don't think so," Russell answered with a smile. "I was looking for the marshal's office," then quickly added, "I haven't been here in twenty years. I'm amazed at how the town has grown."

"I suppose it has. I wouldn't know about that." The clerk reported. "I've only been here a few years. Came up from Fort Worth. But the story I got about this place is that there used to be a restaurant here and it had a fire quite a few years ago that took out a couple other businesses. After the fire they built this building."

"Do you know where the marshal is?" Russell asked.

"Well, we ain't got a marshal. We got us a police captain, though. The police station is over on Fourth Street near Tyler. They may be able to help you."

"Police station? Thank you. I'll head over there."

Russell stood for another moment trying to envision the fledgling town of twenty years ago. He crossed the street and walked a couple of blocks to the old ranger's office. The old red brick building was still there and hadn't changed much, with the same plaque on the brick wall and the same brass star on the same white door. Russell went into the office and was surprised to see that it looked almost exactly like it did when Charlie shoved him in there so long ago. The only difference was that the map of Texas on the back wall had been replaced with a newer one.

"Good morning. Can I help you with something?" a young ranger asked.

"Well, I don't know," Russell began. "I'm trying to locate an old ranger who used to be here by the name of Turlock. Do you know anything about him?"

"Turlock? Didn't know him. But, I heard a few stories about him. Just a minute."

The young ranger walked to the door that had COMMANDER painted on the frosted glass. He knocked and walked in, closing the door behind him. A minute or two later he called to Russell and ushered him into the commander's office.

"My name's Captain Sanders," the commander said, "I hear you're looking for a ranger named Turlock."

"That's right, Captain. Charlie is an old family friend and I haven't seen or heard from him since I left here some twenty years ago," Russell explained.

"Could I ask your name?" Captain Sanders asked.

"Oh, I'm sorry. My name is Russell Hicks. He used to just call me Hicks."

"Well, glory be!" the captain said. "I never thought you'd show up."

His remark caught Russell by surprise. *How could he possibly know about me?* The captain walked over to a safe that was unlocked and standing open and pulled an old, stained, and well-worn envelope from the safe.

"I don't know much about Turlock," the captain said, "All I know is what I heard. He was gone by the time I got stationed here."

"Gone? Gone where?" Russell asked.

"Well, I'm sorry to have to tell you this, but your friend died some twenty years ago. His cabin was burnt down and they found his body inside the burned out cabin. I'm sorry. A few days after the fire, this envelope arrived by stage addressed to HICKS at this office, that's all." The captain handed Russell the envelope. "That's you, ain't it?" Russell nodded and accepted the envelope. "Damnedest thing. Nobody knew where it came from or who sent it. It sat around here for a while, waiting for someone to pick it up. Somebody finally opened it and all they found was a badge and a note in it. Nobody knew what to do with it. Eventually, somebody just tossed it in the safe and never got around to throwing it out."

"Dead?" Russell said quietly. He remembered that night. He remembered Mac's body. Charlie wasn't dead, Russell thought. He just wanted everyone to think he was. He carefully opened the envelope. It was apparent that it had been opened many times before.

The only contents were Charlie's badge and a note that had two series of numbers written on it.

"With the badge, an' all, we sort of figured it might have had something to do with Turlock, but we didn't know what. Nobody knew what the hell those numbers meant," said Captain Sanders. "Officially he was listed as deceased in the line of duty, but somehow, somewhere, his records were lost. No one can find out anything about him. It's like he never existed."

Russell smiled. *You clever bastard.* "Can I keep this?" Russell asked holding up the badge.

"Sure," said the captain. "Those numbers mean anything to you?"

"Not at all," Russell replied. "I can't imagine."

Another lie. Russell knew right away they were longitude and latitude coordinates. But he knew wherever Charlie was hiding, he wanted to stay hidden. So he wasn't going to let the rangers know anything. "Well, I guess I'll be on my way. Thanks for the information, Captain." Russell rose, the two shook hands, and he headed for the door. "Oh, would you know anything about a Marshal Cook who was here about twenty years ago?"

"Only met him a few times. I didn't know him all that well," the captain said. "He was a real nice fellow and a good lawman from what I heard. They wanted him to head up the police force that was being formed, but he didn't want any part of it. He left town shortly after I got here. The stories say he came into some money and went into northern Arizona and became a constable in a small town there. I couldn't tell you for sure."

Russell thanked the captain again.

"Sorry I had to be the one to tell ya' about your friend. And sorry I couldn't be more help to you," the captain said.

Russell smiled and left the Ranger's office. Charlie never missed a thing. Even though he made Russell promise to never come back, he knew he eventually would. He unfolded the note and looked at it again.

37.168156   -104.531

All he had to do now was figure out where those numbers pointed. Russell wished he had his data cell. Then he remembered he was wearing a computer. He could use the time belt for teleportation. He would keep the same time, just change the space destination. He wondered if Marshal Cook had found Charlie and left Amarillo to join him.

Russell walked to just below the stockyards and hid behind a storage shed. He didn't see anyone around. He initiated the time belt and saw the blue-green glow around him. He punched in the coordinates on the virtual display, watched the timer count down, closed his eyes and he was gone.

When Russell awoke, he was amidst a forest of trees and plants. The sun was filtering through the branches, and the sweet smell of pine filled the chilly air. Most of the trees were some kind of fir or pine trees. Through the trees he saw an ever changing topography of rises and slopes. He was definitely in a mountain region.

"Where the hell am I now?" Russell said out loud. "Leave it to Charlie to find some out of the way place in the mountains."

He leaned against a tree, wondering which way he should begin walking. Just before he started out he heard the loud shrill of a whistle off in the distance. It sounded similar to a train whistle, only higher pitched. It was coming from off to his left and down the hill. He headed in the direction of the whistle. The whistle sounded again.

As he climbed down he came across a set of railroad tracks. He turned to his left and walked the tracks in the direction of the whistle. Around the next bend he came upon a number of buildings for some sort of a mining operation. He noticed a team of pit ponies towing several small low-slung cars out of the mine. The cars were filled with a black shiny rock. Russell stepped off the tracks and kept walking toward the mine.

When he reached the mine entrance, he stopped at the gate and read the sign hanging above the gate: RIFENBURG COAL MINE. *So that's what coal looks like.* He's heard about coal, but it had been banned for centuries in his era.

People were scurrying everywhere. The steam whistle he heard must have been some kind of signal to the workers. Russell waited for the horse-drawn train to finally clear the tracks and then he headed toward the largest building, thinking it may be the main office.

"Hold up there, fella," came a voice from behind him.

Russell stopped and turned around. The voice came from a large, burly man walking toward him wearing a bowler which barely covered his short-cropped hair. He wore a collarless grey cotton shirt and wide green plaid suspenders. Russell stared at his large red handlebar moustache. He had never seen anything like that before. The muscle-bound watchman carried a large nightstick that he probably didn't really need.

"Now where do ya' think you're sportin' to?" he continued in a broken Irish accent.

"I'm not really sure," Russell stammered.

"Ah' don't believe I've seen the likes of you around here before." The man gently poked the nightstick on Russell's chest.

"You haven't," Russell said. "I just got here and I'm trying to find a friend who might be around here. I was going over ..."

"An' who might that fella be?" the man asked.

"Well, his name is Charlie Turlock. He's about 5-10, maybe a little stocky, and should be in his 70's by now. I haven't seen him in about 20 years. He used to be a Texas Ranger."

When he said ranger, the watchman's eyes widened.

"An' who might you be?" the watchman asked.

"My name is Russell Hicks. I'm an old family friend of Charlie's. Do you know him?"

"No. I don't know anyone calling themselves by that name. But there's an old pay master here who says he used to be a Ranger. Fella goes by the handle A.J. Campbell. He's been pretty sick lately. He won't let anyone take him to Trinidad to see the doctor. Kind of crazy if you ask me."

"Trinidad?" Russell asked.

"Aye. Trinidad," the watchman said a little annoyed. "It's the town down the hill that you came in here by."

"Oh, right, right. And where can I find this A.J. Campbell?" Russell asked.

"He's been staying in the cook's cabin down the road a piece." The watchman pointed in the direction of a few buildings tucked up among the trees.

Russell thanked the man and walked toward the wooden buildings. He was wondering how he would find out which one was the cook's cabin. He was hoping it would be evident.

"You be careful, now, Mr. Hicks. I'll be lookin' after ya'," the watchman called after Russell.

"I'm hoping you will," Russell replied over his shoulder.

The news that Charlie was sick struck a sad note with Russell. He had a hard time keeping a neutral face with the watchman. Now he could feel tears welling up in his eyes. This had to be why he'd had such a strong feeling to come back and find him.

Russell reached the few wooden structures and went inside the largest one. It was a long narrow building with two rows of wooden tables and benches running its entire length. This had to be the food hall, Russell thought. At this time of day it was deserted.

"Hello?" Russell called out. There was no answer. He walked through the hall to a door at the opposite end that opened into a small clearing where two small almost identical structures stood with a well between the two cabins. These must be the cabins the watchman was referring to.

Russell knocked on the door of the first cabin. There was no answer. He opened the door and looked in at the meager furnishings; two cots, a small wooden table with one chair, a washstand and a bucket. A wooden box sat on the floor at the foot of each cot. Russell closed the door, turned around and came face to face with the business end of an old shotgun.

"What are you doin' snoopin' around here?" the small elderly man at the other end of the shotgun demanded.

His sudden appearance startled Russell and he gasped and threw his hands up in the air.

"I ... I ..." Russell stammered.

"Speak up, there," the man ordered.

"I'm looking for the old paymaster named Campbell!" Russell blurted out.

233

The old man lowered the shotgun a bit and backed up a step. He wore a severely stained collarless white cotton shirt and Russell assumed this man had to be the cook. His bald head had very thin scraggly white hair around the sides. He looked very pale and withered.

"You know this fella Campbell?" the old man asked.

"I'm not sure," Russell said. "Can I put my hands down?"

The old man nodded.

"What do ya' mean you're not sure?"

"Well, I'm looking for an old friend of mine named Charlie Turlock," Russell explained, "but I haven't seen or heard from him in twenty years. I think he may have changed his name to A. J. Campbell."

Russell heard something drop followed by someone coughing. He and the old man both turned to look at the open door of the second cabin.

"Campbell's in there," the old man said, "but I tell ya', he's pretty bad off. He's been sick for a spell now, but it took a real bad turn here a week or so ago. I've seen this before. He ain't long for here, you know? Are you his kin?"

Russell shook his head. "Just a friend."

The old man shook his head and slowly ambled back to the second cabin with Russell alongside.

"Damn shame," the old man muttered. "He's a real nice fella, too. Just a damn shame."

When they reached the cabin, the old man pushed the door open and stepped aside to let Russell go in.

"I'll leave you two alone so you can talk." The old man turned and walked toward the food hall.

It was dark inside and it took a minute for his eyes to adjust to the dim light, but Russell could see right away that the old man lying on the cot was indeed Charlie.

Charlie looked up at the stranger standing in the doorway and raised his head and put his left hand up as if to shield the light. "Who are you?" he said with a raspy voice. "What do you want?"

Russell slowly walked in and pulled a chair close to Charlie's cot. He sat down and smiled at Charlie. Charlie squinted his eyes.

234

Russell took a long slow breath. The old man's thin hair was pure white and very long. Charlie's right hand appeared crooked and withered. He was pale and his eyes were cloudy.

"Charlie? It's me, Russell."

Charlie's eyes widened and he looked closer. Suddenly he let out a laugh and a cough at the same time. His eyes filled with tears and he began to cry. He reached out and held Russell's face with his left hand. "You came back, boy. I knew you would," Charlie mumbled in between his sobs. After a while, he settled down. "Help me sit up."

Russell pulled Charlie up into a sitting position on the edge of the cot. They both sat in silence just staring at each other savoring the reunion.

"You must have gotten my note." Charlie smiled. "I'm surprised the captain held on to it all these years."

Russell nodded. "I was a little surprised myself. You made me promise to never come back. Yet you knew I would."

"I knew you couldn't stay away. This place kinda gits in your craw, don't it. I just didn't think it'd take you this long to come back."

Russell smiled and after a minute motioned to Charlie's right hand. "What happened to your hand?"

"Mac Sherman's curse," Charlie said. "He always said he wanted to mark me like I marked him. I suppose he did just that."

"Did you see a doctor?" Russell asked.

"Yeah. I saw a doc when I got to Tascosa. The bastard wanted to take the damn thing off! But I wouldn't let him. I can move it some, but most of it ain't got no feeling in it." He moved his arm from side to side to show Russell its limited mobility. Russell just nodded. Charlie coughed a bit and took a deep raspy breath. He could see that Charlie was having a difficult time breathing.

"Why A.J. Campbell?" Russell finally asked.

Charlie smiled. "That's my real name. Archibald Jackson Campbell. I finally decided to start using it after my so-called death."

"Well then, why Charlie Turlock in the first place?" Russell asked. "Where did that name come from?"

"Well, that was sort of a mistake." Charlie looked off to the side, past Russell as if he was in deep thought trying to visualize a distant memory. Finally, still staring off in space, he said "When I took that jacket off that dead soldier right after I got here in '62, the name stitched on the inside of the jacket was "C.TURLOCK". I didn't even know the name was there. I headed west and stayed hidden in the woods for about a week. I finally came across a blacksmith and his family in West Virginia. He spotted the name inside the blouse and asked me what the "C" stood for. I didn't know so I invented Charlie. From that point on he called me Charlie. It stuck. That's where the name came from."

"It's real good to see you," Russell said. "How are you feeling?"

"Not well. I'm dying. Lungs are shot. Probably from all the bad air here at the mine with the coal dust and all. Hell, boy, I'm over 70 years old. Most men in this era barely make their 50's. Most miners are lucky to see 40. I'm an anomaly."

"Why don't you see the doctor or let these people help you?" Russell argued. "You can't just die."

Charlie didn't answer. He nodded, smiled, and patted Russell's hand. They sat in silence for a moment while Russell waited for an explanation from Charlie that never came. Then he understood. There was nothing that could be done for Charlie, especially in this remote area in the early 1900's.

"You're all grown up. How long's it been? " Charlie asked, trying to change the subject. "You should be a pretty important physicist by now."

"It's been over twenty years, Charlie. And yes, I'm a doctor of physics now."

"Twenty years," Charlie repeated. "You still teaching?"

"I'm getting ready to leave when I get back. I got a real good offer from the government to go back and oversee the establishment of teleportation ports. It's all going public. Just like you said."

Charlie nodded with a smile on his face and kept looking at Russell.

"Should I call you Archie from now on?" Russell asked to break the silence.

Charlie chuckled. "You can call me whatever you like."

"Did you ever see Hanna or Amos, or Morgan again?" Russell asked.

"Yeah, I saw Cook a few years after I left. He said he and Morgan figured out right away that it wasn't me that died but kept it to themselves. He remembered me talking about Trinidad and tracked me down up here. It was good to see him. I hadn't seen Hanna or Doc. I felt real bad about Hanna. She was a real special lady. I didn't want to hurt her, but I had no choice. She was the one I missed the most. Had it been a different situation I'd a probably stayed with her. But, it had to end this way with her. I heard that her restaurant burned down about ten years ago and she packed up what was left and went back to Illinois to be with her sisters. Amos said that Morgan left town with some money he mysteriously received and went to California."

"Is Cook here?" Russell asked.

"No, no. He stayed here with me for a few days, but said he was moving on to northern Arizona. He got some money himself and was looking to get away somewhere. Haven't heard from him since."

Russell shook his head and smiled. "Why Trinidad and coal mining?"

Charlie told Russell the story of Frank McCrudy and how he was wrongly sent to prison, and how Charlie befriended him while he served his time over his five year sentence. When Frank got out of jail he'd come here to work for his brother who was a shift boss here. Charlie said Frank told him he could get him a job so that's why he came to Trinidad. Russell sat taking it all in. Then, Charlie changed the subject again.

"Does Campbell ring a bell with you?" Charlie asked.

Russell thought about it and then remembered a student. "I remember a Theodore Campbell. He was a student of mine a few years back. Brilliant fellow. Really took to the science well."

"That's my father." Charlie smiled. "My father thought you were a genius. He couldn't stop talking about you. If you remember him then you might remember a Sarah Jackson in the same class."

Russell thought but couldn't place the name. He shook his head.

"No matter. But she was my mother. I never really knew her. Dad said she was a sickly girl and she died shortly after I was born." Charlie began wheezing and coughing. He reached out to Russell and held his hand. "I got to lie back down."

Russell helped Charlie lie back down on the cot. Russell held on to Charlie's hand as Charlie tried to catch his breath. In a minute he settled down and was again breathing better.

"Let me get you some medicine or something to help you," Russell argued.

Charlie shook his head. "You still don't understand, do you?"

Russell stared at Charlie with a blank look on his face. Charlie said "I don't belong here. I never belonged here. When I go, there can't be any trace of me. I have to preserve this time the way it happened. As paymaster here, I made sure my name never appeared on the pay records. When I go, that old Cook outside promised to put me in an unmarked hole in the ground. It has to end this way. You have to understand. You, me, and anyone that travels back to the past don't belong. It ain't right! They just don't belong!" Charlie started coughing and took a few minutes to calm down and catch his breath. "You'll eventually move into a position where you can stop time travel all together. Remember this." Charlie turned away and closed his eyes to relax and catch his breath. There was a silence between them as Russell considered all that Charlie just told him and the things he had said twenty years ago.

"You got time to stay a while?" Charlie finally asked, breaking the silence.

Russell smiled as a tear formed in his eye. "Charlie, I got all the time in the world."

He sat holding Charlie's hand.

ABOUT THE AUTHOR

Edward Gates was raised in Cincinnati, Ohio. After serving in the military during the Vietnam Conflict, he was educated at the University of Cincinnati.

A Systems Engineer by trade, he spent over thirty years writing technical and training manuals, presentations, speeches, and sales media. His career took him and his family to Atlanta, Georgia and eventually on to Southern California where he lived until he retired in 2012. Currently, he and his wife reside in Prescott, Arizona.

Edward has a passion for writing and has always written stories and short scenes. He has been actively involved in theater for well over 30 years and has written a stage play entitled BUSTER'S WIFE. The play was a finalist in the McKinney Reparatory Theater new-play competition in 2013. He has also completed three one-act plays and is working on another two-act stage play.

A RANGER'S TIME is Mr. Gates's first novel. A second novel about the life and times of Charlie Turlock is currently in the works.

Contact information: email at: edgatesjr@edwardlgates.com
mail to: PO Box 12578, Prescott, AZ 86304

To see current projects, follow Mr. Gates on his website: edwardlgates.com

53023001R00153

Made in the USA
San Bernardino, CA
12 September 2019